VALKYRIE CROWNED

This book is a work of fiction.

While reference might be made to actual historical events or existing locations, the names, characters, places and incidents are either the product of the author's imagination or are used fictitiously, and any resemblance to actual persons, living or dead, business establishments, events, or locales is entirely coincidental.

Manufactured in the United States of America
Acelette Press

For my eternal dragon

CHAPTER ONE

KIRBY

The hotel shifted under Kirby, the tremors escalating to a rolling shake. Dust spilled into the air, clogging her lungs and clouding her vision.

She met Brit's gaze. Just a few minutes ago they'd been talking. Reconciling. Brit, apologizing for the past, and Kirby, finally accepting that she meant it. A side effect of having masqueraded as Brit and lived inside her head for weeks.

Now fear replaced adoration on Brit's face.

It had only been a few days since Kirby was on the TOM campus and felt a similar quake. However, this was worse than when Loki killed half of Kirby's former classmates and unleashed a new-old god, determined to destroy the world to find his imprisoned sister.

If that quake destroyed most of the buildings on The Order of Mistletoe campus, this one would bring the hotel down around them without effort.

Kirby couldn't let that happen. There were so many lives here, and none of them had anything to do with the furious god making the ground tremble. She couldn't let them die for someone else's sins.

"Don't do it." Brit approached her when the shaking paused.

Kirby was already reaching deep inside, to grasp the ethereal shield she could summon as a Valkyrie, and protect as many people as possible. "I can't do nothing. Do you still feel him in the air?"

Brit could sense certain magics, especially those with malice and ill intent. "Yes." She clenched her jaw. "But you pushed too hard last time. If you pass out, you can't save anyone, including yourself."

The ground shook again, with no build-up this time. The building rattled violently beneath them, like they were stuck in a paint mixer.

She and Brit had survived lethal gunshots and worse. A building falling on them wouldn't mean death. But Kirby couldn't say the same about the mortals here.

Kirby focused on the power that flowed through her. In her mind, it was water sparked with lightning. She pulled the desire to protect and spun it outward, like unfurling a building-sized cape.

Darkness licked at the edges of her vision. Her shield didn't feel as steady as last time, and she needed it to be stronger.

She tugged every strand of power she could find and spun them into a massive web, letting it flow out more and more with each heartbeat.

"Kirby." Brit sounded like she was screaming through water.

Kirby would stop when she knew everyone was safe. She just needed a little mo—

Chapter Two

Gwydion

Gwydion had lived through enough natural disasters that they didn't usually faze him. This quake was different, though.

It wasn't just the stuttered surges of violent shaking he didn't like, though it threatened to tear this tiny house apart. There was a foulness to the magic causing this tremor. A tainted poison that polluted the earth Gwydion had an affinity with.

It hurt to push past the darkness and stabilize the wooden beams holding this place up. Trees had memories—even re-purposed ones—and these spoke of the heartache, the looming madness, and the suppressed lust that had lived within their walls for the last few years.

A visceral reminder of Kirby's journey to awakening in this life. Of the time she spent training as an assassin, because Starkad insisted it would be best if she learned to protect herself. Of the time after he pulled her from the same place, because the experience nearly destroyed her. And of the time Starkad and Kirby lived in this home, him denying her answers, affection, and anything but the most basic kindness and care.

Anger would have to wait, but Gwydion could fix Starkad with a furious glare. Which was as unhelpful as everything else they were doing.

Starkad vanished. *Poof*—he was gone in a blink.

The shaking stopped, and the toxicity in the ground vanished.

Gwydion stumbled at the shift in stability. "*Starkad,*" he forced enough power into his shout, for it to carry through the entire house. It was tempting to believe Gwydion had wished him into temporary oblivion, but the reality was likely far more nefarious.

This had happened on the TOM campus. When the shaking stopped, everyone was gone, except Kirby, Gwydion, Min, Brit, and Starkad. There was no telling at the time if Loki had taken the other students, or if it was Gluskab—the assumed source of all the quakes—or a third god.

Gluskab was supposed to be a god of good and life and order, but when his sister, a goddess of chaos, was sealed away by the gods, the lack of balance drove him mad. He'd asked Hel for help sleeping as well, until he could release his sister, and they could rain destruction on the world together.

Gwydion searched the house for Starkad. Not that it took long.

Gwydion was alone here.

He dialed Kirby's phone. When he didn't get an answer, he moved to Min. Brit. Nothing. Starkad. A ringing sounded from the device sitting on the table near the front door.

Gwydion's concern spiked. He kept cycling through their phone numbers as he turned on the news.

The local channels were starting to talk about the quakes.

The tension twisting every inch of Gwydion insisted this was worse than it appeared, and it already looked pretty bad.

An alarm blared through the house. The high-pitched noise was a sharp pulse at the top of hearing range, piercing and shrieking and drawing on every battle magic he knew.

CHAPTER THREE

MIN

Min left his hotel room. He moved closer toward the exit each time there was enough of a lull in the quakes for him to do so.

Death permeated the air. Most of it foul and belonging to Gluskab, but the loss of life grew with each new tremor. Not just within the building, but also through the entire city. Far too much death to be a result solely of this disaster.

As he descended the stairs, he found a woman in her late teens huddled in the corner between floors.

She clutched something to her chest, and tears streamed down her face.

"You need to go." He kept his voice kind and reached for her.

She shook her head and jerked away. "He's not moving. He's my best friend, and he just stopped—" She sobbed.

"Who?" Min gently pulled her arms open.

She cradled a toy collie. Tendrils of death circled the small dog's body, lingering uselessly now that they'd sucked away the creature's life.

Rage, potent and terrifyingly unfamiliar coursed through Min. He was a god of life, and that meant accepting that the circle had to close and all lives ended. However, this one hadn't ended on its own. It had been stolen. Viciously ripped away.

"He's okay. Just scared." Min spoke through the violent shaking around them. He held out his arms. "May I?"

She hesitated.

"I won't hurt him. You have my word." Min leaked a hint of soothing into his tone.

She opened her arms wider.

The building around them creaked, dust falling. Min covered his head with his arms, and used his body to shield the young woman and her companion.

A large hunk of concrete struck his back, and he clenched his jaw to hold back a roar. The injury healed as quickly as it formed. Several more slabs struck him, one knocking his phone from his pocket and another crushing it.

When the quake paused, he straightened again, careful to not let any of the darker, death-tinged debris fall on her. He held out his arms again.

She handed him the collie.

Min cradled the dog in one arm and stroked his fingers along the creature's ear. "You need to wake up, little one." The words were for her comfort. "Please." And a little for his own. "You have friends here, who need you still." As he spoke, he let his power drift along the tendrils of death, obliterating them, and breathing life back into the tiny body.

The dog's leg's kicked, his eyes opened, and he yelped a greeting.

"*Benedict.*" Fresh tears tracked through the dirt on the woman's cheeks.

Min handed her the collie. "See? He'll be fine. We need to go."

She nodded. Cradling the dog to her chest, she stood.

Min escorted her to the ground floor, made sure she was safe, then raced back inside to evacuate anyone else he could find. His primary concern was Kirby. And Brit. But they would be doing this as well—helping people. Ensuring as few lives were lost as possible.

As one of the quakes stopped, the rancid scent of death in the air evaporated. It didn't take the sadness of casualty with it. Min mourned all those gone. He couldn't bring thousands back to life. The puppy was a miracle as it was, still with a breath of life, and Min exhausted a lot of energy turning that into more.

He stood at the back of the crowds milling in confusion and grief on the streets. He couldn't see Kirby or Brit. They might not stick out to most of these people, but he was always drawn to Kirby's presence.

Min should stand out to Kirby and Brit, as well. He towered over most people here.

Another presence tickled his senses, though. Another god. One of war. Fallen civilizations. But so many fit that definition.

Min turned, desperate to locate the source.

Chapter Four

STARKAD

Starkad's surroundings vanished in a blinding flash that sent pain rocketing through his skull.

As the brightness faded, trees swam into view instead of living room furniture. It was night here, rather than afternoon. What the fuck?

He patted his pockets, but his phone, wallet—everything—sat back on the table by his front door. He'd become so domesticated.

The position of the moon in the sky and the brightness of the stars said he was nowhere near home. Not that they had trees this tall, vibrant, and ancient in many places in The States. He turned his head toward the sky again and sniffed the air.

Correction—this was *home*. Norway. Where he and Kirby had been created. Where he'd lived for centuries. The comfort that sank into his limbs was disrupted by the nagging thought, *But I shouldn't be here.*

More critical was the need to get back to Kirby. Make sure she was all right. That quake had been Gluskab. No question. And if he'd come to Chicago, it was either for Min or Gwydion, or for the god who had made his home in underground Chicago.

A low growl reached his ears, and his wolf surged forward. He'd made a similar noise more times than he could count.

He spun to see another wolf, this one the size of a large SUV, squaring off with him, teeth bared and body tense.

CHAPTER FIVE

BRIT

Brit should be focusing her concern on the fact that she was in an actual fucking prison cell. Her hotel room had vanished, and concrete walls replaced the luxury.

However, she was too worried about Kirby to give much attention to anything that wasn't an immediate threat.

Kirby had been teleported—*blinked...* whatever—with Brit, but she was unconscious on the floor. Her skin was pale, and her chest barely moved with each shallow breath.

Brit knew intermediate first aid and triage. Useful skills in the field, but Kirby didn't exhibit any injuries. There was nothing to treat.

It took about thirty seconds to explore the small box they were locked in. Three by three meters. Steel door with a tiny window. There was nothing in here besides her and Kirby. No bed, toilet, bucket… This wasn't meant to be a long-term cell.

If some random god intended to execute either Brit or Kirby, they were in for a surprise.

The thought didn't erase the fear mounting inside Brit.

She settled on the floor again, pulled Kirby's head into her lap, and trailed her fingers through Kirby's hair. "Please wake up," Brit murmured. *I don't want to do this alone.*

The air in the room shifted, and a faint hum reached Brit's ears. She laid Kirby down as gently and quickly as she could, and stood, every sense on full alert.

Something magical—a thick, heavy power— flowed over her. There was the god.

"Brit Hauge, remain standing and put your hands behind your head." The voice seemed to come from nowhere.

The last name was foreign to her. TOM stripped students of their last names when they *adopted* them as children, to sever ties with their past and their identity.

Brit complied with the order, putting herself between the door and Kirby. This was likely the safest way to see what happened next.

Two soldiers with guns stepped into the room. It didn't matter how many more were in the hallway. The doorway provided a funnel, and as long as one of them had extra magazines, she only needed one gun to take down a company of men.

The soldiers were dressed in full body armor, including masks. That still left half a dozen spots she could hit to wound or kill.

Both had their weapons pointed more at the ground than at her head.

Fucking armatures. She twitched her foot.

They raised the weapons, fired, and hit her in the knees.

She couldn't bite back the scream of agony, as bones shattered and she collapsed to the ground.

CHAPTER SIX

MIN

Min focused on the energy of the new arrival and relaxed. The woman who stepped into view wore a smile, torn jeans, and an *Anarchy in the UK* T-shirt. She could be sixteen or thirty.

But her age was measured in centuries or millennia. He returned Freya's—Aya's—smile. She wasn't the face he'd been hoping for but was always a welcome sight.

"Min." She gave him a quick hug.

He kissed her on both cheeks before releasing her. "Aya. I hate to be rude, but I assume you're no more here to catch up than I am."

Aya shook her head. "I've been looking for you and your companions. My brother and I both have. We can only find you and Gwydion."

"Kirby and Brit were here, in the hotel, when the quakes started." Concern surged through Min. "I can't locate them now. You don't sense them at all?"

Once upon a time, Kirby had been a loyal believer in Freya. Had prayed to her. A god could typically pluck their followers out of a crowd, regardless of said god's other gifts.

Aya shook her head. "I believe there's a good chance The Followers of Urd have her."

"That's good." Min's relief was short-lived at Aya's frown. "That's not good?"

Her frown deepened. "It's not good."

CHAPTER SEVEN

GWYDION

If Gwydion knew anything about Starkad, the high-pitched alarm was a proximity warning for the house or something equally as paranoid. Not that Starkad's paranoia wasn't justified, but Gwydion wouldn't have thought to install such a thing.

Then again, he wouldn't have thought to put in fake windows with steel barricades behind them.

The knock on the door was barely audible over the screech of the alarm. Was there a way to turn off that noise? Probably. Just like there were probably cameras, so he could see what was going on outside.

Since Gwydion didn't have access to any of the security features, he was the only person in the house, and he wasn't in the mood to play soldier, he answered the door.

Seeing Freyr—Frey—on the other side wasn't enough to eliminate all the stressors Gwydion was dealing with, but it was nice to not add to the list.

The young woman by Frey's side was unfamiliar, though. She was Brit's age—mid-twenties—with black hair, an oversized black sweater that showed off the tank top underneath, and a... ballet skirt over cut-offs? "Do you need to get that?" she asked.

Great greeting. This was almost a broken intro to a bad joke. *A god and a girl show up on a porch...* "Nah. I like it. Soothes the soul."

"Good to see you." Frey's chuckle fell flat. "Are you the only one here?"

"Whom else did you expect?" Gwydion didn't know what to make of any of this.

The woman looked past him. "Starkad? Kirby? It's their home, right?"

"Are you a friend?" Gwydion didn't get the impression either Starkad or Kirby had many friends. He didn't even know how they presented themselves to neighborhood. Did they play the doting suburban couple for the neighbors? Unlikely, given the nature of their relationship before Kirby regained her memories of her past lives.

"This is Dahlia. Dahlia, meet Gwydion." Frey passed around introductions.

Not that they did Gwydion any good. "Charmed, I'm sure. I'd invite you in, but I'm still waiting for you to tell me what the fuck is going on. I assume you're not dropping by for tea and biscuits."

"We think FU took Kirby," Dahlia said.

Gwydion focused on her. Did she have any idea she was in the presence of two gods? Frey seemed to know her well enough he'd brought her to visit. "Who are you? More than a name."

She dragged in a deep breath. "I'm what your girlfriend probably calls a Noble. Or a cunt. Not sure about that. I'm not with TOM anymore. Not that you'd take my word for it. Not that you care. You probably care. I stumbled on a series of prophecies that aren't in any of the printings I've found, and they talk about all of you, and would you *please* let me turn the alarm off? I swear it's piercing my brain."

"I don't have the code." Gwydion was still processing everything else she said. "I do care. You're right; she'd probably call you a cunt if you're a former classmate. Give me one good reason I shouldn't execute you right now." He hated when violence had to be the first option. Some day, he'd like a world where it never was, but as long as the gods freely threw around loyalty to acronyms like *TOM* and *FU*, this was the only option.

"You have my word that you can trust her," Frey said.

Not all gods' word meant something, but his did to Gwydion. "All right."

"Are we good now? Good. Invite us in? Thanks." Dahlia pushed past Gwydion, pulling a tablet and a cable from her messenger bag. She paused in front of a photo of Kirby that hung on the wall. She took down the photo to reveal a seam in the wallpaper, and pressed her thumb along the edge, until a small door *snicked* open.

An alarm control panel sat inside. She plugged her tablet in, jabbed at the screen in a rapid-fire series of taps, frowned, and repeated the process.

Silence settled over the room.

"Starkad is going to be furious that was so easy." Gwydion shouldn't have said that with so much amusement.

"Easy?" Dahlia snorted. "I'm a fucking master. I didn't see you doing it. Besides, I always had the impression most things pissed off Starkad."

Starkad had been a combat instructor for most of the Nobles, and it sounded like she knew him. She certainly carried herself with the confidence of an elite trained assassin.

"Thank you." Gwydion made sure his sincerity showed. "The quiet is much better. And forgive my lack of hospitality, but why would The Followers of Urd have Kirby?"

Dahlia's easy smile vanished. "One of the prophecies I don't think anyone has seen says the last Valkyrie will be no more. And I'm under the impression that FU is all about making sure the prophecies happen."

Chapter Eight

STARKAD

The wolf facing Starkad down was Fenrir. He and Starkad went all the way back to Kirby's original life, but Fenrir was furious about some of Starkad's more recent decisions.

When Starkad said that some of the gods didn't like how he'd played both sides, with TOM and FU, it was an understatement. He'd spent decades just wanting a fight. It didn't matter who was asking or what their cause was, as long as he could get his claws dirty, and that indiscretion tended to piss of… well… most immortals. It was the one secret he still kept from Kirby. She might not forgive his lack of discretion.

The way Fenrir faced him now, ready to strike with any misstep, he wasn't feeling forgiving. Unlike Starkad, whose mind was more wolf than man when he shifted, Fenrir remained in full control of his consciousness.

Fenrir bared his teeth and lunged.

Starkad rolled to the side, maneuvering to put trees between them.

"Now you avoid a fight?" Fenrir's voice was in Starkad's head and all around them, rather than spoken. Being self-aware didn't change the fact that he had a wolf's vocal cords. He charged again.

Starkad should have an easier time avoiding such a large beast, given the trees. But they didn't seem to slow the wolf down.

Starkad struggled to hold onto rational thought. In his mind, jaws snapped to get out. His chest rumbled with a primal need. If he let the wolf out, he wouldn't have control. It was unlikely he or Fenrir would die, but the wounds would be serious. "I don't want to hurt anyone."

"Then you've come to the wrong place."

"I didn't choose to be here." Starkad kept moving, weaving between trees. Keeping Fenrir in sight, but with an obstacle between them as much as possible.

"You just happened to appear in my path?"

"I doubt it was a coincidence, but it wasn't my choice. I was at home, and then I was here." Starkad kept the explanation vague on purpose. Details would wait.

"You're lying." Fenrir attacked again, dodging a tree, moving like a blur, and coming up on Starkad's back.

Starkad rolled but wasn't fast enough. A claw caught his side, tearing flesh as if it were paper. His shout of pain melted into a howl, tearing from his throat. His canines cut his tongue.

23

Fenrir pivoted before Starkad could recover, flying through the air to knock him to the ground. Giant paws stood on Starkad's chest, stealing his breath and calling to him to fight back. *"Which of your temporary masters wants me dead? Is this for money, or simply to eliminate me?"*

Chants of *fight, kill, devour* thrummed in Starkad's skull. "I don't do that anymore."

"Right. Your Valkyrie has changed you." Apparently sarcasm carried over the alternate means of speech. *"Does she know what you became while she was gone?"*

Starkad's control slipped further, his chin and nose growing.

"Fight back." Fenrir pressed his teeth to Starkad's throat.

Starkad was close to doing exactly that. No matter which of them got hurt worse, he'd regret it. Fenrir had never been the enemy, but Starkad was, for a long time.

It took an immense force of will, to keep the growl from his response. "No."

The weight vanished from Starkad's chest, as did the pressure from his throat. Fenrir in human form stepped back a few meters as Starkad hopped to his feet.

Fenrir's lack of clothing showed off a well-built frame, covered in tattoos. His dark-blond hair was cut close the ears, rather than being the long braids so many warriors wore centuries ago. Even nude, he was an imposing presence.

The temporary ceasefire didn't mean the battle was over. Starkad kept his guard up and his stance battle ready.

"Why are you here? The truth this time," Fenrir said.

How long had he been in this isolated piece of wilderness in Norway? Weeks? Months? Was he up to date with current god events? "There were a series of quakes—of the act-of-god variety—and then I was here. That's the truth."

"You finally pissed off the wrong deity?"

Starkad gave him a dry smile. "Not me. I've never met Gluskab."

Fenrir's laugh stopped abruptly. "You're serious."

"You know the name."

Was that concern etched onto Fenrir's face? "Aya helped imprison his sister. How did he—"

"Loki. Not on purpose." Not that Starkad thought Loki was above initiating genocide. "He sacrificed followers on sealed grounds."

Fenrir shook his head. "Fucking idiot. You're fortunate you don't have a bloodline to embarrass you."

Loki was Fenrir's father, and Hel was his sister. He'd severed ties with the family centuries ago, though.

"Why are *you* here?" Starkad asked. He didn't keep tabs on most gods, but Fenrir and Frey owned a club and the surrounding property in underground Chicago. Their presence—their *ownership* of the city—was the reason Starkad settled there with

Kirby. Frey made it clear that neither TOM nor FU was welcome near his territory.

"The modern world gets to be too much sometimes," Fenrir said. "I'm here to clear my head."

"So how did I get here?" It was a rhetorical question. Neither of them had that answer. "You have a phone?"

Fenrir patted his naked thighs. "Left it in my other pants."

Starkad chuckled dryly. This wasn't a vacation for Fenrir. "You've been living out here." Hunting as a wolf. Losing himself in nature.

"Jealous?" Fenrir smirked.

"A bit." Starkad stepped back, keeping his posture as non-threatening as possible without dropping his guard. "I'll leave you to the Call of the Wild. I need to get back to town." Call home. Make sure Kirby was all right.

"I'm not letting you out of my sight." The casual tone vanished from Fenrir's voice, replaced by threat. "A good story doesn't return all that erased trust."

Starkad didn't figure it would. He'd hoped, but he had a lot to atone for.

A new scent filled the air. A muddy power. The nearby trees rustled. Starkad went rigid, and so did Fenrir.

The sound of a suppressed gunshot reached Starkad as a bullet tore into his shoulder.

Chapter Nine

Brit

Brit bit the side of her fist to keep from screaming again. She sat on the concrete floor in a puddle of her own blood, agony shooting through her. The wounds on her knees had already clotted. The bone of her shattered kneecaps was regenerating quickly.

That didn't make it hurt any less.

"You could have complied. You chose not to." The voice sent ice racing down her spine. *Vidar.* Power and threat spilled from the god who stepped into the room. Even if Brit were standing, she'd have to look up—and up—to meet his gaze. His dirty-blond hair was pulled into a clean ponytail at the base of his neck. The long hair was a sharp contrast to the pinstriped suit that accentuated his trim but muscular frame.

Brit didn't want to feel awe at his presence, but the compulsion to kneel at his feet was potent. The

Order of Mistletoe was responsible for far more than just the campus where Brit and Kirby were raised and trained. Their board of directors consisted of a dozen gods—presumably eleven, now that Hel was dead. Brit didn't know every god on the board, but Vidar had been a good friend of Hel's, and was occasionally involved in ceremony on the TOM campus.

Most students prayed to Hel. Worshiped her. Brit had always put her faith in a different member of the board. It didn't matter that life with TOM was behind her, Brit still reached for Vidar's name first when she was stuck. Needed help. Was terrified.

She forced herself to stand, regaining her balance after a few wobbly seconds.

"Don't make me restrain you further," Vidar said.

"You already had them shoot me." Wait. If he was here, were these TOM grunts? The students and soldiers taken from campus?

Vidar gave her a thin smile that didn't reach his eyes. "They shot you to immobilize you, knowing you would recover. Which you have."

"Swell." Brit returned his unamused look. "Why are we here?"

"One of our Nobles recently brought new information to light."

The woman who joined Vidar in the doorway was pale, with long auburn hair. Magnus. She wore a corset and jeans, the same as she had so many times on campus. The full-finger ring on her right middle finger, complete with a stainless-steel claw, was new.

Magnus and her partner, Dahlia, had been some of the few Nobles Brit genuinely liked. They weren't fighters—in fact they were the only Nobles who scored low marks in every single combat area—but no one in the world was better at digital espionage.

"I've missed you, Kitten." Magnus's greeting was sad, but friendly.

I can't say the same. The snide retort stuck in Brit's throat, despite the whole we-were-just-magically-kidnapped scenario. She *had* missed Magnus and Dahlia. "Same. And *Brit*, please." *Kitten* was her call sign as a TOM Noble. Hel insisted that giving each other nicknames would bring the Nobles closer together. Build camaraderie.

She'd also actively discouraged some of them from being named. Brit didn't have a call sign until after Kirby was gone. Kirby picked one up after the Nobles were told she was a Valkyrie, long after her time with TOM. Magnus and Dahlia had never been given alternate names. It was always implied they were Nobles, but not quite as much so as everyone else.

Magnus smiled. "I'd take the time to catch up, but you probably want answers."

"Answers would be nice, yes."

"W—I stumbled on a set of prophecies that aren't in any of the known books. None of the translations. As far as I can tell, very few people know about these," Magnus said. "One of them says that the last Valkyrie will be no more."

A new flavor of fear sliced through Brit. The prophecies of Urd had been written thousands of years ago. A large number of them implied a changing of the guard—so to speak—among the gods, where old gods would die and new would take their place. But Kirby wasn't... She couldn't die again.

"We brought you both here to keep Kirby safe," Vidar said.

Brit snorted a laugh. "TOM has never given a fuck about our lives."

"Untrue." Vidar was calm. Cool. "Hel didn't want either of you dead. Ever. She wanted you to remain part of the team."

"She wanted us submissive and brainwashed." Kirby's voice—despite the exhaustion in it—was a welcome relief to Brit.

Vidar *tsk*ed. "Hel was misguided. She also didn't know this information."

"So that excuses what she did to us? How she treated us?" Kirby's question mirrored Brit's thoughts.

"We do what it takes to accomplish our goals." There was no apology in Vidar's retort.

Should Brit laugh or cry at how black and white he made the whole thing? "And we've become one of your goals?" she asked.

"The Order of Mistletoe exists to keep the original powers alive. You're here to keep your Valkyrie safe."

"From whom?" Kirby asked.

Magnus tapped the claw from her ring against her chin. "The Followers of Urd."

CHAPTER TEN

STARKAD

The hole in Starkad's arm hurt a lot more than it should, even for a bullet wound. It wouldn't kill him, though. Whoever shot him either had bad aim or wasn't shooting to kill.

And their scent lingered in the air. "Go find them." Starkad bit off the words.

Fenrir hesitated.

Starkad wouldn't be surprised if he was left here to deal on his own.

And then Fenrir was sprinting away, cutting a straight line though the trees toward the scent and the source of the shot.

Starkad pressed his back to a tree, putting the trunk between himself and the presumed location of the shooter. He wrapped his fingers around the wound, and swallowed a roar of agony at the light touch. This wasn't right.

"They're gone." Fenrir had returned. "I was closing in, and the air shifted. The scent vanished."

"A god?" Why would a god shoot Starkad?

Fenrir shrugged. "Unless you've pissed off the fae, too."

Currently, the queen of the fae was grateful to Starkad. "I guarantee I haven't. And I don't say that lightly."

"Uh-huh. I'm not going to ask who wants to hurt you; we don't have all afternoon for the list. Can you walk?"

Starkad stood. "It's a hole in my arm. They didn't shoot my legs off."

"I have a cabin about five kilometers from here, so I don't walk back into society naked when this is over. You can use the phone. Dress the wound." Fenrir focused on Starkad's arm. "That doesn't look good."

"It's not as though it's going to kill me," Starkad said dryly. A thousand years ago, Kirby had granted him immortality. He'd tried since then to shed the gift, but it wasn't going anywhere. "Which direction?"

Fenrir jerked his head, and they fell into step beside each other. Starkad had no illusions that this was a friendly walk. They exchanged wary looks more than they did conversation.

The trip should have been no-impact, but there was a lot of stumbling over underbrush in the darkness. By the time the cabin came into sight, Starkad was winded and had broken out into a cold sweat. He didn't have the focus to appreciate that the interior of the building was modern and comfortable—the polar opposite of *roughing it*.

Fenrir managed to keep his attention on Starkad while he pulled on clothes. "That doesn't look so good." He nodded at Starkad's arm. "I've got some bandages."

Starkad stripped off his shirt, and another shock of agony squeezed the breath from his lungs. He glared at the wound. Blackness spread out, snaking through his veins and drawing a roadmap under his skin. This looked a lot like a wound Kirby had described. "Bandages aren't going to help."

"You know what this is."

"I know TOM has bullets that cause something very similar."

Fenrir growled. "You brought TOM down on me?"

"I told you I'm not here because I want to be. Kirby was shot with one of these." Starkad would rather work toward getting the fuck out of her, than argue.

"Kirby?" As Fenrir talked, he dug through a duffel bag. "Did it... Is she...?" His concern sounded genuine. It probably was. He hadn't encountered Kirby in this life, but they'd been friends in several of her previous ones.

The incident had been less than a week ago, and Starkad still had that potent taste of almost losing her again in his mouth. "She survived." Thank the gods. "I didn't see the injury, but it's my understanding it was meant to kill her. Cut her off from her powers."

Fenrir extracted a cell phone. "Can you shift?"

No reason to remind him that Starkad wouldn't be in control if he did. What happened would happen. Starkad didn't have to reach deep for his wolf.

The bones in his face should grow and stretch, while his limbs did the same. Instead, agony screamed from the bullet hole. Nothing else happened. "That's a distinct *no*."

"If she survived, you should too. Nothing kills you. What saved her?"

"Min." Starkad was almost reluctant to admit it hadn't been him. "God of life, and all that. I don't think they meant to kill me. I'm far more of a burden to you alive but seriously injured."

Fenrir shook his head and jabbed at his phone. As he listened, his frown deepened. Impressive. Several more swipes at the screen were followed by a fierce scowl. "You're not the only one who vanished in the quake. Kirby is gone too."

"Someone called to tell you that?" Starkad's fear and rage cranked up, amplifying the pain in his arm.

"Aya and Frey were looking for your friends. We know a young lady, Dahlia, who has information about Kirby."

Starkad knew Dahlia as well. TOM assassin. Deceptively kind. Far more dangerous than she appeared. "I don't trust anything she has to say."

"I don't give a fuck what you think." Fenrir tossed the phone on top of his bag. "I trust her, and that's more than I can say for you. I can't call them back, though. No signal."

That wasn't right. "There was enough of a signal for them to leave messages."

"And now there's not."

This was getting worse with each passing moment.

CHAPTER ELEVEN

KIRBY

Kirby shouldn't be surprised to hear The Followers of Urd wanted her dead, but shock and fury mingled with the exhaustion that made her limbs feel like lead weights. She really shouldn't have done what she did in the hotel.

She didn't regret it, though. Even one more life saved was worth some weariness.

She wanted to ask Vidar a long list of questions. How did she and Brit get here? Where was *here*? Why the fuck did he care about Kirby?

Only one question seemed critical. "I worked for FU for years. Why would they turn on me now?"

"You worked for *us* for years," Vidar said.

"You betrayed me first." A childish retort, but she was tired.

Vidar's smile chilled her. "We punished you. The same way we would have anyone who was found guilty of the things you were. Everything that came before and after was your choice."

Which was a whole giant pile of bullshit. They'd known she didn't commit the crimes in question, regardless of the lies fed to those who passed judgement on her. Hel had spent years both raising Kirby above her classmates and making sure everyone else resented her for it. Isolating her.

Kirby wouldn't argue with Vidar, though. It wouldn't produce any results, aside from her frustration.

"Nothing?" Vidar looked amused. "Very well. I'm sure FU is as grateful for your accomplishments on their behalf as we are. But you should know by now a body is only as useful as the most recent prophecy. Did you really think your current employers were more altruistic that us?"

Min and Starkad wouldn't work for FU. Not if they knew. "I did assume, yes."

"You were a means to an end. For us. For them. Just because their goals are different doesn't mean they accomplish them differently. They kill to ensure the prophecies happen, and that puts you on their list now."

"That's not right," Brit argued. "They save potentials. Keep TOM from executing them."

Vidar raised an eyebrow. "How many of those lives did you take? And now you're defending them? They trade one life for another. Each potential saved is a god destroyed in their place."

37

It wasn't even close to the same. One was direct execution because of something someone wrote thousands of years ago, and the other was allowing people to make their own choices and live their lives.

"Right. Whatever," Kirby said.

"You don't have to believe me." Vidar shrugged. "You'll learn the truth soon enough on your own." He clapped. "Right. Would you like a tour of the place?"

What? "Are you going to cuff us and prance us around the facility like trophies?" Kirby searched for a reason in his offer, and that was the best she could find. "What's to stop us from leaving?"

The soldiers with Vidar leveled their weapons at her and Brit.

"You shot me when we arrived. You know that won't kill us," Brit said.

The sneer that covered Vidar's face was his most terrifying expression yet. "The bullets that struck Kirby on the old campus? All of these soldiers have them."

"I haven't been on campus in years. And I was never shot there." Sometimes it was handy to have been trained in the art of complete and total bullshit.

"I have the survivors. I know you were there. Besides, your blood was spilled, and your magic radiated through the campus as I was taking them. The bullets won't kill all immortals, but they'll kill most, and they *will* ensure you see a fourteenth life."

At least he'd tipped his hand quickly. He must not be the master of deception Hel was.

"You said you brought us here to keep Kirby alive." Brit saw the same flaw in his words.

38

Vidar nodded. "I did. FU will destroy you. *Is no more* implies your obliteration. If we shoot you and don't reverse the damage, you'll be reborn again. I wish to see you survive, but I won't sacrifice my existence for yours."

"At least you're honest about where you draw the line." Sarcasm oozed from Brit's words.

"I'm not Hel. I'll tell you directly what I want."

Kirby suspected that wasn't true. He might not use the same deep-seated manipulation tactics as Hel. Then again, he might. Time would tell if they stuck around here. "So... What? You think you'll tell us your story and we'll all be buds and want to hang out with you?"

Vidar's chuckle was chilling. He had the evil-villain laugh down. "No. I don't trust you any more than you do me. Let me rephrase my offer. Would you like to see your prison for however long is needed?"

"We'd love that," Kirby said flatly. Regardless of the fact that she didn't intend to stay long, she wasn't going to turn down a tour of the facility.

Vidar waved his hand, and the cell door opened. He turned his back on Kirby and Brit—arrogant bastard—and walked out of the room.

Two soldiers urged Kirby and Brit forward and fell into step behind them. The light brush of Brit's fingers over the back of Kirby's hand meant Brit would take point.

They moved into the hallway, and Kirby's gut twisted in on itself. This was too much like the TOM campus. As they moved down the corridor, then up a winding ramp to the next floor, her discomfort grew.

The layout in this building was nearly identical to the administration building, where a handful of holding cells sat in the basement.

Why wasn't she free of this place?

They reached the main floor, and bile burned up her throat. She'd been here less than a week ago, in Loki's office upstairs. "What'd you do? Recreate the entire TOM campus?" She failed to keep her voice light.

"It's not identical, but there are a lot of similarities," Vidar said.

Why wouldn't this place just go away? Kirby wasn't doing this again. She wasn't getting involved with TOM for *the greater good*. Not even for her life.

She bumped her toe against the side of Brit's leg, enough to be felt but not enough for it to make either woman's step falter.

Brit moved aside.

"We'll be leaving now." Kirby only had one real magical attack. She could inflict the pain of all of her deaths on a single person. She'd feel the agony too, but she'd been practicing ignoring that. She dragged up the pain and focused on Vidar.

She fired as he spun.

He held up a hand, and magic crackled around him.

Kirby's attack flooded her with an intensity she wasn't used to, stealing her breath and forcing grief to her heart. She stumbled to her knees, the burn reverberating through her body.

CHAPTER TWELVE

MIN

Min knew Frey owned a modern burlesque club, but had never made visiting a priority.

From the street, the building looked like any other windowless brick shell. The entire block was an unassuming shade of beige. The door Aya unlocked, with the vibrant blue-to-purple logo that said NEON, was the only indicator of what lay on the other side of the walls.

"It looks different at night, when it's open," she said as she let him in.

Frey, Gwydion, and someone named *Dahlia* would be joining Min and Aya soon.

Gwydion had been able to move himself and anyone with him from one place to another by opening a gateway into the faery realm, and then an exit someplace else. However, entrance into the other plane had been granted by Aeval, Queen of the Fae, and she'd since then revoked access, so she could focus on healing her people.

The lobby held more of a hint of the business beyond, with dark wood and leather seats, wood-paneled walls, and an actual neon NEON sign near the host podium.

Over the centuries, Min had watched the evolution of clubs meant to speak to and sate human sexuality. His own ceremonies had been epic events, brightly lit, with laughter and vibrancy radiating from everyone and everything.

Frey's fertility celebrations had probably been similar in the beginning, but a god evolved with the world around them, or they faded. The main room here was more darkness, even with the lights turned on. Black walls; black-stained bar, tables, and chairs; and a dark stage.

The fact that the patrons were seated separately from the dancers spoke to how taboo pleasure had become in modern society. Even the lust and desire trapped within the walls were peppered with the foul taste of guilt.

Then again, Min invested heavily in the internet and technology, to ensure people could indulge their kinks and fetishes from the safety of their own homes, never having to admit them if they didn't wish to.

"We're to make ourselves at home." Aya stepped behind the bar and grabbed a bottle from the top shelf. "Would you like anything?"

Drinking in this place would feel too much like mourning. "No, thank you."

"Suit yourself." Aya brought the bottle to a larger table at the edge of the room and picked a seat.

Min joined her, and they made polite small talk.

How are prayers?

How's faith treating you?

Any big surge in followers lately?

He wanted to dig into the details of what was happening. Why The Followers of Urd would want Kirby. What these prophecies were. Gwydion would want to know too, and Aya said she didn't have all the answers, so the interrogation would wait.

The others arrived a short while later. Min stood when he was introduced to Dahlia, and she stared at him with wide, eyeliner-rimmed eyes. "I knew it was you. I don't know why no one listened. But I *knew*."

"I beg your pardon?" Min studied the woman. Most people radiated life or death, depending on which they respected or feared more. She was startlingly neutral in that department. Curious.

She furrowed her brow and stared back. "Tech investor. One of the most private billionaires in the world. Super-imposing in person. *Wow.* When our... *their*—TOM's people—were killed? Failed missions? You were almost always in the same city. I told Hel, and she said you couldn't be involved. Then again, she was selective about what she heard me say. *Gods*, what a bitch. I mean... Sorry. I ramble when I'm nervous."

She was quite practiced at it. Almost as if she knew how to use the rambling to her advantage.

"You're TOM," Min said. That was the most important part of her statement. He was curious why she'd been tracking him, and whether she knew he was responsible for relocating potentials. If she had the same kind of training as Kirby and Brit, she wouldn't tell him unless it suited her purposes.

"Was. Don't shoot." She held up her hands with a laugh. "I'd like to say I got out, but no one left with the kind of flair Kirby did. I shouldn't call a suicide attempt and being rescued by a double agent of an instructor *flair*, should I? Insensitive. Sorry. I just kind of walked away when Hel died. Or rather, I would have, if it weren't for..." She dragged in a deep breath. "Doesn't matter. You're on their shit list too, so I'm in amazing company."

Min glanced at Gwydion, who shrugged. "She grows on you," Gwydion said.

"Indeed." Min didn't dislike Dahlia. A few months ago, he would have appreciated her enthusiasm. It made him uneasy that his first impression now was one of distrust. He'd spent weeks pretending to be a TOM soldier, and while he no longer shared the thoughts of the person he'd been impersonating, enough of the mindset lingered that trust no longer came naturally.

"Why were you looking for us? The full story," Min said. Dahlia wasn't the only one who made Min suspicious, and that bothered him more. Aya and Frey were old friends of Min's; he should trust them.

Frey dropped into the seat next to Aya, grabbed the bottle of gin from her, and took a long swallow. He gestured around the table. "Have a seat."

Dahlia took the chair next to Frey. Gwydion and Min sat together, with some space between them and the others.

"As I said before"—Aya took back the booze but didn't drink—"Dahlia uncovered some prophecies about the last Valkyrie. About all of you. When she told Frey, we agreed it was important you knew."

Min heard Kirby's skeptical *uh-huh* in his head.

Gwydion leaned back in his seat. "Last time we went to Aya for help, she was very distinct in your *no*. And now, just like that, you care?" He and Starkad had asked her for help, learning how to destroy Hel.

"Kirby is a faithful believer." Aya's smile was too pure. Too sweet.

"*Was.*" Min didn't buy their intentions for a second. Six months ago, would he have hesitated to believe them? Probably not. "You sought us out in the middle of a god-induced quake, because you were suddenly concerned about a single voice who *used to* worship you?" He would move heaven and earth for Kirby, but Freya had refused to help when fate said earth was in danger. Her about-face made no sense.

"Do you know who's responsible for the quakes?" Frey asked.

Min nodded.

Aya jerked visibly, and Frey grunted. Did she kick him under the table?

Frey glared at her. "We're going to tell them everything, anyway."

"All right." Aya sighed heavily.

Dahlia's silence was more disconcerting than her babbling. She alternated between studying her nails and fiddling with her hair. However, Min suspected she was listening and processing everything.

"Aya helped imprison Malsumis," Frey said. "The bond created between the gods who did so prevented her from speaking out against any of them, including Hel."

Aya took another drink. "I wanted to help. I wasn't physically or magically able, and I'm sorry for that. With Hel gone, that bond is broken."

"Going by all of the not-so-natural disasters striking around the world, Gluskab is looking for everyone responsible, and he can't have my sister," Frey said.

Gwydion looked between them. "And this has what to do with us...?"

Min had the answer, though. "You're offering information in exchange for protection."

"For an alliance," Aya corrected him. "I will not cower."

"I will." Dahlia raised her hand. "I found all of this. I'm giving it to Frey, in exchange for keeping me away from TOM, and he's using it to protect his sister. In other words, please don't kill me or tell anyone you heard this from me. I'm the terrified little mortal in this situation."

Gwydion nudged Min and met his gaze. Between Kirby's last life and this one, they'd traveled with each other for a few decades and spent a great deal of time together off and on over the centuries. They could say a lot without exchanging a single word.

And they were on the same page this time. Min gave him a faint nod.

"It should go without saying, but in case it doesn't, we only speak for ourselves. We'll help," Gwydion said.

They would have, regardless. It was hard to ignore centuries of friendship for a single bad decision. However—"I make no apologies when I say finding Kirby is more of a priority than protecting you. You knew she and the others were gone. How?"

Aya dipped her head. "You're wrong when you say her faith is in the past. I feel her, as I do any believer. Or I did, until the quakes started."

"And I knew the instant you all set foot in my city," Frey said. "I've known since she and Starkad moved in. I suspect the fact that I'm here—that most gods aren't interested in fucking with me—is why the two of them settled here. I also felt Starkad vanish, along with Brit."

"To be fair, they were looking for y'all before people *poofed*," Dahlia said. "The missing Valkyrie just gave them extra leverage."

Min raised an eyebrow, but amusement threatened inside. Gwydion was right; she was growing on him. "And you believe Urd took Kirby and the others because of a prophecy."

"A series of them, but those are the basics." Dahlia pulled a tablet from her messenger bag and made a series of swipes on the screen. "Because you're dying to know, this one is called *The Valkyrie and Her Court*. Since there's only one Valkyrie, and apparently you people orbit her…"

Min scanned the screen.
Life and death bind them

With the highs and lows
The aches and joy
And when she finds the balance in it all
The last Valkyrie will be no more

For a prophecy that started on a high note, it certainly didn't end well. Min couldn't ignore the trepidation tightening inside. "And you believe The Followers of Urd have Kirby to ensure the prophecy happens."

"That *is* what they do." Gwydion's retort was heavy.

Min would have liked to argue. He'd worked with The Followers of Urd for a long time, helping them relocate potential gods that TOM wanted dead lest they replace the current gods. Those altruistic actions didn't mean they were above taking an opposite approach if it meant achieving their goals. Urd herself never would have stood for such a thing, but no one had seen her in centuries, so she wasn't here to say otherwise. "I can speak with my contact there, to see if there are any murmurs about Kirby."

"No offense, but you're not exactly…" Frey winced.

"What?" Min asked.

Aya's smile didn't reach her eyes. "A dishonest person."

"Why would I take offense at that?"

"It means you're not the right guy to go poking around and asking questions with any degree of subtlety." Dahlia sounded like she spoke from experience. She probably did.

48

So did Min. "I understand that. I've had a shift in perspective, when it comes to some things, and I can do what I need to. My contact won't meet with anyone else in this room."

Frey studied him, eyes narrowed and brow furrowed. "Gods are like zebras—we don't change our stripes."

"I spent some time on the TOM campus, and I took on the form and mind of a soldier to do it. There are things the mind can't unlearn." Min wished he could.

Dahlia's jaw dropped, and a range of emotion from shock to grief splashed across her face. "You were there? When? It was when things blew up, wasn't it? Can you tell me what happened?"

Min gave her a brief rundown of capturing the other Nobles, and how Loki had executed them.

Sadness sank into her, dragging her entire frame into her seat. "I may not have shared their beliefs, but I grew up with them." Dahlia let out a bitter laugh. "I always wondered if Loki would be our downfall."

"I'm sorry." Frey covered her hand and stroked his thumb along the back of her knuckles.

She sniffled. "They would have come after me, anyway. I guess I'm safer this way, but... it hurts."

A lot more people would die if Gluskab wasn't stopped.

Min kept the thought to himself, but he couldn't ignore the heavy weight of that reality.

CHAPTER THIRTEEN

STARKAD

Starkad needed to find civilization. Find a phone with a signal. Get back to Kirby. "Point me to the nearest town, and I'll get out of your fur."

"About forty kilometers to the South West."

As Kirby would say—*fantastic. Not.* Near enough for Fenrir to reach on foot, but far enough it would be a painful hike for Starkad wounded and in human form. Especially through the heavy forest, with a sniper potentially hunting him.

If Starkad was right, though, they didn't want him dead, just distracted. Which meant, if they returned, he had to worry more about staying on course than about being mortally wounded.

His shoulder twinged, taunting him. "Enjoy your hunt. I'll be on my way."

"Fantastic." Fenrir's retort was flat.

Starkad pulled his shirt back on, ignoring the scream of protest from his body. He paused with his hand on the doorknob. As a human, he had better senses than most, but they weren't as good as a wolf's. He couldn't smell or feel anything outside, aside from the forest. "Are they still gone?"

Fenrir sniffed the air. "Yes." As Starkad opened the door, Fenrir tensed. "No."

A bullet dug into the frame, sending splinters flying and peppering Starkad with wood shrapnel. He slammed the door shut.

He wiped the back of his hand across his face, and pulled it away streaked with blood.

Fenrir sniffed the air again. "They're back. Several of them."

Just like that?

"Did they just appear out of nowhere?" Starkad was asking himself, as much as Fenrir.

"*You* did. Seriously, whom the fuck did you piss off?"

"The same person you did, I assume. Whoever sent me here didn't pick the spot you were by mistake. There's a reason I appeared in front of you." Starkad moved to the window on a next wall. The tactics of this attack made him think they were surrounded. He cracked the window. Another bullet bit into the side of the house.

Not the window, though. He was right—they weren't shooting to kill. The intention was to keep Starkad and Fenrir distracted.

"Maybe they hoped I'd destroy you, so they wouldn't have to." Fenrir was snide.

"Or that we'd beat each other into exhaustion."

"They didn't shoot me."

Touché. "So why didn't you?" Starkad asked.

"Destroy you?" Fenrir moved to the rear of the cabin. "I'm not you. I loathe the decisions you've made, but whom I war with is a conscious decision based on my beliefs, not on whichever side lets me kill the most." He cracked the door. Another gunshot and another hail of splinters.

Starkad wasn't buying the too-righteous-to-murder-him line. Not completely. "You've thought about it."

"I'm still thinking about it. But if they're here for both of us, I have to bank on your seeing them as more of a threat than me."

"Everyone's a threat right now." Starkad couldn't shift, but he could still pull a trigger. "I need a gun."

Fenrir growled.

"What now?"

"I'd rather confront them face to face," Fenrir said. "Rip their throats out with my bare teeth."

Starkad understood the sentiment. "If you don't have any firearms in the house, that's a great way to get one."

"We're hunters, not assassins. We don't hide in the shadows and pick people off from a distance." Disdain hung heavy in Fenrir's words.

If only life were that simple. "I'm a creature of war, and this is war."

"No. This is the kind of battle Loki loves—deception and hiding in the shadows. You're a berserker; you were created to toe-to-toe, face-to-face with your foes."

And Starkad had. For centuries. His drive to immerse himself in the fight, to not feel anything else, was why Fenrir was wary of him. It didn't change the fact that wars were fought in the shadows now.

Fenrir sighed. "As much as I hate it, that kind of sneaking around is what we need right now. Tell me what to do."

"I'd suggest we test their perimeter to find the weaknesses, but if they have a god helping them, everything can change in an instant." This was easy. A mindset Starkad fell into without hesitation. "We'll assume there's one team per each door and window. Tree line is closest on the East, so we'll exit that door. I'll go first—draw fire. You find the muzzle flash, and run toward it once they're focused on me."

"I'm not faster than a bullet, and they've already proven theirs incapacitate you."

True. But— "This is about catching them off guard. You're faster than they are, and they don't want to kill us. Just keep us here. Use the shadows, hit them before they know what's happening, and bring me back a fucking gun."

On the one hand, it would be nice if the weapon included some of whatever rounds had hit Starkad. But if their effect was cumulative or if the bullets were hard to make, it was unlikely the snipers had them. In the short term, that was good. Less chance of Starkad or Fenrir taking another of those shots.

"And then?" Fenrir asked.

"I take out the rest of them, and I'm armed and on my way." Starkad spoke through clenched teeth as another spike of pain hit.

"Reinforcements?"

Starkad had to make a lot of assumptions with this plan. He hated not having all the details, but he and Kirby had operated with less over the years. "It's not a video game with unlimited bad guys. They only have so many soldiers, and sending them in wave after wave means they have a lot fewer."

Fenrir shook his head. "It's a shitty idea."

"It's a shitty situation. Do you have a better idea?"

"No."

"Then let's do this."

Starkad opened the back door and stepped outside. A quarter-sized crater exploded in the side of the house, next to his head. Fenrir-wolf dashed past, a blur of nighttime heading toward the source of the gunfire. Another *plink* of a suppressed gunshot accompanied a cloud of dirt. Fenrir was long past that. He might not be faster than a bullet, but in the darkness, with the short distance between the house and trees, he was almost impossible for the human eye to track or lead.

A series of soft *thunks* filtered from the trees, accompanied by a handful of grunts.

Starkad had to admire the soldiers' commitment to not screaming and giving their position away, even in the midst of dying.

Fenrir returned quickly, and he and Starkad secured themselves inside again. Dark red dripped from Fenrir's fur and left paw prints everywhere he stepped. He dropped an AUG at Starkad's feet.

Starkad did a basic weapon check. Time was of the essence. The magazine was the 42-round variant, with only five shots fired. The ammo left should be enough. If it wasn't, the hole in Starkad's arm was a reminder he had more to worry about than running out of bullets.

They took positions near the first window—fortunately the cabin didn't have many—and enacted a similar plan to before. Starkad drew the fire, and Fenrir located the source. With a target in mind, Starkad knew where to look when he popped his head back up in the window. He tracked the muzzle flash and the silhouettes it left behind, and squeezed off two shots.

Another pair of *thunk*s sounded from the treeline.

Celebration would wait until everyone was gone. And probably until the agony in his shoulder subsided. Each recoil from the rifle jarred him, sending daggers of pain slicing along his skin.

They cleared the remaining exit points—windows and doors—with sharp efficiency. Then did another sweep to ensure no one else waited in the shadows.

Adrenaline still raced through Starkad's veins, but his throbbing limb dragged him to the floor with a gasp. He couldn't do another round of firing. Willpower would only take him so far, before he blacked out from the pain. He knew that from experience, and he'd pushed past his limits tonight.

Chapter Fourteen

BRIT

Vidar watched Kirby and Brit, eyebrow raised. "Do you have that out of your system?"

"Yes." Brit spoke before Kirby could. "For now, at least." This wasn't the time or place to fight, and whatever made Kirby forget that...

Brit understood, though. This place looked so much like home. No, not *home*, the past. Kirby looked more like *home* than anything. It wasn't the time for the thought, but Brit couldn't help it.

"Kirby needs to sleep." Magnus sounded concerned. "I'll get them a room." There was a unique blend of deference and command in her tone.

Vidar nodded. "Take them with you." He pointed to six of the soldiers. "Give our guests a room in housing." He focused on Brit and Kirby. "We'll speak in the morning. Please keep in mind, I'm not Hel. I have a great deal of respect for your skills and who you are. There's no competition here. Not like that."

"Thanks for the recruitment speech." Brit didn't try to hide her sarcasm. "We'll be sure to not take it into consideration."

"Keep in mind, Sergeant Hauge, your time here will be a bit prison like at first. You know how it goes—you can have freedom or security, but you can't have both. Rest well." Vidar turned on his toe and strode away.

Brit hated gods.

"Let me show you the digs," Magnus said lightly. "You'll love it. It's almost like we never left."

"Swell." Kirby slipped her hand into Brit's and squeezed.

The sweet gesture sent a rush of familiarity and warmth through Brit, but the way Kirby leaned her weight into it marred the experience with concern. This wasn't about making a connection; Kirby needed to lean on her for support.

They stepped from the main building, and Brit's gut twisted in on itself. She hid the reaction. This wasn't identical to the old campus, but it was too fucking close for her comfort.

"I miss the trees." Magnus was conversational. "So far the weather isn't as intense here, though."

"Where's *here*, approximately?" Brit asked.

Magnus glanced at them with a smirk. "Not the northeastern part of the US. I could get more approximate, if you'd like."

"Nah. We're good." Kirby was mostly upright, but every few steps she wobbled.

Brit supported her. Their path was taking them straight toward where Noble housing was on the old campus. Odds seemed high it would be the same here.

"So what have you two been up to?" Magnus's question sounded like casual small talk, the way Brit's about location had. This was all low-level interrogation bullshit, though. If a detail slipped, anything that could be used to learn more, any of them would stash it for future reference.

Brit plucked an answer out of thin air. "I've been teaching English as a second language to Martian refugees in New Mexico."

"Oh, *wow*." Magnus sounded genuinely fascinated. "Area 51?"

"Nah. An *actual* Top Secret black site. I could be shot for even talking about it," Brit said.

Magnus tapped her claw against her chin. Interesting tic. Intentional or not? "I probably shouldn't ask you more, in that case. Kirby?"

"I'm a chaplain in Kuwait. US Army." Kirby's answer wasn't fabricated at all. According to Min, that was her last life.

"I didn't realize the army had a lot of Freya worshipers," Magnus said.

Kirby squeezed Brit's hand more tightly. It was hard to tell whether it was because of the Freya comment or the fact that they'd just stepped into a building that might as well be their old apartments.

"It's more of a nondenominational thing." Kirby's light retort defied the tension vibrating through her grib. "You know, I won't yuck your yum, as long as your god doesn't try to kill me."

They stepped into the elevator, and Magnus pushed the button for the fourth floor. "You and I always had some differences of opinion. I hope we can still be friends."

"I'm sure we can." Brit and Kirby spoke at the same time, but Kirby's retort held a lot more sarcasm.

This wasn't right, though. Not just the creepy recreation of a place that had been turned to rubble less than a week ago, but also Magnus's behavior.

Brit had always liked Magnus and Dahlia. They were genuine. Not the phony make-everyone-think-you-like-them that most of the Nobles practiced, but actually kind. Fun. And they'd never struck her as zealots.

Maybe it had all been an act, but pretending to not be brainwashed by the cult one was trapped in didn't seem like the smartest thing to pretend.

They reached their floor. The walk down the hallway was half-eerie-flash-to--past, half-march to their execution.

They stopped in front of room 404—Kirby's old room number. Magnus unlocked the door, then pocketed the key. "There's food in the fridge and cupboards. Clothes in the dresser. If you need anything, there will be guards outside your door. Just ask them."

"Thanks." Brit had lost all desire to fake sincerity. The room they were shown into was identical to Kirby's old room.

It wasn't decorated the same, but Kirby had the biggest room of any Noble. Partly because of her position, and presumably as another of Hel's manipulations.

"See you in the morning." Magnus closed the door behind them, and the audible clicking of a lock sound filled the air.

Kirby leaned her back against a nearby wall, and her shoulders slumped. Exhaustion shone in the lines on her face and the dark circles under her eyes. "She didn't even give us the grand tour."

"Rude, right? I guess we'll have to show ourselves around." In other words, time to take a look and see what they'd been handed. Brit both hated that the double talk came so easily, and adored that she and Kirby still had that connection they'd shared as partners.

It was a basic apartment. A kitchenette, small living room, and bedroom with bath. The bedroom was where Brit stalled.

Last time she was in this room—no, just a room like this—with Kirby, she'd known she was going to betray the woman she loved. This campus was a replica, and missing the people who made her old life miserable, so the triggers weren't there. But this room... this woman... Brit wouldn't fall into it, but fuck she wanted to.

All of the food in the kitchen was either vacuum sealed or canned. Nothing gourmet, but edible and nutritious. "So great to be back," Kirby said sarcastically, as she eyed the shelf full of beans and peaches.

There were two sets of dressers. Brit checked the top drawer of each. White cotton bras and panties. "Is it just me, or is it creepy someone else went underwear shopping for us?"

"Creepier that they're the right size." Kirby fingered a lingerie label. "If there are uniforms in the other two drawers, I *will* try to kill myself again." Her laugh fell short.

Brit stared at her, not sure how to respond.

"Kidding." Kirby's weak smile shifted to too bright in a heartbeat. "Do you think we have the full security package in this place?"

"One assumes." Brit agreed the suite probably had full-coverage cameras and mics.

What was in the drawers wasn't as important as what was eating at Kirby. It seemed unlikely she'd open up to Brit even under good circumstances, but here, with an audience...

Then again, the *here* was probably the issue. If Brit hated being reminded of that last night the two of them spent together on campus, it had to be devouring Kirby.

"I'm sorry." Brit's lungs squeezed tight, as she let the memory and guilt linger. "Nothing I can say feels sufficient. It was my decision—"

"You were under duress." Kirby's tone was tighter than her casual dismissal.

True. Mark had told Brit her life on campus would never get better if she didn't sell out Kirby. He assured her Kirby would recover. But Brit's life got worse, and that night, Kirby tried to end her own.

For years, Brit thought Kirby succeeded. Brit had no idea Starkad had rescued her. Taken her away from all of this.

Brit had been pressured, but she'd also been selfish. "I wish I could do that night—the next morning—over again." Saying the words left her throat raw and the confession took a chunk of guilt with it. She'd rarely dared let herself think that, let alone admit it.

"In a way, you can. How many people get that kind of second chance? Don't sell me out in the morning." There was no more fakeness in Kirby's voice or expression. There was no more of any emotion.

"Never again." The assurance wasn't enough. Could it ever be?

Chapter Fifteen

KIRBY

Being here shouldn't hurt like this, driving into her thoughts and gnawing at her soul. It had been years. Kirby should be able to shrug off the past like shedding a jacket.

Instead, the past played out bright and vividly in her mind. The hurt. The betrayal. The doubt. The press of a cool razor against her wrists. The thick, dark red of the blood.

Brit watched her with pained concern. It was genuine—Kirby knew that, after living in Brit's head, as well as she knew what kind of duress Brit had been under back then.

But the present overlapped with an intensely vivid memory of Brit sitting with a review board of gods, calling Kirby a monster. Accusing her of abusing her power. Shattering everything they had.

"Kirby?" Brit kept her distance, and concern bled into her voice. She wasn't wearing a mask anymore.

Did seeing how she really felt make things better or worse?

It was a struggle to keep these emotions below the surface. Kirby wanted to hug herself. Shiver until it all went away. Better—she wanted to be back home. Safe. Away from this bullshit. She met Brit's gaze. "The *attack* I have, that allows me to inflict pain on someone else." The one she'd tried to use on Vidar. A stupid move, because she felt what he felt.

"I remember it."

Brit would. Kirby had used it right after she discovered who she was. After the memories of her past lives came back. "It's the pain of every one of my deaths. I recognize them individually. Being shot by bullets. Arrows. I died of Tuberculosis once." She dragged in a shuddering breath and forced herself to step outside her head. "And I remember how much my heart and body hurt, as I bled out on the shower floor. The shower that looked identical to that one." She nodded to the bathroom.

"*Fuck.*" Horror splashed across Brit's face.

Kirby couldn't have conveyed a more appropriate emotion. "Starkad thinks he saved my life that night." No one knew this. She hated to think about it, because of the emotions attached to that specific death. But being here, the memory was impossible to ignore.

"I died before he got here. But I came back. If he hadn't found me, I assume I would have awoken to exactly what Hel wanted—a Valkyrie she could manipulate and control." Or maybe Starkad saved her in more ways than just taking her away from here. Maybe it was his showing up that brought her back.

Brit crossed her arms with a shiver. "I don't know what to say."

"You could apologize again." Kirby let her voice go flat.

"I'm so—"

"Don't. Just... Please. I know you're sorry. Hearing it again won't make any of this easier to accept." Kirby thought being in Brit's head, feeling her remorse and her side of the story, had made things better. It certainly told Kirby that Brit was sincere. That she'd changed. But apparently it hadn't healed all of Kirby's thoughts about the past.

"Then what? Anything."

Kirby needed to not feel this. Not now. When she was somewhere safe and could process, but not in this den of vipers. "Get me through tonight." She needed new memories here. Or a distraction. Or something. "And don't betray me in the morning."

Kirby kissed Brit hard. Desperately. Crushing their mouths together and pouring herself into the physical connection. If Kirby blocked out the past, this felt right. Incredible. The kind of kiss that she could lose herself in until it consumed her.

They broke apart with a gasp, but didn't pull away from each other. Brit glided her mouth to Kirby's ear.

"—audience?" Brit was breathless, the heat of her question falling softly against Kirby's skin.

Kirby didn't give a fuck who watched. This wasn't about their captors. "Do you think I care? Do you?"

Brit shook her head. "I just want to be with you."

"So fucking obsessive and unhealthy."

"That I love you, or that you're trying to fuck away the pain?" Brit didn't pull away.

"Do you want to stop?"

"No." Brit's kiss was as intense and desperate as the Kirby's racing thoughts.

It was breath. It was life. It bordered on insanity and Kirby found it both harder and easier to remember how much she used to trust Brit.

How much she still wanted to. Needed to.

Kirby trailed her fingers down Brit's sternum, never breaking the hungry kiss, and slipped under the waistband of Brit's jeans. The fresh contact with skin cranked Kirby's need higher. She pushed up the bottom of Brit's shirt, wanting more of that physical connection.

Brit grabbed her wrist. "Stop." There was no force behind the word.

Kirby pulled away, her mind a jumble of lust-clouded confusion. "What's wrong?"

Brit tugged her closer again, leaving millimeters between them, but not making contact beyond her grip. "This place fucked us both up. I don't deny that. And dealing with the scars hurts like hell. I can't even imagine…" She sighed. "I want to be with you, in every way, but I swore when I left that I'd never be someone's outlet again. Not even yours."

"So that's what Meatloaf meant," Kirby said softly. The reference was easier than forcing her thoughts into line.

Brit furrowed her brow. "What?"

"Forget it. That part, anyway." Kirby sank onto the edge of the bed. "And I get it."

"I'm sorr—"

"*No.*" Kirby kept her tone firm. "Not for this you're not. I am, though." Reality was crashing in around her again, but not as hard as she'd expected. Through it all, she could see a light that hadn't existed before. A reminder that the past shaped her, but didn't define her. "I'm sorry."

Brit squeezed Kirby's hand. "Ask anything else of me, and you can have it."

Kirby didn't question that for an instant. After all they'd been through, the lies and betrayal and death... She believed Brit was being sincere.

"*Self destructive.*" The word slipped softly past Kirby's lips. It was better than a sob, and it was only meant for Brit's ears. Kirby didn't care if the world wanted to watch her fuck, but TOM wasn't getting in her head again.

Brit pressed closer. "I wasn't going to—"

"It's what Starkad called me." So many times.

Brit's growl was low but threatening. Almost like a wolf's.

Kirby twisted her lips, to hide her sardonic smirk. "I know you think that after he took me away from here—the other *here*—he and I fucked non-stop, like the closeted lovers we must have been on campus." Kirby wasn't guessing. Brit had all but spoken those thoughts several times. "But we weren't—either one of those things. He kept me at arm's length for so long…" At least this part of the story didn't hurt the way it used to. Kirby understood now that the circumstances had been unique.

"After everything the two of you shared in the past?" Brit laced her fingers with Kirby's and traced a thumb over the back of her knuckles. "I mean, Min told me a little when he was explaining your curse and how each time he fell in love with you. Min adores you intensely, by the way."

Kirby was aware. "Starkad thought he was doing me a favor by not loving me while I didn't have my memories. And—*fuck*—it hurt at the time." Why was she dumping all of this now? Here? To Brit?

Because Brit needed to understand her. She couldn't climb into Kirby's head, but if she listened… If she heard…

"You've forgiven him, though." Brit's question was a blend of hopeful and snide.

Neat trick. "We worked through it. Since I regained my memories, I've spent a lot of time denying my pasts. I don't want the actions of some other me to define who I am now. But the longer her—*their*, my—memories live in my head, the harder it is to distinguish this life from past emotions. I can see now why I loved Starkad. Gwydion. Min. And I don't want to fight it anymore."

"What does that mean for us?" Brit asked.

"You assume there's an *us*."

"I hope. Possibly more than anything I've ever hoped for, including top sniper marks." A hint of teasing slid into Brit's voice.

A smile slipped out without Kirby's permission. "You have to be okay with me and them. They all are." She'd never put that into words before. Not now or in the past. Min and Gwydion always treated it like a given—that they'd both be by her side—and she'd never lived long enough before to piece the same together with Starkad. "They've been here for centuries, and I won't choose."

"I just want to be a part of your life. Not like a loyal puppy. Not the way I saw myself before, in your shadow. I want to be by your side."

Kirby hadn't realized how much she needed to hear that. "We make a better team as equals."

Being in this clone of her childhood *home*, there was the one good memory rushing back. One that made it so much easier to remember the good with Brit.

Until the trial, until Kirby was stripped of her rank, took her own life, she and Brit had been brilliant together. Always came out on top.

But with furious and vengeful gods running rampant, and people believing Kirby was on her last life, the stakes were a lot higher if she and Brit failed this time.

CHAPTER SIXTEEN

STARKAD

The orange sunrise peeked above the mountains, bathing the forest in a stunning wash of light. Sitting around here wasn't doing Starkad any good. The longer he waited, injury growing worse each second, the worse the hike back to town would be.

"I'll go," Fenrir said. "I just need an outside line, and I can bring someone back here to get you."

"If TOM comes back while you're gone, I'm fucked." Starkad hated that he couldn't handle this on his own. "And if they hit you in the forest... Similar problem."

Fenrir sighed. "Fine. We'll trek back together."

Conversation was sparse as they headed into the forest. The bodies were gone. Efficiency at its finest.

There was no clear path, but Fenrir didn't hesitate choosing his direction. Starkad wasn't so steady. With his energy sapped and a steady thrum of pain making him stumble, even making it a meter was like crawling through molasses.

He refused to be dead weight. He stumbled over fallen brush and wove through low-hanging trees. It was a chore, though.

With dawn flowing from a faint glow to early-morning sunshine filtering through the leaves, it was easy to tell how much time had passed.

This was taking too long. Starkad loathed feeling like deadweight.

If he could access his wolf form, he'd heal faster. He'd have the strength in his legs to run. Losing his sensibility, going feral, seemed like a small price to pay for getting out of this quickly.

Fenrir would—probably gleefully—stop him from hurting anyone if it came to it.

The sunlight faded as they hit a thicker patch of trees. The underbrush grabbed at Starkad's feet and legs, leaving long scratches through denim. His arm pulsed in agreement with the aches.

He reached deep, past the pain, to grab his wolf. His body screamed in protest, and he stumbled. Mentally, he brushed something. He stumbled, and his wolf whimpered as it slipped out of his grasp.

If he could just reach a little deeper and push past the distraction of pain, he could shift. He couldn't do it while they walked, though. Both actions required too much attention.

He and Fenrir continued forward.

Starkad hit another buried root and stumbled again.

"Let's take a break." Fenrir settled onto a nearby rock.

"If you're tired." Starkad gave him a tight smile.

Fenrir pulled his phone out, studied it, and shook his head. "Still no signal."

Of course not. Now probably wasn't the time to rib Fenrir about not having inherited his father and sister's ability to teleport.

Instead, Starkad focused inward again. It was easier to reach for the wolf this time. He coaxed, like talking a terrified pup out from behind the couch. His body roared with protest, and the wolf receded.

He had to push a little deeper, though.

Just a little closer.

Almost there.

And then he grasped it by the nape of the neck. He shoved past the agony and yanked.

The tug ripped free a scream of pain that became a howl.

Pain.

Hunger.

Rage.

Death.

"Starkad?"

Predator.

Friend?

Fenrir.

"Follow," friend-enemy commanded.

Starkad chased.

CHAPTER SEVENTEEN

KIRBY

Kirby wasn't surprised to be woken by a knock on the apartment door, but that didn't stop her gut from lurching on a wave of flashback.

"I'll get it." Brit squeezed her hand, and climbed from bed and yanked on some clothes.

Kirby did the same. "No. We don't do anything without each other while we're here."

"Flip a coin for who takes point?"

Kirby patted her empty pockets. "No coins. Rock, paper, scissors?"

"You guys up?" Magnus's call carried in from the living room.

Right. They couldn't have opened the door for their visitor if they wanted to—they'd been locked in for the night.

"I have your back," Brit said. "We're up," she called.

Kirby forced her feet to move, one and the other, and repeat, without stalling, while Brit followed.

Magnus stood in the kitchenette, three coffee cups in a carrier on the counter. "I wasn't sure how Kirby likes her coffee. Build your own?" She pointed to a paper bag next to the drinks.

Kirby's mind froze. There were no campus police demanding she accompany them. No terse orders. But her brain chanted *wait for it.*

"Chocolate?" Brit stepped around her, brushing the back of her hand.

The barely-there touch was enough for Kirby to shake off the haze and stuff it away.

Magnus slid one of the cups across the bar top. "Plus caramel and extra whipped cream. I *do* remember how you like it."

Brit grabbed the drink and took a long swallow.

"It's still hot." Magnus winced.

Brit shrugged. "I wanted the caffeine more than those taste buds. They'll grow back in a few seconds."

Interesting approach, since Brit would feel the burn regardless.

Then again, Kirby didn't judge when it came to how people liked their pain. She joined them, and dumped copious amounts of sugar into her coffee. "No food? Is today's plan to overload us with sugar and caffeine until we crash?"

"The two of you were always capable of a sugar binge without help." Magnus's tone was playful. And she was right.

"Fair point." Brit nodded.

Magnus sipped her drink more slowly. "I thought we'd go get breakfast. Catch up, away from prying eyes and cameras."

"If you're there, you *are* the prying eyes," Brit said.

"Yeah, that's true."

"Tell me someone didn't recreate that entire little town that the campus was next to." Kirby wanted to be joking, but a slice of fear said this was all so surreal, her fear was possible.

Magnus studied her. "No. Not that it matters, because we're not going into town. What's your favorite city for fun? Or for food, if the two are different for you."

So many of Kirby's memories were attached to loss and grief, and it would be wrong to mar the truly bright favorites by sharing the moment or the place with anyone working with their captors.

"Salt Lake City," Brit said.

Kirby and Magnus looked at her with disbelief.

Magnus fiddled with her finger-ring. "That place is repressed as fuck."

"Not if you know where to look." Not that Kirby'd had much time to explore, but she'd done her research before going in. "It's also—"

"Got fantastic cake shops, and I never really got to try any." Brit looked at Kirby. She was trying to convey something in her expression. With her eyes.

The only thing Kirby remembered about cake shops was the one where she'd tracked down Brit. The primary setting for Hel's torturing Kirby, when she required Brit to shoot her over and over again in a dream-like world, to prove Brit's loyalty.

"It's early there. I doubt the cake shops are open." Magnus grabbed her phone and scrolled. "I can find us an outdoor café and bakery, though."

"That'll work." Brit was still watching Kirby.

No it wouldn't. That would suck.

Or would it? Kirby had ascended in Salt Lake. Regained her memories there. It was also the last mission she or Brit had done in a city. Though it was more than six months ago, the memories lingered near the surface of all the intel and prep-work Kirby did for her visit. It'd be the same for Brit.

"There's a place near one of the universities. Opens early. Serves amazing chocolate croissants. At least, I've heard. I didn't get a chance to go." Brit frowned.

Magnus held up her phone to share a series of images. "Outdoor patio? Gaming café?"

"That's the place."

"We're not sitting outside." Kirby might be a bundle of stress-teetering-on-destruction, but her training was ingrained in her.

Magnus pocketed her phone and took another sip of coffee. "Because someone might shoot you? One—you'd survive. Two—if we wanted to shoot you, we wouldn't take you off campus. And three—Vidar and I aren't stupid. No one else is going to pay any attention to us. I've been hooked up."

Kirby knew the trick; Gwydion did something similar. It had its flaws, though. "That kind of soft illusion doesn't work on everyone. If people are looking for *us*, they'll find us." Besides, Vidar didn't have that kind of magic, and Magnus didn't have any kind of magic.

"They won't. Are we going or not?" Magnus fiddled with her ring. She did that a lot. TOM training had beaten the obvious tells out of all of them, which meant she'd wanted to draw attention to the jewelry since last night.

"Chocolate croissants it is." Kirby wasn't going to learn anything, sitting around here. If Magnus was taking them out in public, Vidar allowed it for a reason.

Magnus held out her hands, and Brit and Kirby each took one. The apartment vanished, and an outdoor café took its place.

The relief that breathed through Kirby was tangible. Each breath came more easily. The tension in her neck loosened.

They stood in front of what had once been a house but now had a cute neon sign out front with a cartoon girl sitting on a coffee cup.

No one else was here yet. That was nice. Easier to see people approach. Less of a chance for collateral damage.

The interior was an odd combination of computers and tables to dine at. More sugary cuteness, straight out of a story.

Brit ordered them a plate of pastries to share, as well as more coffee.

"You still want to sit inside?" Magnus asked.

Kirby did, but more than that, she wanted to see how this safety of Magnus's worked. "It's a gorgeous morning, and I could use the fresh air."

Brit nodded her agreement.

They picked a table at the edge of the dining area, and all of them nibbled on sweets for a moment.

"Where's Dahlia?" As she asked, Kirby watched closely for any tick from Magnus.

Magnus's upper lip twitched. "Gone." She bit off the word.

Most Noble teams were well matched. Partners were as close as siblings or lovers, depending on the relationship. Magnus and Dahlia might as well have been sisters. The hurt in Magnus's voice was the one thing Kirby didn't question about this exchange.

Magnus waggled the finger with the full ring. "You're wondering why I want you to notice this. I've been waiting for you to ask, so I can tell you this was a gift from her. Your question works just as well, as a segue."

Min was right—it was stressful talking to people as mired in this lifestyle of deception as Kirby was. That included any back and forth she had with herself.

"Consider yourself asked," Brit said.

"She gave it to me as a promise." Sadness lingered in Magnus's reply. "That we'd leave TOM together."

If Dahlia was gone and Magnus was still here, it didn't seem like Dahlia was the one to break the promise.

"You're just admitting that?" Brit had chocolate on the corner of her upper lip.

Kirby reached to smudge it away with her thumb before she processed what she was doing. A spark raced between them, and a smile ghosted across Brit's face.

"The agreement was to leave Hel's TOM. Loki's. He's certainly a master of deception, but..."

"He's a shitty strategist. Yeah. Definitely not a military man." Kirby's laugh was a notch too high, as she tried to slide into casual, rather than stare at how Brit looked with the morning sun glinting off her hair and the flush of pink in her cheeks.

"The agreement was we'd find another god we believed in. One we could fight for. That's always been Vidar. You get that, don't you?" Magnus looked at Brit.

Brit shook her head. "I used to. Turns out gods are assholes the same way people are. They just have more power."

"Vidar is different." Spoken like a true believer. "You've seen for yourself he's not like Hel."

No. He was like salted-caramel asshole, instead of butter-pecan asshole. "He stuck us in a room identical to my old one. That was out of the kindness of his heart? There was no manipulation there?"

"It's still the biggest room in the dorm, and there are two of you." Magnus shrugged.

Good story. With so very many holes.

"Speaking of campus— What happened? Please tell me the truth." Pleading bled into Magnus's voice.

Brit sipped her coffee slowly. "I worked for Hel directly for a very short while before she was destroyed. I knew that her death would the fate of most people on campus."

"We couldn't let them die." There was no reason to lie about it, though there were some details Kirby wouldn't share unless called on it. She hadn't touched the food or coffee. "So we found a way back onto campus."

"*You* did." Magnus focused on her. "Every person there knew you were a shoot-on-sight target."

"She does a great impersonation of me." Brit grinned.

Kirby didn't adjust her posture or voice at all. "Look, I'm Brit. Howdy, howdy, howdy."

Magnus snorted with disbelief and laugher. "Fine. Keep your secrets. You may not believe me when I say this isn't part of the pitch to keep you here, but I missed you. Both of you."

"Same." Brit sounded sad.

Magnus looked at Kirby again. "No love?"

Kirby smiled. "If I had to be tracked down by one of the few remaining Nobles, I'm glad it was you." It would be wonderful to fall into old friendships, but these weren't the circumstances for that to happen.

"I'll take it." Magnus grinned. "What's it like, being immortal?"

"It's a pain in the ass." Though it was better than dying. Kirby suppressed a shudder as memories of so many deaths licked at the edge of her senses.

Brit nodded. "That pretty much sums it up."

"But… I mean… You get special powers, don't you?" Magnus asked. "One of you is a fucking Valkyrie. That can't be all bad."

"I can breathe fire. Shoot lightning from my fingertips," Brit said with a straight face.

Magnus's eyes grew wide. "Really?" She frowned. "Not really."

Brit grabbed a fork and jammed it into the back of her arm, hard enough to shake the table and splash coffee out of the cups. Her entire face screwed up in agony.

Magnus gasped in horror.

Blood pooled up from the four holes that appeared in Brit's skin. She grabbed a napkin and wiped it away, to expose that the wounds were already pink with new skin and closing up. "I heal." Pain strained her voice. "The same way I did in the cell. That's it. That's all I got."

Magnus shook her head, and the shock vanished from her face. "But Kirby tried to do something to Vidar. Some sort of attack."

"I can do a few things. Any Valkyrie can." Not the *project their deaths on a target* thing, though maybe. Hard to say, since the other Valkyries had stayed dead. "We weren't created to kill, but I can fight. Like normal, stuff we learned in school fight. The one magical attack I know, the one I tried to use on Vidar, is debilitating to me as well. Oh, I do have wings."

Magnus gasped and clapped once. "Can I see?"

"Not in public." Though it seemed like no one was paying attention to them. Whatever Magnus used to hide them was good.

Magnus worked her jaw and traced her thumb over the ring. "When we get back to campus?"

"All right." If they made it back to campus. Kirby didn't intend to return.

"What else can you do?"

Kirby would wonder if Magnus's fascination was fake—a way of extracting information—but Vidar knew what Valkyries were capable of. Kirby wasn't special in that regard. "I heal. Not just myself, but I can heal others." Except those encased in another god's magic, like Brit.

Inspiration struck. Kirby nudged Brit. "Remember how the mission went down in Salt Lake?"

"Oh yeah." Brit's enthusiasm looked genuine.

It couldn't possibly be, if she actually remembered. Brit's mission had been to kill a potential, and Kirby was there to stop her. Kirby did so by firing a grenade into the room Brit was in with her partner, Mark. The explosion disrupted their mission, drew too much attention, and put the entire city on high alert.

Kirby was going to try to do the same now, but by alerting the gods, instead of the people around them.

As long as Brit understood a lot of heads were about to turn in their direction, she didn't need to know the details.

"Don't do that," Magnus warned.

Kirby adopted an innocent expression. "Do what?"

"Seriously?" Magnus was exasperated. "We all had the same training. Don't do this double-talk bullshit. Don't fuck with this outing, please?"

"We're not. Are we?" Brit looked at Kirby with fake curiosity.

Kirby shook her head. "Nope."

Magnus sighed. "Salt Lake was the last time we saw Brit as *Brit*, aside from her brief stint with Hel. The two of you never did a mission there together. That explosion made national news as a terrorist threat. Don't blow us up. I'm the only one who won't survive something like that."

"I won't blow us up. Cross my heart." Kirby didn't trust Magnus, but she wasn't ready to kill her.

Magnus's scowl deepened. "I know you don't believe me, but I'm trying to win you both over. I genuinely want you to join us. This is a new system. A new structure."

"Which literally looks almost identical to the old one," Brit said.

Kirby didn't know if her plan would work, but she wanted Brit to be prepared. She nudged her partner's foot gently. "No blowing things up. I'm serious," Kirby said. "The other thing I can do is make a shield. I did it on campus, to keep people alive."

"That does seem pretty benign." Magnus looked hesitant to agree.

Kirby extended the shield to encase Magnus. "It's invisible. Flexible. And around you right now." She picked up the same fork Brit stabbed herself with, and threw it.

She was fast.

Magnus wasn't. She gasped and flinched as the fork bounced off the empty air, less than a millimeter from her shoulder, and clattered to the ground. She raised her eyebrows. "I didn't feel a thing."

"It comes in handy." Kirby extended the shield, rather than contracting it, and nudged Brit harder this time. The goal was to push the barrier through whatever Magnus had, keeping them hidden.

Magnus winced, then cringed. She shook her head a few times, as if trying to get rid of something. "What was that? Why did my ears ring?"

Because it worked. "Don't know. Never seen it do that before. It's like anything magical. It can clash with other magical things."

"I don't hear any explosions." Magnus was hesitant.

"I promised you." A bullet bit into Kirby's shoulder, and another into the sidewalk next to her. "Shit."

The women turned the table toward the source of gunfire and ducked behind it. Kirby extended the shield again, since the PVC wasn't going to protect them from anything except being seen.

"—the fuck?" Magnus asked.

Kirby held up her hands. "That wasn't me. I promise. We need to go. *Now.*" And hope whoever was hunting them wasn't trained as well as they were.

CHAPTER EIGHTEEN

MIN

Frey owned the entire block NEON sat on, including several luxury apartments that no one would suspect existed from looking at the outside of the building. He'd offered rooms to Min and Gwydion for as long as they needed.

Gwydion had excused himself to start making phone calls.

Min had other tasks to accomplish.

After centuries of waiting, Min had perfected the art of searching for Kirby. However, the overnight delay made him *twitchy*. Every hour that ticked away was another that she was in danger.

Thanks to decades of investments and working in the industry, Min had countless contacts in technology. He called in several favors to track trends across the globe. Unusual and abrupt weather patterns. Deaths. Plagues. Especially in those locations where gods who'd helped lock away Malsumis were located.

It helped keep track of Gluskab, and at the same time might reveal where Kirby was. And Starkad and Brit as well.

Morning approached, and with it his appointment with Lance—a long-standing member of The Followers of Urd. Aya could teleport and was *unwilling to sit around and do nothing while that bastard Gluskab hunts me down.* So she took Min to Barbados.

Lance ran a private security firm, and he did a large amount of his training in this facility. From the outside, it was an unassuming hut at the edge of the forest.

Upon knocking on the front door, the experience changed. A pleasant female voice came over an invisible intercom to ask for their information.

Min told her they had an appointment with Lance, and they were buzzed in. He knew from a previous visit it wasn't so straightforward. Cameras and various heat sensors had watched them approach, checked them out, and done facial recognition on them, all before they reached the door.

This was high tech anyway, but the fact that Lance was a dragon and older than humanity made the setup more intimidating.

As they stepped inside, instead of a living room they were in a modern reception area. White leather seats, frosted glass tables, and a sleek desk were laid out. The receptionist gave them a polite smile, and gestured to a door to her left. "You're expected. Head on down."

"Is he for real?" Aya muttered as the rode the elevator down. And down. And down.

"Quite."

They reached their destination, ten stories underground. Lance was waiting for them when the elevator doors opened.

"Glad you called." Lance's tone was pleasant, but his smile didn't reach his eyes.

Min was used to the forced sincerity, but he hoped life never wore on him the way it had Lance. Not even a thousand years from now. "Thank you for making time for us."

"Of course." Lance gestured down a concrete corridor. "Join me in my office?"

There was no indicator that they were walking through a massive box built in the water, under the island. Lance's people trained here. This was nothing like the TOM campus, which was more of a military school setting, meant to prepare students to blend into society while they learned to kill.

This was an underground bunker with no warmth. The faint plink of gunfire, and the muffled grunts and shouts of hand to hand combat barely reached them through the heavily insulated walls.

There were only three dragons, as far as anyone knew. Lance and his sisters had taken various forms through history, and in the past had frequently been seen as the villains, as they pushed to keep Urd's prophecies from being obstructed.

This time around, saving lives helped things fall into place, but looking back, Min shouldn't be surprised that they'd order Kirby's execution if they felt it was necessary to make the visions happen.

The realization made Min's blood run cold.

"I see you're dealing with a lot of quakes in your brother's part of the world." Lance's tone was conversational as he glanced at Aya.

She nodded. "The destruction is horrific."

"Hmm. It's a shame." His tone was cool. Removed.

Min didn't care for the callousness, but he was here for information. He wouldn't change Lance's perspective or get what he needed if he lost his temper. The prophecies The Followers of Urd were enforcing now centered on Ragnarök—the destruction and rebuilding of the world.

Any disaster, even if Urd hadn't mentioned it, brought things closer to that conclusion.

Min couldn't fathom the mindset. He was so tied to life on this world, that the disruption of it caused him physical pain.

"How's your Valkyrie?" Lance asked him.

Cutting straight to the point made things easier. If this was Lance's way of making Min think they didn't have Kirby, it was a thin pretense. Min and Lance had discussed Kirby before, because she worked for the organization via Starkad.

What if FU had used their knowledge of her TOM training to capture her? Min couldn't tumble down the *what-if* path. "She's wonderful. I can't tell you how grand it is to have her back. Alive."

"Is she around, then? I'd love to meet her," Lance said.

He'd never made that request before. Never seemed interested. "She's with Starkad. Most times, I'd rather not know what they're up to." Min hoped she really was with Starkad. She'd be safer that way.

"Ahh, such a delicious contradiction." Lance almost sounded reverent. "The god of life who loves a harbinger of death."

"She's not." Aya's retort held an edge.

Lance raised an eyebrow. "Oh? If she's there, so is death. Always, but especially now."

"Correlation versus causation," Aya said. "Kirby is balance. Everything about her keeps a foot in both life and death."

Lance's expression slid back to neutral. "I didn't realize you were a fan."

Neither did Min.

"It's hard not to respect someone like her." Was that awe in Aya's voice?

Lance's phone chimed, and he glanced at the screen. "Well, when she's back, let her know she has another fan. We'll have drinks. Excuse me." He stepped far enough away his voice was muffled as he answered the phone.

"She's back," Aya said softly as she glanced at Min, shock on her face.

"She's where?" Lance's question on the phone drifted back to them.

Kirby. "Can you take me to her?" Min kept his question quiet.

"I don't know what kind of situation she's in," Aya said.

"I don't care. Take me."

Chapter Nineteen

GWYDION

Gwydion stared at the original prophecy text Dahlia had uncovered, versus the translation courtesy of Frey and Aya. It was unlikely they'd misinterpreted something between the two languages, but the meaning may have changed.

It didn't matter how long he stared; the only thing he could do was guess at alternate interpretations. NEON was still closed. He, Frey, and Dahlia were sitting in the main room, lights on, trying to find anything that could help... anyone.

"That kind of focus, I'd expect you to have figured out how to manipulate time and space by now." Dahlia's tone was light. She took the chair across from him at the table and slid him a can of Red Bull.

Not usually Gwydion's thing, but it was the thought that counted. "If I could do that..."

"You'd what?" Dahlia asked. "Serious question. If you could manipulate time and space, what would you do?"

Gwydion stared at condensation dripping down the can, as he tossed the question around in his head. There were so many things in his past that he'd wished at the time had happened differently. But they all brought him to here and now. If he changed anything, what would he surrender instead? "I don't know."

"No?" Dahlia popped the top on her drink and took a long swallow. "You don't have some grand plan to right all the wrongs? Remake this place in your image?"

"That would be a remarkably dull place. I'm great and all, but I work better with an audience."

She laughed. "I've never met a god like you before." Words offered so casually, as if meeting gods was an everyday occurrence.

"Funny?"

"Relatable," Dahlia said.

It wasn't a common trait among gods. "I've never met a Noble like you."

"Ex. Know a lot of us, do you?"

"More exes than currents. Don't you usually travel in pairs?" It was a question Gwydion had since last night.

Her expression slipped. "We do. But Magnus and I had a difference in opinion."

"About what? If I may ask."

"What qualities make a god worth knowing." Dahlia's smile was back, but it didn't reach her eyes. "She wanted someone to worship; I'm over that."

Gwydion was over being worshiped. "I understand."

His phone rang. *Kirby?* The screen said the call was international. Norway? "Hello?" He couldn't keep the hope from his voice.

"S'me."

Starkad.

"Is Kirby with you?" Not the most polite thing Gwydion could have asked, but the two of them had surrendered *small talk* decades ago.

Starkad's growl wasn't quite human. "No. Not there?"

"No. You, she, and Brit vanished during the quake. How the fuck did you get to Norway?"

"Don't know. Come fetch."

The fractured speech was a bad sign. It took a serious threat to push Starkad to shift.

"I've got this," Frey said.

Gwydion looked up to see him on the phone as well. He vanished, and reappeared seconds later with Fenrir and Starkad. Fen must have been who Frey was on the phone with.

"I changed my mind," Gwydion said. "If I could alter time and space, I'd learn how to teleport."

Dahlia took in the scene with a neutral expression. "Don't blame you."

Starkad whipped his head in her direction with a low, threating growl, and strode across the room.

Fuck. Gwydion stepped between him and Dahlia.

"Not a friendly." Starkad spoke through clenched teeth.

"She's with us." Fen joined them. He kissed Dahlia on the forehead. "Hey, Duckie."

She stepped closer to Fen and farther from Starkad. "Welcome back."

"She's a Noble. The fuck is she doing here?" Starkad demanded.

"She's—" Gwydion's gaze landed on Starkad's arm. The limb was twisted and black from the shoulder down. "What the hell happened to you?" Gwydion stepped closer, examining without touching, and his medical training took over. "I need supplies. Scalpel. Gauze. Staples." He'd prefer an operating table, but with field triage, one didn't always get what they wanted.

Fen sighed. "*Shit.* It didn't look that bad before. The teleporting must have made it worse."

"It's not going to matter." Dahlia's confidence was gone, replaced with a timid tone. She was half-hidden behind Fen. "If that's a wound from a TOM bullet, the only thing that *might* help is amputation, and even then it's iffy. *Gods*, how are you still standing?"

Starkad cracked his neck and rotated his shoulder. "It doesn't hurt anymore. It doesn't feel like anything. Why the fuck is she here?"

Frey emitted a faint glow, the same color neon as the club's sign. He was pissed. "Fen told you we vouch for her."

"Did she tell you who she is?" Starkad looked at Gwydion.

Gwydion wasn't interested in being in the middle of this battle. He understood that TOM graduates were trained to lie, but he preferred to trust what his gut said about a person over non-stop paranoia. He hated that the last pair of Nobles he, Brit, and Starkad ran into had died. Brit had her reasons for killing them, but the deaths were still tragic. "We already covered that. Noble. TOM. She brought us some important information, and I'm more concerned about your arm," he said.

Starkad knocked Gwydion's hand away. "What does she want in return?"

"For you to not kill me?" Dahlia said meekly.

"She has a new prophecy." Gwydion needed something to diffuse this situation. "About Kirby. Where she might be."

Starkad snapped his jaw shut. "Where?"

"The Followers of Urd have her." Dahlia could barely be heard now.

Starkad roared and slammed his fist—the bad one—through the closest table. That wasn't right. Starkad was strong, but not punch-holes-through-two-inch-solid-oak-like-it-was-paper strong.

CHAPTER TWENTY

MIN

The world that materialized around Min and Aya came with a hail of gunfire.

Kirby, Brit, and another woman their age were crouched behind a table. Min and Aya ducked to join them.

Not that the table was big or sturdy enough to offer any protection. Copper-jacketed lead was evicted from Min's skin the instant it pierced. It was like being pelted with tiny pieces of hail—irritating, but more inconvenient than anything.

"What are you doing here?" Kirby demanded.

Min wasn't offended by her tone—she'd probably hoped for a combatant to come to her aid.

Brit surveyed the landscape. "And did you bring an assault rifle? Carbine? They're not that far out. I'll take anything with a rifle round."

"We're looking for you, and now that we have you, we're leaving," Min said. He placed a hand on

Aya's shoulder, as she did the same to Kirby and Brit.

The gunfire paused.

Why were they still here?

"They're reloading. Run," Kirby barked.

"This way." The other woman directed them behind the buildings and up a small back street. She led them into a local church "They won't find us, as long as no one does anything stupid." She directed a glare at Kirby.

Kirby held up her hands. "Your spiffy *we'll be incognito, I promise* magic failed. Don't blame me."

"I do blame you."

This wasn't the time to argue. "What happened?" Min asked Aya. "Why are we still here?"

"Maybe you shouldn't have dropped into a war zone with a goddess of war who refuses to fight." Kirby's tone was snide.

Aya gave a soft *huff.* "I have my reasons for what I did, and I'll ask your forgiveness when we're clear."

Min didn't like sitting here. Waiting. "Why are we still here, then? Take us back to NEON."

"I can't." Aya's bravado vanished. "I've been trying. I'm stuck here."

They ran into something similar on the TOM campus, when Kirby had been undercover. This wasn't good.

Brit nudged the other woman. "You're hiding us, aren't you? Let us leave."

"I can't. I'm trying to go, myself." Her dark-rimmed eyes were wide with panic. "Something else is keeping us here."

"Even if our pursuers can't see us, if we stay here, it won't take them long to find us via process of elimination." Kirby surveyed the area. She gestured down the hall. "Out that way. Brit, keep an eye on Magnus. Min, watch my back. You"—she glared at Aya—"don't get in our way."

Gunfire shredded the wooden doors and sent stained glass flying. Everyone ducked behind the nearest pillars, half-walls, or benches, though the shrapnel slammed into an invisible wall before it hit any of them. Kirby stayed close to Magnus. *Interesting.*

"For fuck's sake." A soft glow radiated around Aya, growing brighter until it was nearly blinding. A horizontal spread of spears appeared in a half circle, floating in the air in front of her.

You can't just kill these people. The protest died on Min's tongue. *These people* were trying to kill them.

"They're wearing class four body armor," Brit said at the same time Kirby muttered, "So you do remember how to fight."

Aya's glare at Kirby was withering.

Kirby stared back, unflinching. "She needs targets. I'll cover you. Find a spot where you can see."

Brit crouched and sprinted across the room. A few bullets struck the air in front of her, but not her. She slid into position behind a thick wooden post. Each time she popped her head out, another hail of gunfire rained on her position.

After six rounds of that, she ran back. "Two at ten o'clock. Behind the Chevy. One in the copy shop.

97

Two more in the building across the street, second floor, two o'clock."

Aya flicked her hand and the spears flew away, seeking their targets.

Min felt five lives snuff out in rapid succession, and suppressed his grief at the death. "She got them all."

An eerie calm settled over the church.

"I still can't leave," Magnus said softly. "Something's keeping us here."

Aya held out her hands. "Let me try again, now that the enemy is gone."

They all joined hands, except for Magnus who stepped back.

"Are you coming?" Min asked. It was difficult to believe Kirby would leave an ally behind.

"No," everyone else said at the same time.

Aya shook her head. "It doesn't matter. I'm also unable to leave." Her voice was heavy with resignation.

"Maybe you're trying to take too many people." Magnus's timidness had vanished. "Could you go alone or with just Min?"

"My magic doesn't work that way." Condescension bled into Aya's retort.

Magnus didn't look concerned. "You seem surprised it's not working at all. How can you be so certain its behavior hasn't changed?"

Aya raised an eyebrow. "Vidar and Hel may have raised all of you to not fear the gods, but unlike the others, you're mortal. Yes, I know who you are."

"Not a secret." Magnus shrugged.

"If I *can* leave, I'll return promptly with backup," Aya said.

And she was gone.

"I don't believe we've been introduced," Min said to Magnus. "I seem to be the only one here who doesn't know you." Though she knew him enough to use his name.

"She's TOM." Kirby stepped between them. "Supposedly FU wants me dead, so TOM is *keeping me safe.*"

Min wanted to argue the ridiculous notion, but coincidences were stacking too high for him to write off the idea.

Magnus rolled her eyes. "I was, until you shattered my wards. I wanted to go for pastries and catch up with my sisters. You had to bring the heat down on us."

Where was Aya? She should have landed in NEON in a blink, and at least Gwydion would have been ready to go that instant.

"We should go before the police show up." Magnus nodded toward the back of the church.

Where were the police? A hail of gunfire had broken out here, and there were no sirens. In fact, there were no other people. This wasn't a large city, but it was still a city, mid-morning, in the middle of the week.

"Are you certain you can't take us from this place with whatever you used to bring us here?" Kirby asked.

Magnus shook her head. "Why would I stick around if I didn't have to?"

"That's the question, isn't it?" Kirby eyed her with suspicion. "Brit?"

"Point. Destination?" They'd moved on from questioning Magnus and were making plans for next steps.

Min knew all of that without questioning. It didn't occur to him immediately that there was anything odd about their conversations. "We need to stay local."

"Our hunters know we're here. Staying isn't smart," Kirby said.

"But no one knows where we are right now." Min looked at Magnus. Apparently she was responsible for keeping the world from looking in their direction. "As long as it stays that way, we need to be where Aya and the others can find us again."

Brit shook her head. "We can't just sit and wait."

"What do you propose?" Min was open to reasonable alternatives. "We don't have a magical way back to Chicago, so we can fly or drive. By the time we get there, they may be here." There was no way to tell why Aya hadn't returned with reinforcements. "If they come back here, where will Starkad look for you, Kirby?"

She dragged in a deep breath. "The house is near, within walking distance. If Magnus-I-don't-know-why-we're-stuck-here keeps us hidden with her mysterious magic, it's probably safest."

Brit frowned. "*The* house? The one where..."

"You shot Mark, yeah. That house." Kirby was already walking north. Min followed, as did Magnus.

Brit strolled in a position a few steps ahead, and Kirby fell back the same distance. It kept the four of them close enough to speak, let the women keep an eye on Magnus, and didn't completely block the sidewalk. Though Min got the impression no one would notice them enough to find them in the way, regardless.

"There's nowhere else?" Brit asked. "Firing range, maybe?"

Kirby's chuckle was dry. "Seems like it's the week for us to face our demons. Starkad and Gwydion know where it is, and they'll look there if Aya brings them here and they can't find us. The only other people who know are TOM." She glanced at Magnus. "Am I right?"

Magnus smirked. "I know where most of Min's properties are, or I can pull a list quickly. I haven't shared all of that information with the top, though."

If Magnus and Dahlia had that kind of knowledge—the ability to track Min, despite how well he'd covered his tracks—they must have been TOM's most dangerous team, regardless of whether or not they were armed.

Kirby drifted in a casual weave that took her closer to Brit, their feet lightly colliding before Kirby fell back.

Min tensed, prepared for whatever they planned next.

"Don't." Magnus sighed. "Taking me down doesn't drop the wards, and it means you have to carry me. Killing me brings Vidar here. Now. Trust me, I'm better company."

Other people walked along nearby sidewalks, but none came close to their group. It was as though the four walked in a giant bubble.

"You could be lying," Min said.

She glanced at him. "You're far more suspicious than I expected. Go ahead and find out. I'm not currently a threat, and you've picked the destination. Vidar? He's a threat if something happens to me. FU? They're a threat."

Lance had been alerted to something at the same time Aya and Min had been. The gunfire Min appeared in the middle of felt like too much of a coincidence.

"What are you hoping to accomplish?" Min expected deception. He recognized the women's behaviors and non-verbal cues. That didn't make it any easier to trace it all back to a conclusion.

"I've already explained myself. I want Kirby and Brit back at TOM. Vidar has his reasons, I have my own, and they don't happen to contradict each other." Magnus frowned and worked her jaw.

That felt like a lot of information to reveal, but Min wasn't practiced enough in the nuances of these people's deceptions to know why.

"What are Vidar's reasons?" Kirby asked.

"You'd have to ask him."

If Min wasn't satisfied with that answer, it was impossible that Kirby or Brit would be.

"But *I* want you to come back," Magnus said. "I miss you. You're my sisters."

Kirby glanced at her, brows furrowed. "You could stay with us."

Magnus sighed. "Look. Go play house, or whatever. Get it out of your system. I'll be back in a few hours, and you can tell me what you've decided. I'm not going far, and I'll know if you leave. You'll make the right decision."

Chapter Twenty-One

Starkad

The wolf lingered. Starkad was himself again—he could think, speak, process complex thought—but that primal *need* to hunt lingered near the surface. The pain in his arm had vanished, but the appendage felt more like wielding a familiar weapon than it did like his arm. Sparks raced through his veins. The world barely made sense.

Especially standing in a tacky club he'd sworn he'd never visit, facing a pair of gods he'd rather not associate with. He'd known Frey was in the city. It was why Starkad ultimately settled here with Kirby. No one looked too closely at Chicago. No one could, because it was Freyr's realm.

According to Gwydion, they'd been roped into an agreement to protect Freya, the goddess who turned her back on them when they asked for the same. The story was, Aya couldn't help them before because helping to seal Malsumis away prevented her from speaking against any of the other goes who were part of the ritual.

Starkad's wolf didn't want to buy it, but he leashed the reaction. It was a good enough story to believe.

Now she was out with Min, trying to find Kirby and Brit.

None of that explained why there was a Noble here. Starkad wouldn't go through Fenrir to get to her. Not now, at least, given what he and Fen just went through. But Starkad was furious that she'd hacked his home security system, and even more bothered that Gwydion seemed to have accepted her so quickly.

In fact, the only thing Starkad understood completely was the snarling in his head. *Kirby.*

The air crackled, raising the hairs on the back of his neck, and Aya appeared in the middle of the room. Alone. She met his gaze. "We found them. Min is with them. We need to go now."

Fucking right, they did. Starkad's questions and concerns would wait. He stepped toward Aya.

"Your arm." Gwydion reached for him.

Starkad fixed him with a glare, and a growl rumbled up from his chest. He didn't give a fuck if this made his arm worse.

Gwydion took Aya's hand instead of pushing the issue, and Starkad did the same.

Nothing happened. What were they waiting for? "Let's go." Starkad's command was rough.

"I'm trying. I can't." Aya clipped off the words. "I can't feel Kirby anymore."

"You know where she was. Take us there."
Starkad just needed to contain his frustration a little
longer.

Aya shook her head. "There's a giant black spot
where she was, as though that part of the globe—half
of Utah—has ceased to exist. I'm not physically
capable of traveling there. Something is stopping
me."

Frey joined them. "Maybe with both of us.
Show me." He rested a hand on her shoulder.

Nothing. The glare of neon on dark tile didn't
even flicker.

Frey stepped back with a shake of his head. "It's
like that part of the world has been ripped away. It
doesn't exist."

"This is ridiculous. Did a part of the world just
vanish, Dahlia?" Starkad didn't want to ask her, but
if he remembered anything about her, she was
digitally plugged into everything.

She looked as startled to be addressed as he was
that he had to address her, but she shook it away and
turned to her tablet. The longer she typed and jabbed
at the screen, the deeper the creases in her forehead
grew. "No. Everyone's talking about quakes and
floods and all sorts of unnatural things, but nothing
unusual is coming out of Utah."

"But *something* is coming out of it," Gwydion
said.

"Yes. Normal stuff. Streaming. Chatting.
Signals by the billions."

Starkad wasn't in the mood to figure this out.
"If it still exists, we can get to it. Take us to the edge

of the blank spot." They'd walk in, the way they did on the TOM campus.

"I'll wait here, in case anyone comes back." Frey stepped away.

Fine with Starkad. They needed fighters on this trip.

NEON vanished, replaced with dry, hot air. Freedom, fouled by magic. Starkad wrinkled his nose. Dirt spanned out in every direction, blending into red-rock mountains, pausing at the scrub brush and freeway, and then continuing.

"Where did you find Kirby?" Starkad asked.

"Salt Lake," Aya said.

Gwydion had his phone out and pressed to his ear. "Min's not answering."

Based on the scenery, they were hours away from their destination, even driving at top speed. "On the TOM campus, teleporting was possible inside the barrier. A few steps forward, and we can finish the journey." Starkad could almost taste their destination. His Valkyrie.

Aya stepped away from them and strolled several meters, before walking back. Her expression wasn't promising. "The void—whatever it is—it follows me. It's like it encircles me. In there, nothing around me exists. I only know the two of you do because I see you."

"According to my GPS, we're about four hours out. Let's go rent a car and drive." Gwydion jerked his thumb toward the freeway.

Instinct wanted Starkad to shift again. To run. But they were more than ten times farther from their destination than he and Fen had been from town in

Norway. It felt ridiculous—*pedestrian*—to rent a car and drive, when they were working with gods who could fly and teleport. But life was ridiculous sometimes. They headed toward the freeway and followed the signs to the closest town.

"Your arm looks worse." Gwydion probed the blackened flesh.

Starkad jerked away. That was the least of his concerns. "It feels fine." It didn't quite. In fact, it didn't feel like anything. He was breathing, though, and could fight and shift.

"I never realized you were a masochist," Gwydion said.

A strained laugh escaped Starkad's throat. He was the ultimate masochist. The sadist in him had spent centuries torturing him, in favor of losing himself.

Gwydion glared at him. "Just because you're fine now doesn't mean you will be later. Next trip could take that arm off. Dahlia said those bullets could kill you."

"I'll deal with that when it happens."

CHAPTER TWENTY-TWO

KIRBY

There weren't many places that held negative associations for Kirby. Sure, she had a lot of bad memories, but most of those stemmed from a campus that should no longer exist. Which for some unfathomable reason had been recreated someplace else.

The odds of her landing in a second bad-memory place in twenty-four hours seemed astronomical. Yet here she was, searching the house where her memories came back, for security reasons. The house where Brit landed solidly in her life again. Where Kirby discovered what Starkad had kept from her. Where—

"Are you all right?" Min's soft question startled her.

"Mm." She struggled to grasp enough thoughts to put them in words that would make sense. The house was as clear as it could be. She didn't think for a moment that Magnus had just let them walk away, but that meant any external threats were most likely held at bay.

Kirby wandered back into the living room and perched on the edge of the couch. "Apparently, I can't escape my ghosts," she said as Brit returned from her own search.

"Boo?" Brit gave her a dry smile. "Rest of the house is clear."

"I'm sorry." Min settled next to Kirby, his thigh pressing into hers.

The closeness was comforting. Part of her wanted to be pulled into his lap. To curl up there and vanish from the world until the end of time.

She sank back, letting the cushions swallow her. "The memories here aren't as bad as there. At least here..." The words that rose to her lips tasted melodramatic. But they were true. "That last night, I was a part of TOM. Before Starkad pulled me out. When I—" *Killed myself.* "That was the end of my life." Literally. Emotionally... "What came after... I wasn't living; I was surviving. Questioning. Lost." But this house— "I was reborn here." Kirby gestured broadly.

Min was a part of that, with his kindness showing her what such a thing was like when there were no strings attached. Brit played a large part in Kirby's re-emergence into living, as well, though not in such a positive way.

Kirby looked at Brit. "When you shot Starkad... Mark..."

"I still don't know why you let me live." Brit made herself comfortable in the chair near the couch.

Min rested his hand on Kirby's knee, drawing slow passes with his thumb. It might be a warning, for her to temper her words. It felt more like reassurance and support.

"I've lost track of the number of times I've asked myself that," she said. "The best I've got is that I'm currently glad I didn't make a different decision."

Brit's smile came easily.

Min shook his head. Was he judging Kirby after all, for struggling with a question like that? He couldn't be.

"Yes?" Kirby asked.

"It's nothing." Min squeezed her thigh.

"It's obviously something."

His smile was soft. "I've tried for so long to understand the two of you and the way you toss around conversation about death so easily. I still can't think in those terms, but I know why you do, and I don't judge you for it."

That was the first time he'd ever said something like that and Kirby believed him. She leaned her head against his arm, focusing on the electricity that flowed between them.

Brit played with a loose thread on the arm of her chair. "It's funny—for everything they taught us growing up, how to live was never really on that list. Not how to live for ourselves, anyway."

"They really didn't." Kirby hadn't thought of life at TOM in those terms before. "In fact, it's been so long since I have—I mean *really* lived—that I don't remember how either."

"Longest you've ever made it?" Brit asked.

"Before I died? Not counting my first life..." Kirby wiggled her fingers, pretending to count on them. "How old am I?"

Min slid his hand under hers, raising both to kiss the back of her knuckles. His silent support was soothing and alluring.

If Brit was bothered by the display of affection, it didn't show in her expression or movements. "Ever wonder what it would have been like to be normal?"

"Sometimes. More than sometimes. For a long time, I pretended things were normal with Starkad." Living in the suburbs, pretending to be a happy little family.

"You wouldn't be happy with *normal*. Either of you." Min's tone was low and thoughtful.

Brit shook her head. "No. Not knowing what I know now."

Kirby had thought she was happy in her past lives. Technically, that meant she was, but as she looked back, something had been missing. More than just love. Depth. Reality.

"Not to make this dark by bringing up your death—though who are we kidding, it's already floating in the shadows"—Brit's chuckle was flat—"but if you hadn't hit immortality in this life, if your death started the cycle all over again, how many more lives do you think until you fell in love a fifth time? A sixth? I assume the collection of lovers grows as time goes on."

Kirby had never thought of her lives in terms of who she fell in love with. Or that they were all immortal, even if they hadn't started out that way. "Mathematically speaking? Three more lives. Do you think I've deprived someone of their immortality, or would have fallen in love with a god next?"

"Maybe Magnus could do the math on that for us. She does love her data." Brit was subdued, but not in bad spirits.

Min adjusted his position, to grab Kirby's hips and slide her into his lap. The warmth of his chest pressed into her back, and his presence was a shield from the world. "I'm willing to make that sacrifice." His words rumbled through her.

She had to process what he meant. "You'd have a random stranger, one, two, maybe three hundred years down the line, give up their immortality for mine?"

"Without question. I'm not taking their life, just removing their chance at eternity, so I can keep you in mine."

That was almost too sugary. Kirby was fond of extra sweet, though. "Do you think this ever ends? Not my reincarnations, but... these wars? Prophecies? In-fighting among the gods?"

"It doesn't." Min's answer wasn't the let-down she expected. "It takes different shapes, but it's always there."

"The question is, can you turn your back on it, once you're not directly a part of it?" Brit said.

Kirby hesitated. "I want to live. But I want the same for others."

"No one says you can't have both." Min sounded perfectly reasonable. "There's always downtime, especially in centuries-long wars. Now is a perfect example."

"But there's so much darkness in the uptime." Kirby could live in the shadows, but some days it was exhausting.

Min trailed his lips along the back of her neck. It was a comforting, no-demand gesture. "You've never had good times?"

The question was likely rhetorical, but it was worth lingering on. "Those six months in the fae realm."

Brit's frown was hard to interpret.

Kirby selected another good memory. "Ordering cake to a random hotel room, in a random city, and trying every flavor. Some of them with the help of kisses." That had been the night, years ago, when she and Brit confessed their feelings for each other.

"You don't hate that memory?" Brit was surprised.

For so long, it had tormented Kirby. "I do… and I don't. I hate what happened to us." The betrayal that came after. So much pain. "But I enjoyed the moment, and I want more of them." That was both easy and terrifying to admit.

"There will be more chances for good memories, even among the bad." Min was infuriatingly right.

Kirby loved it.

"This morning was fun." Brit grinned.

Kirby couldn't argue. "Yeah, it was."

Min's grip on Kirby's hips tightened. "This morning, as in an hour ago? When you were being shot at?"

"Before that." Kirby didn't have to ask what Brit meant, because their cohesiveness was where the fun came from.

"Clicking," Brit said.

"Knowing what you were thinking."

"Instinct kicking in. No second-guessing."

Like the old days. Before it went bad. Correction—before Kirby realized it had always been a little bad. "We make an amazing team."

"When I'm not fucking up," Brit said.

Kirby didn't want to be the one to say it, but she wouldn't argue Brit's response.

"Since we're speaking of the past," Min said, "I've been curious about something. When I found you again, months ago, you didn't remember me, but you remembered the bondage."

And she'd craved the pain. She still did. "*Therapy.* Starkad introduced me to it, to teach me I had control over who and what caused me pain." Physical pain, anyway. "It helped. Until I broke our agreement." She bit back a bitter laugh. "It feels like it was so long ago. After that, pain was an escape, but it stopped healing."

The silence that met her confession drilled into her soul. She didn't owe anyone an explanation, but one forced its way out. "I'm coping better now. With all of it. Not as in, *Oh my god, I've completely recovered*, but facing the past that put me in that frame of mind is becoming easier."

"You could have gone in the opposite direction." Min's tone was without judgment. "Asked some god to numb you. To take away the mental agony."

There had been so many times Kirby wanted the world to stop. The grief. The anguish. The hatred. Life. She was grateful now that it had all continued—the good and the bad. "I'll work through it. It's the only way. Like with Brit. Each time she does something right, it becomes easier to forget why it was all wrong."

"I'm not asking you to forget," Brit said.

"*Forget* is the wrong word. How about, it's easier to remember why we used to be good?"

"In other words, what you're saying"—Min stood her on her feet with no effort—"is you need to do the good things again and again, have them go well, to assure you they're good things." He stood as well, pressing into her back and sliding his palms to rest on her stomach. The embrace was safety and intimacy and promise.

Disbelief mingled with amusement and heat, as Kirby leaned back into him. "I'm sorry. Are you *actually* trying to seduce me? Now? While we're baring our souls and being hunted by multiple gods for reasons that are questionable at best?"

"Yes." There was no hesitation or apology in Min's reply. "You prefer to shoot things, to solve your problems. I prefer fucking. The three of us have the entire house to ourselves, and memories to reshape."

Brit's laugh was strained. "No offense. You're a wonderful guy. But you're not my type."

"My dear, I'm everyone's type." Min's voice was silk and chocolate and seduction.

Kirby bit the inside of her cheek, to hold back her amusement. She knew where this was going.

Pink flooded Brit's cheeks. So unlike her. "You don't... That is... You've got..." She gestured at her crotch.

She must actually respect Min. Then again, Kirby knew that. Brit and Min had formed a bond of trust and friendship, in their time together.

"You have a penis." Kirby didn't want the awkwardness to stretch on too long. "That's what she's trying to say." She felt lighter, like she could breathe. The mood in the room had flowed into pleasant and secure.

Brit shrugged. "It's true. I only play straight when I have to."

"Neither of us minds if you watch." Min was unfazed.

Kirby liked the idea, but not the assumption that Brit wanted to stick around and be excluded at the same time. "That feels a little rude."

"It sounds a lot tempting." Brit bit her bottom lip.

Min twirled his finger, and Kirby's wrists were bound. A whimper escaped her throat. "You're still welcome to join in," he told Brit. "I promise to keep my hands... Well, not to myself, but clear of you."

The desire that raced through Kirby was intoxicating and familiar. Safe but terrifying. She tasted lust, and the anticipation of pleasure. Of pain. It wasn't the same as the first time she'd encountered Min, though. Or even as what she and Brit shared last night.

Kirby didn't want to escape in this feeling. She had no desire to get lost in the moment. She wanted to enjoy the good while it was here, despite the bad out there.

Min fitted a blindfold over her eyes, blacking out the world and sending anticipation spilling inside.

And *gods*, it promised to be good.

CHAPTER TWENTY-THREE

KIRBY

Lips met Kirby's in gentle, hesitant kisses. *Brit.* Kirby's fingers twitched, aching to touch back.

Brit's kisses grew more intense, drawing Kirby into the physical tugging at her heart. Each nip, peck, and nibble carried a new promise. Safety. Love. Brit glided her hands up Kirby's chest, teasing her through fabric, with thumbs brushing nipples, palms cupping breasts, and finally coming up to her face.

Familiar callouses bit into Kirby's cheek, as Brit dragged her mouth down Kirby's jaw to her collar bone, licking and lightly sucking.

The kissing and touching drew on, and Kirby fell into each new caress. This was what they should have been. What they would have been in a different world. What they were now. Partners. Lovers.

When the kissing stopped abruptly and Brit pulled away, Kirby pouted.

Fingers knotted in her hair before she could process a response, and Min yanked her head back. She gasped with delighted pleasure at the sensation. Min pressed his hand to her throat, forcing her chin in the air, and leaned over her to claim her mouth and swallow her moans.

He increased the weight of his touch against her neck, fuzzing her thoughts, as he nibbled her ear, and bit her shoulder.

Brit pushed Kirby's shirt up, shoving her bra out of the way in the process, and licked over a swollen nipple before drawing it into her mouth.

Kirby floated in the haze of strained breathing delicious teasing. She couldn't do anything but fall into the intoxicating blend of sensations. With each breath she dragged in, her head floated further away.

Brit kissed down Kirby's stomach, undoing her jeans at the same time, then shoved Kirby's bottoms to the ground.

Min glided his hand over Kirby's ass, to slip his fingers between her legs and tease her pussy. He brushed lightly, dipping near her opening but not penetrating her.

When Brit molded her body to Kirby's again, it was skin-on-skin. As Brit kissed her, nipped at her jaw and her chin and her earlobe, Min pushed two fingers inside her.

The contrast of light and playful from Brit, and possessively passionate from Min, added to the floaty, lost-in-desire feeling that coursed through Kirby.

"Turns out watching someone else tease you and play with you and make you gasp is a definite turn-on," Brit confessed between kisses. She glided her hand lower, to rub Kirby's clit.

The build-up toward climax was a slow burn of shallow breath and more touches than Kirby could keep track of. She rocked between Min and Brit, wrapped in them. In pleasure. When that first shudder of orgasm clenched inside her, her legs wobbled, but they kept her upright.

As she came, her body shuddered with desire. With completion. She tightened around Min's fingers and ground into Brit's touch, not knowing when it was too much. Not wanting the moment to end.

Her knees buckled, and Min's hands feel to her hips, supporting her. Cradling her. "How are you, Huntress?" His voice was both distant and buried in her thoughts.

She nodded and gave a tiny laugh as she struggled to find her voice. "Good. Really good."

"More?" Brit's question brushed Kirby's ear.

"Yes." Kirby nodded.

Min guided her forward, and coaxed her to her knees. The fingers knotted in her hair this time were more gentle—Brit. Her knee rested near Kirby's shoulder, heat radiating between them.

Kirby didn't need eyesight for this anymore than the rest of it. She was between a seated Brit's legs. She vividly remembered this. Wanted it again.

She dragged her mouth up the inside of Brit's thigh, kissing, licking, and ticking enough to draw a light giggle. When Kirby reached her destination, she scaped her teeth over skin and the thin landing strip that would be as pale as the skin it sat on.

She dove her tongue inside Brit's pussy, savoring every gasp as sigh. *Goddess* she missed those sounds.

As Brit fingered her own clit, her fingers occasionally bumped Kirby's nose, and she ground into Kirby's face. Brit tightened her grip in Kirby's hair, and her hips bucked.

Kirby recognized the tiny whimpering mewls that said Brit was close to climax, and increased her attentions, licking harder, feeling muscles tighten around her tongue and tasting a fresh rush of honey.

Brit pulled away with shaky laugh, and her body relaxed away from Kirby.

Before Kirby could tease a bit more, draw another shudder, maybe coax out another orgasm, Min lifted her to her feet.

He kissed her. Devoured her. Shared Brit's taste with her. Intimacy and desire wrapped around them. As he danced his tongue with Kirby's, he slid his fingers inside her again, meeting no resistance. She was wet, slick, and ready for more.

He pumped in and out, striking the right spot inside, and she rocked against him.

When Min pulled out, a disappointment sparked with anticipation, lighting a fire under her skin.

Min moved behind her to press his body to hers. He was naked, hard, and unyielding. He guided them back, then pulled her into his lap as they sat, stretching her out as he buried his cock inside her.

He withdrew almost to the tip before plunging back in, increasing the pace and shortening the thrusts until he pounded hard against and in her.

Brit was back, sucking on Kirby's breasts while Min kissed along the back of her neck. The penetration, the touches and bites, the moans and sighs of her lovers, filled Kirby with need and security.

Another orgasm built inside, drawing out until she wanted to jump to feel that sensation of climax. When she tumbled in, all other thought fell away. There was nothing here but pleasure and love and a new flood of connection when Min spilled inside her.

This was everything. And Kirby would fight anyone who tried to destroy it.

CHAPTER TWENTY-FOUR

KIRBY

Lying like this, tangled up with Brit, Min pressing into her back, it was easy for Kirby to ignore the rest of the world. Especially the voice that played on a non-stop loop, as it listed the ways Brit had betrayed her over the years.

It was easier for Kirby to remember the good now—what things were like with Brit before it all fell apart.

As nice as it was to ignore the outside world, it hadn't stopped turning while the three of them indulged in nostalgia and—incredible—sex. Kirby needed a direction. She understood Min's insistence they wait here, but she only had so much patience for it.

"Call Gwydion again." As Kirby made the suggestion, she reluctantly extracted herself from the warmth and security. It was tempting to move this into the bathroom. Take their time in the shower together. But that meant sacrificing their ability to hear. To react.

So did what they'd just done, and Kirby refused to do anything with the lingering memories but enjoy them. It didn't mean she could wrap herself in this cocoon. She tugged her clothes on, and Brit did the same.

"No answer. Not from him, not at NEON." Min dressed more languidly.

Kirby didn't know that name. "*Neon?*"

"Frey's club. Gwydion's there with another of your TOM *friends*, Dahlia—"

Brit snapped. "I found her. Oh fuck."

Kirby didn't have to ask Brit to elaborate. She was thinking the same thing. There were too many coincidences. "So we get split up, literally moved to various corners of the world, while one partner works one group and the other works us." She'd bought Magnus's sadness this morning. Thought that whole Dahlia-betrayed-me shtick was real.

Kirby shouldn't have run from TOM. If she'd stayed, she could have started to unravel some answers.

"I didn't care for Magnus, but I trusted Dahlia when she said she left the organization. She's a good person," Min said.

Kirby bit her tongue, to hold back the retort that he wasn't always the best judge of character.

Min's expression darkened. "Consider for a moment—does this situation become less dangerous if both women hold the allegiances they say they do? Not everything is a conspiracy, and sometimes that makes things just as bad."

Kirby's argument died on her lips. He had a good point. "That doesn't mean I'm writing off the Dahlia-and-Magnus-still-working-together idea. I almost guarantee Magnus is the reason we're stuck here and can't call out to any of our allies. " Which also meant Magnus was nearby.

"Don't dismiss either theory," Min said. "Every option is possible until disproven. That's part of training."

He had an infuriatingly good point. Kirby had to find Magnus and go back to Vidar. She needed answers.

"Not without me," Brit said.

Kirby stared at her. "I didn't say anything."

Brit raised an eyebrow. "Magnus has answers, and we're not going anywhere unless she lets us or we kill her. We don't know if killing her will change anything, since it's not her magic, and neither of us likes that idea anyway. Which means we play her game until we know more."

"I wouldn't go back. That's ridiculous." Kirby's lie had no weight behind it.

The way Min watched his phone, frown etched on his face, he might not have caught it. "Something's not right," he said.

Besides the fact that they couldn't reach any of their allies? "What is it?"

"Gluskab's *natural* disasters have stopped." Min scrolled. "There was a non-stop string, and now nothing."

"Maybe he's recharging?" Brit didn't sound like she believed it.

126

It was possible, but even a lull felt like a bad sign. An eye-of-the-storm kind of situation.

There was a knock, and tension ratcheted through Kirby. She moved quickly to the room with the cameras. No surprise, they were out.

"Magnus is back," Brit said.

Kirby had suspected that would happen sooner or later. She was already moving toward the front door, Brit at her heels.

"You can't return to Vidar with her." Min stayed back. "This is your chance to be done with TOM."

Walking away from TOM for good was a wonderful thought. "They want me for a reason. They're keeping us here for a reason. I need to know what that is, or we're not done with them." She answered the door before he could argue.

Magnus was on the front step, looking irritated. "Do you have whatever this is out of your system?" Her voice was strained, despite her casual posture. "Because we need to go *now*."

"You're nervous." Kirby could take this opportunity to probe her defenses. "Vidar have something wicked planned for you if you come back alone?"

"Presumably. But I can't afford to stay here. Something's coming, and I can't hide myself or you from it. If I stay, I won't survive. If you stay, you won't get answers, and you will get dead."

After the shoot-out this morning, there was definitely *some* threat out there. "You want me? Just take me. Like before."

Magnus shook her head. "If you don't want to be there, it will be one fight after another on campus, and no one has the time or energy for that."

"Then they're coming with me." Kirby was going to yield, but she'd feel a lot better with backup.

"Brit, yes. Your god? Not a fucking chance."

Kirby shrugged. "Both of them, or no deal."

Magnus rolled her eyes. "I'm calling your bluff." Panic wove with her words. "Just you and Brit. The clock is ticking fast and loud. You have five seconds to decide."

CHAPTER TWENTY-FIVE

MIN

"Deal. Just us. Let's go." Kirby gave Min one last glance, then she, Brit, and Magnus vanished from the room.

Min moved to the doorway. If he called Gwydion now, would he get through?

"Is she with you?" The question was shouted, carried on a guttural tone.

Min looked up to see Starkad, Gwydion, and Aya approaching on foot and wearing a matching set of scowls. He waited the few seconds until they were closer than yelling range, and shook his head. Might as well answer the question now, so they could take action quickly. "She was. She left with someone from TOM. Returned to camp—"

"You let her leave? With *them?*" Starkad half-shifted in a blink, face elongating and teeth growing pointed. He closed the distance between him and Min just as quickly, growling and snapping and pausing so closely to Min's throat, his hot breath falling against Min's skin.

Min stood his ground. "I argued my case, and she made her decision."

Starkad's growl deepened.

This was time wasted. Min twirled his finger, magically binding Starkad's wrists and carrying him back a few meters.

With a bite and a jerk, Starkad snapped the invisible restraints. The shock of having the spell shattered shook Min, rattling in his thoughts. No one had ever done that before. Min reapplied the bonds before Starkad reached him again.

And again Starkad broke loose, sending a shower of sparks into the daylight. His growl was feral and the threat of death sparked in his eyes.

Each time Min held him back, Starkad broke loose to attack again, until they were surrounded by a midday fireworks show, caused by a clash of magics and wills.

"*Enough*," Gwydion barked. "What the fuck?"

Starkad stepped back, chest heaving with restraint, but he looked otherwise unwinded.

Min felt drained. He'd poured more energy into the brief struggle than he realized. What had happened? Starkad wasn't that kind of magical creature. He shouldn't have the strength or power to break through Min's defenses.

Gwydion looked between the two of them. "Nothing? Honestly, I always thought it would be me, standing where Min is, when this happened. But it's not getting us anywhere."

"I didn't want to let her go," Min said. "She chose this, and if you'd been here, you wouldn't have been able to stop her either."

"I would have found a way." Starkad spoke through clenched canines.

Aya stepped forward. "If you're done with the dick-measuring contest, we should get back. I can see NEON again. Whatever removed this part of the world from the rest is gone."

"His arm." Gwydion nodded at Starkad. "What we should do is get inside, let Min take a look, and then get to work."

Min hadn't noticed the twisted limb before. "Agreed. The deal was that we keep Aya safe in exchange for help finding Kirby. It's as safe here as NEON."

"And here, there are fewer non-combatants." Starkad brushed past Min, bumping him as he moved into the house.

Min stepped aside, to let Aya and Gwydion in, as well. "We have everything we need, and if we don't, I can have it brought in. We also have more information now," he said.

For instance, Kirby told him the campus had been recreated someplace else. The list of places a full-sized school could be plopped down without someone noticing, and have the weather she described, was limited.

"What happened?" Min nodded at Starkad's arm.

"Those bullets TOM has. The ones they used on Kirby."

131

"It looks worse each time he teleports," Gwydion added.

Min only vaguely knew how he'd healed Kirby. He'd see her, the death flowing through her, and done the only thing he could think of—he poured life into it. He hovered his hand over Starkad's arm. "This isn't the same magic."

It was still death, but not the creeping, all-consuming plague-type sensation that had emanated from Kirby. This was more driven. Had more purpose. Was familiar.

"Maybe they've improved the bullets. Changed the formula." Starkad sounded more bored than concerned.

Min shook his head. "Perhaps. I can't say for certain, but it would have to be a drastic change. This feels like it's a part of you. I can't distinguish the bullet's magic from yours."

"If they've changed anything, it's been recent." Dahlia's voice came from behind them.

They spun, to see her standing in the middle of the room with Frey.

"Whatever was blocking you is gone," Frey said. "When I felt Aya and knew the situation was safe, we came."

"Magnus." Min had no doubt.

Starkad growled. "*Great.* The gang's all here."

"You talked to Magnus?" Dahlia's tone softened, and whisps of adoration drifted from her. It wasn't lust or desire, though. It was more of a familial bond. She gave her head a single shake. "Not why we're here. I'm seeing some chatter online. People are looking for yo—"

The door slammed open, cracking against the wall, as wood splintered and plaster filled the air.

"Down on the ground, now." Lance burst into the room, several of his force at his back, all with guns drawn.

Chapter Twenty-Six

STARKAD

Finally. A real fight. Starkad could sate the itch he hadn't been able to scratch.

Even better he got to sink his teeth into the assholes who not only betrayed him—betrayed Kirby—but who brought guns to fight gods.

He let his wolf form take over.

Kill. Devour. Destroy. The words chanted in his thoughts, as he leaped for the nearest soldier, teeth bared and eager to sink into flesh.

Dragon.

Starkad reared up, rage and frustration rushing through him. Lance had assumed his other form too, and he didn't fit in this house.

Lance swung a clawed hand toward Starkad, and the wolf dodged without hesitation. Plaster, wood, and fiberglass rained down around them.

Starkad dodged falling pieces of house, to lunge at dragon-Lance's throat.

A backhand knocked Starkad aside. He landed on his feet, already springing forward again. Lance was strong, but Starkad was fast, and in the crumbling house, he was a lot more maneuverable. *Shouldn't be enjoying this.*

He ignored the whisper of conscience, and embraced glee instead. *This* was living.

CHAPTER TWENTY-SEVEN

BRIT

The house vanished, but Brit, Kirby, and Magnus appeared in the middle of an empty field instead of on campus.

Danger surged through Brit.

"Where—"

"*Shield.*" Brit cut Kirby off.

Flame struck the air immediately in front of them, heat flooding the air. The fire didn't hurt them, though.

"I've always wondered what Valkyrie tasted like." The smooth, seductive woman's voice was more in their heads than reaching their ears. A dragon appeared in the middle of the field, wings spanned as wide as a medium-sized plane and head as big as a car.

"—the fuck?" Brit expected Magnus and Vidar to pull something, but feeding them to a dragon was so far outside the realm of what she could have imagined.

Kirby wrenched Magnus's arm, forcing her toward them and away from the beast. "Get us out of here, *now*," she barked.

Magnus's eyes were wide with fear. "I can't. This isn't me."

Another charge of magical threat sparked over Brit. "*Shield.*"

Once again, flame struck everything around them, but not them. The ground burned hot, and the fire vanished in a blink, leaving a circle of scorched earth.

When Brit had met Artura, she'd asked Gwydion anything and everything she'd ever wanted to know about dragons. He shared their history, incredible stories, and the fact that only three were left. Artura, Lance, and Vera.

The flash of sapphire and gold scales on this one matched his description of Vera. She and Lance protected all things to do with fate, and were the backbone of FU.

Maybe Magnus being more truthful than Kirby suspected up until now.

"Would you like to test that little toy shield of yours against my jaw, Valkyrie, or will you fight back?" Vera asked.

Brit was awed by the entire idea of dragons walking among humanity, but that didn't diminish her disdain for any immortal who wielded their power as a threat. "Do you like to play with your food?" she asked.

"I'd like *to see if the rumors are true."* Vera's tone stayed calm and smooth. *"That the two of you don't lie down and die. That you fight."*

"How are we supposed to fight a dragon?" Fear spilled from Magnus.

Brit couldn't fight. She hated this helpless feeling. Maybe if she had a gun, she'd try. It seemed like a waste of bullets, though. "I'll cover Magnus," she said to Kirby. "You fight."

"Don't you dare sacrifice yourself for her." Kirby looked from Brit to Magnus.

Kirby cared.

Brit couldn't ignore the warmth that flooded her. "I survived a bullet to the brain. I'll be fine." Unless she was chewed up and swallowed. She couldn't think about that right now, though.

Kirby stepped away.

"Wait." Brit had to do this. Today wouldn't be the end, but just in case it was... "I love you."

Kirby glanced at her with a smirk. "I know."

Magnus made a gagging noise.

And then Kirby had wings. A full armor Brit had never seen before, that was intricate and dark. A sword. Kirby didn't have any magical weapons as a Valkyrie—where did that come from?

Kirby flew straight toward Vera, sword drawn.

"Fuck me. That's amazing." Awe mingled with Magnus's terror.

"Get down." Brit tackled her, as Vera's tail swiped over their heads.

Kirby might have the dragon's attention, but Vera was so large that all of her was a threat.

Brit hopped to her feet and pulled Magnus upright. "We need distance and shelter. Don't leave my side."

"I'm an average fighter, I'm not stupid." Magnus kept pace with Brit, as they raced toward the nearest tree line. They ducked into the thin foliage and turned to watch the fight.

Kirby wove and dodged with awe-inspiring skill, sometimes touching down and others flitting around Vera like a raven. But neither of them was making contact.

Every time Vera attacked with magic, Brit felt the charge in the air increase.

This was beyond frustrating. Brit had power—she could feel others and didn't die—but not being able to consciously access whatever lived in her veins was ridiculous. She hated being stuck on the sidelines like this. If she could do *anything*, it would be better.

Vera's slash through the air was followed by a burst of flame.

Kirby dove, but a wing caught her in the shoulder and sent her tumbling to the ground. She sprang to the air again in an instant, but she was moving more slowly. She couldn't do this alone.

Brit needed to help.

The ambient charge in the air faded. Was Vera getting tired? That didn't seem right.

Brit spun to Magnus, but Magnus was gone.

She had abandoned them.

Why was Brit the least bit surprised?

CHAPTER TWENTY-EIGHT

GWYDION

Fight or flight.

Instinct for most creatures.

For Gwydion, a conscious struggle during battle. He gripped the resolve to fight, as the house creaked and groaned around them, and large chunks of plaster fell the floor.

Starkad's lack of hesitation was expected, but this was different. The ferocity and cognizance he attacked with were almost as terrifying as the fact that Lance was the enemy.

At least the dragon had chosen to limit his size to that of a house, rather than growing much larger.

The house shuddered. Gwydion felt the wooden beams sigh, then crack. He wove magical fingers through the beams—there was no reason to worry about destroying the structure, since it was crumbling around them—and grasped everything wooden that he could to weave a shield around himself, Min, Frey, and Dahlia.

Creating and holding the structure strained him like overworking a muscle, but he pushed past the sensation. He glanced at Frey. "Get her out of here."

Bullets bit into the wooden shell, drowning him out. He reshaped it, to account for each new hole, but that wouldn't last long, if the shield disintegrated in a hail of gunfire.

"I can help," Dahlia said. She pointed at the closest gunman, about ten meters away. "Take him out."

Gwydion didn't have a better plan, so he sent a stake through the target's heart—not just for vampires. He tossed up a rolling wall, as Dahlia sprinted out to grab the now-available gun.

"Get me to a better vantage point," she said to Frey when she returned.

She'd made her decision, and Gwydion had other things to focus on. He grabbed more wooden ammo, not needing as much of a barrier now that Dahlia had moved, and picked his next target.

Starkad was holding his own against Lance, but nothing more. Each time the wolf got close, the dragon flung him back.

Gwydion's magic slipped from his grasp, and wood fell to the ground around him.

"Are you all right?" Min sounded concerned.

Gwydion rolled his neck. "Fine." His magical grip had faltered; that was all. He flexed ethereal fingers and grabbed again, ignoring the cramp that ran through the connection.

The ground shook under his feet, and death poured through nature. Rot. Decay. It tasted foul, and he almost lost his grip again.

Gluskab.

The blight rushed over Gwydion, until he couldn't see or think or breathe. He clawed past the corruption. Panic clogged his mind, and he dropped to his knees. A fist squeezed around his lungs. Was this panic, weakness, or the more powerful magic? All of the above, most likely.

Blackness licked at the edges of his vision.

Silence descended.

Gwydion dragged in a deep breath and looked around. He was still conscious. Min and Starkad looked as confused as he felt.

Lance was gone. So were his forces. There was no more suffocating presence from Gluskab.

Gwydion didn't like it. "What the—"

"Aya's gone." Frey's yell clattered over the demolished house. "*Gone*, gone. I can't feel her anywhere."

CHAPTER TWENTY-NINE

KIRBY

This dragon was fucking with her. It had to be.

Each time Kirby got close enough to land a hit—which had yet to do discernible damage—she'd be knocked back. By a wing. A flick of the tail. A claw.

Every action Kirby took in this fight, from flying to the shield, drew power. Fortunately, once she summoned the armor and sword, they were physical. She had no idea where the weapon came from, but it was the perfect weight and length, so she wasn't questioning too deeply.

She had to meter everything else and she had to stay airborne. Standing on the ground, jabbing this beast in the ankle wouldn't do her any good.

Then again, neither did the rest of this. If she found a weak spot, could she drive the sword deep enough to matter? What she wouldn't give, to have some sort of ranged or area attack right now…

Did she want to kill a dragon? It apparently wasn't trying to kill her.

Kirby dove for the crook where wing met back, her shield going up at the last moment. It wasn't soon enough, as a gust of flame knocked her back.

The burns that crackled along her skin healed quickly but left her gasping for breath. If she told the dragon, *Just kidding. Let us go*, would that work?

Considering the dragon brought them here in the first place and threatened to eat her, it seemed unlikely.

A soft *pop* reached Kirby, as she angled herself for another attack. A suppressed gunshot? And then another. Was Magnus armed, after all? There was more than one source. Who was here?

"You brought gunmen?" the dragon growled.

"Of course I did." Kirby's confident retort was distorted by her own shock.

"I see. This isn't your doing."

Kirby alternated her attention between the dragon and the tree line. A squad—maybe two—of soldiers was fanning out, exactly where she'd expect TOM grunts to be.

"Vidar, this isn't your fight." The dragon's casual tone shifted to anger.

Vidar? That couldn't be right. "He's not here. Not for me," Kirby said.

"She's one of us." Vidar's voice echoed in the air, magically amplified.

No. He couldn't be talking about her. Not honestly, anyway.

"She's never been one of you." The dragon's retort echoed Kirby's thoughts.

Kirby should be lunging in and attacking while everyone was distracted, but something wasn't right. Actually, none of this felt right. She touched down, using the pause as an excuse to catch her breath and draw in a little more magic. The latter wasn't as difficult as she expected.

"This is your fight, Valkyrie. Not theirs." The dragon swept a wing across the clearing, and a chorus of screams erupted from the tree line.

Kirby attack, ignoring the chill of terror that raced down her spine. She hit empty air. The dragon was gone. Vanished as abruptly as it had appeared.

"We need to go." Vidar grabbed her arm. The field vanished, replaced with an infirmary.

Kirby clenched her jaw, as she jerked from Vidar's grasp. She'd spent a month here once, when Starkad broke her ankle to keep her away from Brit. Starkad had visited her, racked with guilt. Brit never had.

But it hadn't happened *here*. This was a recreation. A bootleg. Kirby needed to remember that.

As she pushed past the memories, Vidar barked orders for triage, pointing a doctor toward Magnus first. That was one thing *not* in Kirby's past—a god, hanging around the infirmary. Was that concern on his face?

Of course it was. He'd had a notable chunk of trained soldiers put into hospital beds.

The moans, whimpers, and screams of pain made it difficult to think.

Kirby needed to help. No one deserved to suffer like this.

"We don't know what's wrong," one doctor called. "No wounds. No signs of internal injury."

"So sedate and medicate them until you have answers." Vidar snapped off the words. He stayed near Magnus's bed, face etched with deep lines.

Brit joined Kirby. "What do we do?" Brit sounded fine.

A stale wave of doubt joined the cacophony of Kirby's emotions. "I'm glad you healed."

"I didn't. I wasn't attacked. Ever get the feeling everyone knows what's going on except you?"

"Every fucking day. How did Vidar know…?" Where they were. To bring an army. Any of it.

"Magnus vanished during the fight, and moments later, she was back with the cavalry. Can you heal them?" Brit's voice dropped in volume on the question.

Starkad would probably have some argument about letting the enemy wallow in their agony, but Gwydion would already be helping the doctors. Kirby wouldn't let these people suffer, regardless of what the people she loved thought. And not just because these soldiers were hurt when they came to save her. "I can try."

She approached Magnus first, shouldering Vidar aside.

He grunted in disbelief.

Kirby didn't care, as long as he didn't stop her. She wasn't his student or his soldier. She was more than his equal. When she took Magnus's hand, she was met with a glassy-eyed stare of agony.

Kirby turned her concentration inward, drawing on the energy that kept her healed and spilling it into

Magnus. She focused on removing the pain and repairing any damage.

Magnus's grip relaxed, and Kirby opened her eyes. The pain was gone from Magnus's face, and she was flexing her free fingers. Her arm.

"You fixed me." Magnus was in awe.

Kirby was relieved to see her better. It didn't matter that Magnus's motives were still suspect, Kirby didn't want to see her in pain. The healing didn't take anything out of Kirby the way she expected, either.

"Do this for everyone. Please. If you have the strength."

If Kirby didn't know better, she'd think Vidar was begging. She'd planned to help regardless, and she moved to the next bed without pause.

Magnus was on her feet, looking fine. She rushed to another bed, concern in her voice as she chatted with the man who was only half-conscious thanks to the painkillers pumping through him.

Kirby healed one soldier after another. It didn't take as much from her as she expected. She was moving to Grunt Number Six, when Brit nudged her. Kirby followed her pointing, to see Magnus helping her friend out of bed.

"What...?" Kirby muttered.

"She healed him." Brit was quiet. "I watched."

—the fuck? If Magnus could do that, what was Kirby doing? Was this part of the same magic used to hide them? Teleport them?

Kirby finished her task, nursing irritation the entire time. The lies were expected, so why was she surprised by this one? Because she'd believed they needed her help. Bought into Vidar's concern. Magnus's pain.

And she was going to demand answers.

As she and Brit went to find Magnus and Vidar, Kirby ignored the chanting voice that wanted to know why she thought they'd tell her any more than they did before. Vidar wanted her here for a reason he hadn't given her yet, and that meant she had at least a little negotiating power. She also had some serious Valkyrie power.

She and Brit didn't have to go far. Vidar stood at the end of the hallway, talking quietly to Magnus.

"What did you do to me?" Magnus asked, wide-eyed.

"I healed you. I think. Though maybe you never needed it." Kirby didn't try to hide her distrust.

Magnus shook her head. "No. I—"

"Not here," Vidar said sharply.

He led them out a back door, keeping a brisk pace. The portion of lawn they covered was as neatly trimmed as Kirby expected, but the trees weren't right. They were too close—the infirmary had been nudged up near the woods on the old campus—and had been mostly maples and oaks. These were evergreens. Were they on the West Coast? Somewhere besides the US?

She didn't recognize the new building, either. It was a similar brick, late 1900's construction to the others on campus, but brand new to her. The interior was nothing like she expected. Sleek glass, steel, and black leather decorated everything. It was modern and minimalist.

The contrast of brand new versus having her past shoved down her throat was jarring, but a relief. "Nice to see you didn't go full jilted-lover and recreate the entire TOM campus."

"Heh." Vidar huffed out a strained laugh and led them into a small conference room. He looked at Magnus.

She pulled her tablet out, made a few swipes, and nodded.

He gestured to the chairs. "We can talk in here."

Weird. Did he expect someone besides him to be listening? No one sat.

"Is this reverse psychology tactic sixty-nine?" Kirby asked. "Now that we've been everywhere traumatic, let's go somewhere completely unfamiliar and pretend it should instill a false sense of security?"

Vidar pulled out a seat and made himself comfortable. "I barely knew you in your time here. Hel talked about you like a weapon, and to Loki, it was all a game. I don't know what causes you trauma. I'd rather you weren't suffering it while you're helping us. I put you in the room because I hoped the two of you would talk, and you did."

"Uh-huh." Kirby wanted a better comeback, but he made a good point.

"This is falling apart more quickly than I anticipated," Vidar said. "It's time for all of us to stop playing games and come clean."

Brit settled into a chair, expression bland. "Okay, boomer."

Kirby laughed and took the spot next to Brit. Being casual about this whole thing seemed like the most effective approach to frustrating Vidar. Since she wanted answers from him, and he seemed to need much more, it was time for Kirby to call his bluff and *stop playing games*. "I like the sound of it. How about this—you tell us why you're working so hard to keep us around, and then you let me bring in my associates, because your soldiers are mortal and very obviously not equipped for this."

"The attack you tried to use on me, you said it transfers the pain of your death to others," Vidar said.

The redirected conversation was the opposite of *no games*. "Why do you want us here?"

"Can you do the same with your other powers?" Vidar asked.

"Why do you want us here?"

Vidar raised an eyebrow. "You wrapped a shield around Magnus earlier, to keep her from getting shot. When you healed her, she was able to do the same for a short time. What else can you do that with?"

Ah. He was under some delusion she could make his soldiers more powerful.

Could she? Not that she would for him, but if she could share this with another individual. Brit, maybe? The notion clawed at her with doubt and hope and tasted acidic. "I doubt it. When there were more than me, did you ever see a Valkyrie do something like that?"

"I saw a Valkyrie grant her lover immortality because she couldn't bear to watch him die." Vidar stared at her, unflinching.

"I didn't give Starkad my power. I simply refused to take him to Valhalla."

150

Vidar's expression was marble. "You think Odin punished you for *that*? Refusing to grant Starkad a warrior's afterlife hasn't kept him alive for a thousand years. He's stubborn, and the fight means more than anything to him, but last I checked, force of will doesn't grant immortality. What about the wings? Can you share those?"

"No." Could she? Kirby would hate this doubt, if she wasn't fascinated by the possibility. Whatever she'd done to Magnus hadn't lingered. When she inflicted pain on others, she could take it away again. And Brit was right here, a willing subject. Kirby stood and tugged Brit to her feet. "You ready for this?"

Brit was practically humming with anticipation when she nodded. Or that was the electricity that flowed between them. Kirby had no idea how this worked, but focus tended to be most effective when she summoned anything Valkyrie. She pictured Brit with wings. Armor. Glorious and vibrant. They'd fight side-by-side so well.

Sparks singed Kirby's fingers, and she yelped in surprise as she jerked away.

Brit wore a frown, but no wings.

"That's a no go." Kirby forced her disappointment to stay at bay.

"Doesn't your power clash with Brit's?" Magnus asked. "Ever since Hel made her immortal, your magics are incompatible?"

Kirby didn't remember telling either of them that.

151

"I volunteer as tribute." Magnus's words were light and not nearly so impulsive sounding as she might think.

But if sharing was an option, Kirby could revoke it, too. She'd done so before. She wouldn't give Magnus immortality, just the wings, and then yank them away again as quickly.

The entire idea still made her nervous. She exchanged glances with Brit, not having any idea what she wanted to convey beyond *help me keep this from being a mistake.*

Brit's faint nod was reassuring.

Kirby met Magnus at the front of the room, and grasped the Noble's fingers. She summoned the same image she had with Brit, though the warm fuzzies weren't there when she pictured Magnus with glorious wings.

Magnus's gasp and the faint tug on Kirby's hands forced her eyes open. It worked. Magnus floated a few centimeters off the ground, and she wore the brightest grin to accompany the large auburn wings spanned from her back.

Holy fuck. Kirby retracted the gift in a blink, and Magnus landed on the balls of her feet.

Kirby refused to imagine the fallout if even one member of TOM kept and warped what she had. "I'm not doing this for your people."

"You can't fight without them." Vidar sounded smug, like he'd made an inarguable point.

He hadn't.

"I have my own people. I trust them." Loved them. Knew them so very intimately, and not just in a physical sense.

"You shouldn't," Vidar said. "But it doesn't matter how you feel, because they're not here. You came back without them."

Like she'd had a choice if she wanted answers? Which she had now. Vidar wanted her to make his people powerful. "So, what? You'll walk into this battle you're not prepared for, and you think I'll go out of my way to keep your people alive? No. Not my war. Not my problem."

Vidar's smile was more unnerving than his stony-faced expression. "You willingly returned to a campus where most everyone wanted you dead, and you did it to keep those people alive. That wasn't your war either. If I stick you in the middle of a fight, you'll help. It's who you are."

"And your people will die regardless." Kirby wanted to argue that he was wrong, but these were soldiers, trained to follow orders. And a large number of them literally worshiped Vidar. "You don't have many left, even if you don't give a fuck about the individual lives."

"You also still haven't told us why you're invested in this fight," Brit said. "It's not because FU wants Kirby dead. What is it?"

Silence.

Kirby cast her gaze between Magnus and Vidar, who were sharing one of those *should we say this* looks. Would they admit what she had figured out?

Vidar sighed and leaned forward in his chair, staring at his clasped hands. "Freya and Hel aren't the only ones who helped lock away Malsumis. I can't give you all of their names, because they all took the same pact, but Grytha was one was well, and she's missing."

"Your mother." Kirby was so used to the gods fighting among family—Loki and Fenrir for instance—that she forgot some of them were as close-knit as mortal families. "I'm sorry, but that doesn't sell me on taking your side." Did she sound believable? She was already going to help Aya, and she couldn't stand to see the underdog be trampled on, even if they were the enemy most of the time.

"Kirby's right about needing extra help." Brit knew her too well. "We can't do this without her team."

"They're not going to help me, even if I want them here," Vidar said.

"They will if Kirby asks. Especially if what you say is true about her being a target. But even without that, all she has to do is ask."

Kirby heard an edge in Brit's voice—envy mixed with awe and conviction.

Vidar kept his attention on Kirby. "That dragon came for *you* in the field. She said as much. You don't have to believe me, you saw it for yourself." He dragged in a deep breath and let out a long sigh. "All right. I don't like this, but I want Grytha returned safely. I'd rather have as little to do with your *people* as possible, especially Starkad." He said the name with the same level of disdain as every other time it passed his lips.

"Starkad is a warrior. *The* warrior besides Brit. Why are you so opposed to him?" Kirby asked.

Vidar shook his head. "The only thing he stands for is you, and I'm not even certain about that some days. He's dangerous."

Not to Kirby, but Vidar's words left a trail of question marks in her mind.

"You have forty-eight hours to convince them, and then I give up on you," Vidar said. "Not that I'm concerned about *you*."

Curious. "Why not?"

"Because you were a shitty Noble."

Kirby didn't like that those words still stung after all these years. "I was the best."

"But you were honest. Honorable," Brit said.

"Good to your word," Magnus added.

Vidar stood. "Those aren't Noble traits."

Given the number of ways Kirby had been taught to lie in school, she couldn't argue. "I'll reach out once I've talked to Starkad and the others."

CHAPTER THIRTY

KIRBY

Magnus refused to teleport them for this trip.

Not that Vidar would let her. "I refuse to risk her in that den of vicious immortals." He sounded so serious, that Kirby couldn't find the voice to ask where he thought Magnus was now.

Vidar planted them on a street in front of a nondescript building, and nodded at a doorway that simply said NEON on it. "We'll speak in two days," he said, and then he was gone.

Kirby had been into this part of the city several times since she moved to the suburbs with Starkad, but she'd never noticed this building. She looked at Brit, who shrugged.

Kirby kept her armor within mental reach, and pushed inside.

It was a club. An empty one, with all the lights on. Kind of depressing.

"Kirby?" The voice was one she hadn't heard in centuries, but brought a smile. *Fenrir.*

She turned to see him striding toward them. She'd always liked Fen. They were friends in his first life, and in the few times she'd run into him since.

He wrapped her in a giant hug, and she squeezed back. It was nice to run into a friend. Someone she didn't need to second-guess. Did she?

Fen stepped back to study her. "What's wrong?"

"Trust issues." That ran so very deep. She gave him a weak smile.

"Tell me this isn't another lover," Brit said dryly.

Kirby and Fen spoke at the same time. "Definitely not."

Kirby couldn't fathom sleeping with him. She adored him as a person, and if he was here, Frey may be too—this looked like Frey's kind of thing—but there was no sexual attraction.

Fen turned. "You must be Brit."

"Must I be?" She was definitely on the defensive.

Kirby should be too. Unknown situation. God she hadn't seen him in ages. But she couldn't muster the concern. "Brit, Fenrir."

"Ah." Brit's reaction was impossible to read.

"So we were just deposited here..." Kirby didn't want to say by whom, or why. She was already trying to figure out how to make Starkad and the others listen when she explained to them.

Fen nodded toward the doorway he'd come through at the opposite end of the room. "Everyone's in back, except Aya, Freyr, and Dahlia." A shadow crossed his face. "Frey and Dahlia are fetching information."

Min had explained Frey and Aya reaching out to the others. Dahlia being here probably explained why Magnus refused to make the trip. Maybe they actually did have a falling out.

"What kind of information? Where's Aya?" Kirby had always admired the goddess, and knowing what she did now, about how Aya had been unable to help before, rather than just refusing, it was difficult to hold onto that grudge.

Fen's frown deepened. "We were attacked, by FU forces, a dragon, and Gluskab. When the dust cleared, she was gone. We assume Gluskab has her."

Did that happen before or after Kirby encountered the same? "We'll find her." She didn't remember Fen being close to Aya, but he was close to Frey, who held his sister in high regard.

"I know. But not without a serious plan. We got our asses handed to us last time."

Kirby knew the feeling. "I guess we have time to catch up and share intel."

"I'm sure everyone else will be happy to do exactly that." Fen gestured toward the back of the bar again.

Everyone. Kirby's anticipation spiked. It had only been a few days, but not knowing when she'd see Gwydion again. Starkad. That had gnawed at her. She and Brit followed Fen down a long hallway, through an unmarked door, and into something that looked more like a house than a business. He stopped in the doorway of a living room, and Kirby's heart skipped.

She barely had time to register that Gwydion and Min were here, before Starkad was in front of her. He gripped her hips tightly, lifting her to press her back into the wall as he crushed his mouth to hers.

She wrapped her legs around him out of instinct, drowning in the security and intensity.

He bit her lips enough to draw blood and lick it away before the wounds healed. He held her tightly enough to leave marks on her skin. With each heartbeat, the world drifted further away, until nothing else existed.

Fen cleared his throat, jarring her back to reality.

Starkad didn't let up.

Kirby laughed into his kiss. "Answers first, fucking later," she murmured against his lips.

Starkad's growl rumbled through her entire body. The primal sound was as much wolf as human, and it shouldn't be. She didn't care—it was intoxicating. He finally set her on her feet with a gruff, "fine."

Gwydion was by her side, cupping her cheeks and searching her face. "I can't compete with that." His tone was light, but he sounded off.

"Good. Never be anyone but you." Kirby needed his touch.

Gwydion kissed her gently, drawing out the moment until she thought she'd tumble into nothing and love every minute of it. If Starkad was security, Gwydion was safety. An odd distinction, but one would protect if she needed, and the other would keep her away from harm to begin with.

Min's greeting was a more reserved kiss on the back of Kirby's knuckles, but the way he said, "Welcome back, Huntress," made her grin.

Gwydion and Min gave Brit warm hugs as well.

"I'm going to leave you all to talk." Fen looked out of place. "I'm down the hall if you need me, and if there's news, you'll know as soon as I do."

"Thank you." Kirby turned back to the group as soon as he was gone. Her gaze fell on Starkad's arm. She gasped. "What happened?" The limb looked like a twisted blend of truck liner and rotted tree, from shoulder to fingertips.

She reached out tentatively and he turned his hand up to tangle his fingers with hers. It still felt like flesh. Still moved and pulsed like Starkad, which explained why she hadn't noticed during the kiss.

He squeezed her hand, led her toward an upholstered chair, and dropped into the cushions, pulling her into his lap in the process. "We believe it's the same thing that happened to you—TOM bullets. I'm fine. It looks far worse than it feels."

Thank the gods for that, because it looked pretty bad, and Kirby still remembered how much her wound had hurt.

"Vidar says he has a cure," Brit said.

Kirby wanted to hug her for remembering.

Min sat next to Gwydion on a nearby couch. "Speaking of, I was under the impression you were returning to him."

"We tried." Kirby wasn't having the best luck with plans lately. "But a dragon intercepted us, and there was a fight TOM was grossly under-equipped for, and Vidar brought us back here because Grytha was taken, presumably the same people who took Aya. If we help him, maybe he'll heal your arm." The instant the words passed her lips, she realized how naive it sounded. "Yeah, never mind."

Starkad traced his nose up the side of her neck. "It's fine. It's not pretty, but it's fucking useful in a fight."

Kirby leaned her weight into him further. "So we have a god who's kidnapping the gods who locked his sister away because she was dangerous. He appears to be working with a dragon, who also wants me dead."

"We hoped that wasn't true. That Dahlia was wrong." A strain ran through Gwydion's voice. Heavy shadows lingered under his eyes and he looked drained. That wasn't right. They were all tired, but something about him was off.

"*I've always wondered how Valkyrie tastes* is a pretty specific threat." Kirby would be hearing those words for a while. "Wait." She twisted to face Starkad. "TOM bullets—I thought FU was the enemy. Where did you go after the quake?"

"Norway. One minute I was in the living room, and the next I was standing in front of a very pissed off Fenrir, in the middle of the woods. TOM worked pretty hard to keep us there, so whatever Vidar promised you, I'm even less inclined than normal to believe it."

"But why would..." The several instances Vidar mentioned not trusting Starkad rushed back. Would he go to that kind of trouble to keep Kirby away from

Starkad, just to get her help? Vidar had to know she'd find out.

"Speaking Dahlia, what do you think of her?" Brit would be looking for a bar to compare Magnus's behavior to.

Kirby was grateful for the shift in conversation to move on from the glaring stupidity of her putting even the smallest amount of faith in Vidar. She still believed what he said about Grytha, though.

"What do you think I think?" Starkad's tone changed in an instant to menacing.

No surprise there. It seemed unlikely he would warm to any Noble.

"I like her," Gwydion said. "Fen and Frey seem rather attached to her, which is also a good sign."

"I like her as well. Far more than the young lady you were with—Magnus." Min tended to like most people, so the fact that he had doubts about Magnus was more telling than the rest of his response.

Kirby looked at Brit, curious if that answered her question.

Brit shrugged. "I'd be hard pressed to hurt either one of them unless they gave me a reason. They're still... you know."

Kirby did. And the disconnect between wanting her friends from school back, and how stupid it was to trust anyone, especially former classmates, was glaring.

CHAPTER THIRTY-ONE

GWYDION

It was disconcerting to still be in pain even a few minutes after a fight, let alone hours. The fact that he was struggling to grasp his full power was something Gwydion didn't care for.

Having Kirby back, safe and acting exactly like herself helped. All the way down to the fact she said she was working with Vidar. It didn't matter that he'd had a hand in her shitty upbringing and trauma, he'd asked her for help and go figure, she said yes.

Her drive to save the world was both admirably lovable and frustration at its most chaotic.

Gwydion looked up at a knock on the entryway frame.

Fen had returned. "Just talked to Frey. He and Dahlia won't be back for several hours, but they want to see you." He focused on Kirby. "Since you've all been going everywhere since your house and hotel rooms were destroyed, you're welcome to stay here."

"No offense, but a hotel is probably more comfortable"—and private— "than a lounge at a club." Gwydion wouldn't be the only one who wanted some time with Kirby.

Fen was unfazed. "This block, and the three adjoining ones, are more than just a club—NEON is more than just a club. This is a refuge for immortals who are sick of the games gods play. We're not self-contained, but thanks to the various magics, we're close. Follow me."

As everyone stood, Fen paused and shot a pointed glare at Starkad. "But keep an eye on your puppy."

It seemed their time together hadn't brought them any closer. Gwydion might joke that he understood Fen's sentiment, but for all the shit he gave Starkad, Gwydion wouldn't want him gone. Starkad was more than the straight man to Gwydion's jokes. He was part of Kirby's world, and Gwydion's friend.

The group stepped out another door, and into the night. There was sky above them, despite being underground. They were at the edge of a small clearing of grass, tress, and even a stream with a bridge over it.

Shops lined the cleaning. A diner. A florist. A clothing boutique. More. Behind them, the door they'd just come through, was an actual facing for NEON. Somehow, despite the contrasting nature of the club, it fit in here.

Gwydion breathed deep, drawing in as much of the outdoors as his lungs could hold. A spark of replenishment bloomed inside, but he couldn't grow it.

"Feel free to wander. Check the place out." Fen swept his arm wide. He led them down a stone path, past the businesses and into a row of apartments.

The entire place was the perfect blend of modern living and escaping to nature. The type of feeling so many towns tried to recreate, but wasn't quite possible without a little magic.

Or a lot.

A little farther, and they were on a street lined with adorable homes, complete with the lawns, flowerbeds, and white picket fences.

"Idyllic." Starkad didn't make it sound like a good thing.

Fen rolled his eyes. "I know where you were living before. Don't pretend that wasn't the goal." He led them up the walk of one house, and let them inside.

"Not locked?" Starkad asked with disdain. "Next you'll tell me there aren't any security cameras."

"No one is finding this place," Fen said. "Make yourselves at home. We'll touch base after you're rested."

Inside, dark wood wainscoting ran along the bottom of the walls, and distinct, darker paint decorated the top halves. The furniture was clean and new, but the style was more than a century old, with rich velvets that matched the walls and plush carpet.

It was Victorian made new again.

"This entire place—NEON—is amazing." Brit's awe was adorable.

And a good reminder to Gwydion that even someone like her, someone who was raised on death, still saw the new and incredible in the world.

As everyone else settled into seats, Kirby grabbed Gwydion's hand and tugged him away from the group with a chipper-but-terse, "We'll get the coffee."

They reached the kitchen and she planted her back to the wall, facing him and grasping his fingers.

"I'm so glad you're safe." He dipped his head to brush his lips over hers.

She pressed into the light kiss, breathing a spark of heat into the sweetness, and broke away with a tiny smile on her face. "Do you want to know something?"

"Always."

"Even before I had my memories back, I knew instinctively Starkad would tear the world to shreds to keep me safe." Sadness whispered through Kirby's smile, but it vanished again in an instant. "Even when he refused to admit the pull between us."

"You sure you don't want him here instead of me?" Gwydion asked dryly.

She shook her head. "I grabbed the right person, I promise. The instant I met you, every time I meet you, you anchor me. I think that's why I remember when you're around. You're my sanity in a world that stopped being sane a long time ago."

The words warmed Gwydion in a way her touch couldn't. "I could say the same about you." She was the Alice to his Hatter—the core of stability in a word where everyone was mad including them.

She nodded. "Which is why I can tell you're not okay."

"I'm just tired."

"All right. Except you're limping. Among other things" Kirby dropped her hand to his side and nudged the bruise hidden under his shirt.

Gwydion couldn't hide his wince from a pain that shouldn't be there.

Warmth flowed from Kirby into the bruise, healing and sapping away the ache. She moved her hand to his leg next and treated him to a similar sensation.

"Thank you." He *was* grateful, but also concerned that he couldn't do that himself.

Her slight frown implied she felt the same. "What's going on?"

"Something happened during this last fight. Or rather, it *didn't* happen. I couldn't reach all of my power." It was a relief to admit it, and he wasn't sure why. "It's as though a switch has been flipped and I'm running on reserves rather than recharging. As though once I'm spent, there won't be any more."

"You didn't mention this before." Kirby's tone was concerned rather than accusatory. "How long has it been happening?"

"It's new. I was fine on campus. Even when the quakes started, I was me. Maybe when everyone got sent to the four corners of the world, my godliness made a similar trip." It was meant to be a joke. Neither of them laughed.

"What do we need to do to figure it out?" Kirby asked.

The realization struck him—this was why he didn't mind telling her. "What if we don't? What if we let whatever this is run its course, and I sputter out?"

Kirby's frown deepened.

Gwydion didn't mean that the way it sounded. "I'm not saying I want to give up, this isn't a fatalistic thing, but would it be so bad to be like Brit? Immortal, but not a god?" Another thought slid into his head. "There's one drawback, though."

"What's that?"

"I can't fight by your side like this." After so many centuries of war, Gwydion would always choose to heal rather than wound, but, "Something big is coming. I don't know if it's more than Gluskab, but the fact that he and the dragons have made an alliance is terrifying enough."

Kirby pressed into him, cheek to his chest and his shirt clenched in her fists. "I know. And I don't know what to do about any of it. At least I can trust the four of you, though."

Gwydion wrapped his arms around her and rested his cheek on the top of her head. "I won't lose you again. *Never* again."

"Same." Kirby pulled away enough to meet his gaze, not breaking the contact between them. "If the roles were reversed, would you let me go into battle like you are now?"

He wasn't sitting this fight out. "Would you let me stop you? You haven't once held back from a battle—physical or otherwise—because one of us asked you to." Despite being stressful, it was also one of the many things Gwydion loved about her.

"I was made for war."

Aya's words echoed in his thoughts. "No. You were made to be the balance between life and death, and you are that balance."

"Which is why I have to pursue this. Gluskab, Malsumis, they'll destroy that balance."

This was a circular argument. Gwydion wasn't conceding, and Kirby wouldn't either while he was in this kind of shape. "If I could recharge." His thought was born of desperation, but it quickly formed into more.

"Is that possible?"

"I don't know. But there are spots close to home"—his home, the place of his creation, where the land still breathed life into and energized him— "Similar to Stonehenge, but unmarred by swaths of people. If I could spend a little time there."

Kirby nodded. "If it doesn't work, you're not going to into battle with us."

It had to work. As tempting as the thought of surrendering his godhood was at first glance, Gwydion wasn't ready to roll over and give up.

Chapter Thirty-Two

MIN

The moment Gwydion and Kirby joined them, Starkad was at Kirby's side, grabbing her by the waist and pulling her back to his chair, to sit in his lap.

"Possessive much?" Kirby settled despite her question.

"Everyone else has taken your time, it's my turn." The growl in Starkad's voice had been there since he returned with Fen.

It was as fascinating as it was wonderful to Min, for all of them to have been together so much. This had never been the case in any of Kirby's other lives, especially with Starkad.

So Min didn't know if this behavior was typical, but he'd never seen Starkad like this. Physically he seemed fine, despite the glaring issue with his arm. But he was more aggressive with Kirby. More primal, as if some of his humanity had slipped away. And a faint aura of death encircled him—not the kind that was waiting to sink into him, but rather it was as if the cloud waited for its next victim to approach.

"What's the plan?" Brit watched Starkad and Kirby with a faint scowl. Brit was different too. She didn't look as disgruntled as she had in the past, when it came to Starkad, and unlike him, the aura of death around her was fading.

"I need to make a trip home," Gwydion said. "As soon as Frey returns I'll have him take me. It should only be a few hours."

Starkad rolled his eyes. "Do you really think this is the time for nostalgia?"

"Yes." Kirby's playfulness vanished in an it's-not-open-for-discussion tone. She looked around the room, as if daring someone to challenge her. "Until then, we need to be on the same page. Share *everything* you've learned since we were split up. It doesn't matter if you think it's repetition."

Min loathed the life Kirby lived while she was growing up, but this confidence, her ability to command a situation and a strategy, left him in awe. She'd never been more his huntress.

The five of them shared their experiences and knowledge gained from the past few days. One thing stood out as unexpected—the stories they'd heard from both sides held very few discrepancies, including nearly identical prophecies. "Perhaps there's some truth to what TOM is telling us after all," Min said.

Starkad stared back in disbelief. "Or there's no truth to any of it, and they've coordinated their stories." He focused on Kirby. "And you're not going back to Vidar."

"I gave him my word." She twisted in his lap so she faced him. "He brought soldiers to save us, something he has a limited number of. Magnus was already clear. He could have left Brit and I out there and walked away."

"Except there's a reason he needs you, and you can't possibly think he's told you the full story there," Starkad argued.

Brit scoffed. "Uh, duh? How is that any different than these gods?" She gestured broadly.

She didn't understand, but Min found the question insulting regardless. "Frey and Aya, Fen, they've been friends to most of us for centuries. They're trustworthy."

"But they're following Dahlia's cues," Brit said. "Either intentionally or otherwise. Everyone's allegiances are in question. Even you're different, Min. I know that, and I haven't been around long. I'm not saying it's bad, but if you can change, so can they."

A reasonable point. And a disturbing one, since Min had always been what he was. His world was a lot less black and white now, and some of those shades of gray were less than appealing.

Gwydion lingered near the door, leaning against the wall with his arms crossed. "Dahlia walked away from TOM, Magnus didn't. Vidar immersed himself more in the organization, picking up the pieces of a broken cult and reassembling it to be his own. I agree with Starkad—assuming he's told us the full story is foolish."

"Dahlia *says* she walked away." Starkad's agitation was palpable. "Why are we taking her word for anything? Because she's fooled people we like? Because she's endearingly awkward? She's got the same training as anyone else who came out of that place, and she's a Noble."

Kirby extracted herself from his lap and stood next to his chair. He reached for her hand.

"Sometimes when people say they've left TOM, they mean it." Irritation crept into Brit's voice. "You people are hundreds—some of you thousands—of years old. Why is *the pretty young lady lied and fooled us* your go to move?"

"Your leaving didn't make you any less of a threat," Starkad said.

Brit's scowl deepened. "It would've if you hadn't been so insistent I was all bad."

Kirby stepped farther from either of them. Her posture was loose, which would be *relaxed* in most people. For her, it indicated she was on her guard.

"Do you blame me for not trusting you?" Starkad's question was gravel.

"I gave Vidar my word." Kirby's edged tone sliced through the mounting tension. "I don't trust him. I *never* said that, and he knows I don't, but I promised we'd help. The lot of you have already promised we'll rescue Aya, and I'm fine with that. But if Grytha is there, we're not leaving her because Vidar's an asshole."

"Your promise doesn't make *any* of Vidar's story true." Gwydion crossed the room to join them, but his posture was no less defensive. "Including anything he said about Grytha. For all we know she's retired on some island in the Atlantic."

Kirby clenched her jaw. She wasn't naive or stupid. She also wasn't great at hiding her emotion when it came to lying, but she knew how to spot the cues in others. She'd been trained in deception like any other Noble, as Starkad said. And to her, justice and balance meant everything. If she gave Vidar her word, if she was looking for a reason to trust Magnus, she saw something worth working with. Despite being unable to vocalize it. She may not even be completely conscious of whatever let her make the promise to Vidar in the first place.

"Kirby's right," Min said.

Starkad pinched the bridge of his nose. "We can't trust them."

"You don't have to. We won't give them any additional information, keeping in mind that so far most of what we know came from them." As Min spoke, Kirby's expression softened.

"And if that's all culminating in leading us into a trap?" Starkad asked.

Gwydion stood straighter. Looked more determined. "We can trust Frey and Fen."

"Eh…" Starkad led his uncertainty drag into a sigh.

"And if it is a trap, it puts us closer to the source anyway, doesn't it." Brit made it sound as though even being captured was preferable.

It may be, if the group had the resources to get out. They'd survived the first round of being split up and thrown into disarray. Granted, it had been mostly torture free. Even Starkad and his mangled arm came out of it all right.

"Unless the point is to draw us as far from the source as possible." Starkad stood, raising himself to full height. He knew what an imposing presence he was. "We're not doing this without more information."

"I am." Kirby stood toe-to-toe with him. Despite being half a head shorter, she matched the threat and strength he radiated as she stared him down. "Go with me, or stay here and whimper."

Starkad's low growl rumbled through the floor, and the small trinkets nearby rattled. "You're not leaving my side again."

"Then you'll be joining us." A soft black glow licked in coils around Kirby.

As the two stared each other down, the air in the room grew heavy, until breathing felt like inhaling molasses. When did this become a power struggle?

CHAPTER THIRTY-THREE

KIRBY

The girl who was raised by TOM, the assassin taught to be tougher than anyone and to never back down, was terrified right now. Kirby's heart slammed against her ribs and her current incarnation pleaded for her to step away. To not piss off Starkad.

But the Kirby at her core, the woman she'd lost so many lives ago when Odin cursed her, screamed for her to stand her ground. *I'm his equal. I always have been. When did we forget?*

The conflict made her fear that same kind of delicious she craved when she was feeling self-destructive, but this time, without the desire to implode on herself.

The aura Starkad radiated shouldn't be there. He was a creature of magic, but not one who could wield it.

The tendrils of power encasing her were new as well, and with them shielding her, she could anything.

"Hey." Fen's bark disrupted the tension and both walls of power shattered, but the staring match continued. "What the fuck are you doing? I told you to keep him under control."

Kirby took a deep breath, and broke eye contact with Starkad as she turned to face Fen. Starkad would either see it as submission or an insult, though it was more of a *we'll finish this later*. Her apology to Fen died on her lips when she saw the way he was watching them, with a mixture of concern and... fear?

That couldn't be right.

Whatever she'd seen vanished.

"The entire block is rumbling," Fen said. "This is a sanctuary and if you violate that, you won't be welcome here."

Kirby hated the sound of that. She was happy to have Fen and Frey back in her life, despite the short timespan. "I'm sorry. I'll behave. Any idea when the others will be back? Gwydion needs to make a trip."

Fen shrugged. *"Hours* is still the only answer I have."

"Thank you. And sorry, again." Kirby made sure to sound contrite. She scrubbed her face when she left, and kept her attention on the room, rather than Starkad. Easiest way to keep her center. She didn't want to waste hours waiting for Frey, and then more hours waiting for Gwydion to come back, and then even more hours making more plans.

If they could overlap at least two of those, things would move fast. Time to suggest something no one would go for, and hope things didn't escalate further with Starkad. "Magnus can take Gwydion."

Starkad's laugh ended with an abrupt, *no.*

Kirby kept her back to him, and her focus on Gwydion. "It's your call."

"I hate to say it, but I'm not useful if I don't make this trip." Gwydion's resignation rang heavy. "I trust you. If you think this is the right call, I'll do it."

For as much as she'd argued, Kirby still had her doubts. She also needed to make a decision and move forward. Doing nothing wasn't an option. She had her phone out and was walking away as she dialed Magnus, before Starkad could stop her. She half-expected him to grab the device away from her.

"Valkyrie." Magnus's greeting was friendly and cheerfully surprised. "I hoped you'd call."

Kirby winced at the nickname the other Nobles gave her after she was gone. No one else had used it in a complimentary way. "I promised."

"You did. You ready to come back?"

Kirby was intently aware of everyone's focus, and while she loved an audience, this wasn't working for her. She wandered toward the door. "I need a favor."

"For you? Anything."

Though Magnus's reply was brightly enthusiastic, it also sounded genuine. Was the hurt she had when Kirby had ruined their morning outing real? Kirby had wanted to belong for so long, and finally felt like she did. Was Magnus searching for that same connection, and missing it in the friends she'd had?

Was she sincere?

"Gwydion needs a ride, and there's no one here right now who can take him," Kirby said.

"Nope." Magnus *popped* on the P. "Not just him. You're welcome to hang out with your creepy old gods, but if you want me to take one of them somewhere, you have to be there too."

Kirby glanced back at the room, and the sets of eyes fixed on her. "He's not creepy."

Gwydion raised an eyebrow, but he was smiling.

"But I'll go with you. That's fair," Kirby said.

"*No.*" Starkad's roar was loud enough to make Kirby wince. "Not without me."

Magnus sighed. Apparently she heard that. "This isn't a field trip, and Starkad *definitely* isn't welcome."

It was what it was. "Okay. Just me and Gwydion. Thank you."

CHAPTER THIRTY-FOUR

GWYDION

The edge of the woods where they appeared was familiar and intoxicating. The air tasted of fresh mead and woodsmoke and whimsy.

Gwydion breathed deep and held the air in his lungs, letting the sensation permeate him.

It felt good here, but that flood of magic—that re-energizing sensation he'd hoped for—wasn't here.

"This is an in and out gig, right?" Magnus sounded impatient.

Min had been right, she wasn't nearly so endearing as Dahlia.

A maze of stones stood a few meters away, glowing with a faint sheen some would sense, but few would ever recognize enough to see. He needed to lose himself in those for a few hours. "This may take a while. Feel free to hop into town and grab a beer or something."

"I'm not a fucking Uber."

"Please give us some time?" Kirby's tone was almost demure. "I'm not going anywhere. You have my word."

Magnus let out a long sigh. "When you're done with them, can we talk? Just you and me? No tricks, no barriers, no gods at all?"

No.

"Sure." Kirby nodded. "I'll call you when Gwydion is done and then you and I can go get actual coffee or something."

Magnus glared at Gwydion. "You're not going to tell her *no*?"

"As much as I'd like to, Kirby's perfectly capable of speaking for herself."

"Hmm." Magnus raised an eyebrow. "Okay. I'll wait for you call."

When she vanished, a familiar whisper tickled Gwydion's senses. He'd felt it when they arrived, too, but he assumed it was part of the environment. He was too weak to identify the tainted magic around Magnus, though.

"What next?" Kirby slipped her hand into Gwydion's.

He squeezed. "I'm not sure. I hoped just being here would help. This has never happened to me before, so I'm making it up as I go along."

"You know a guy gets to be a certain age, and things change when it comes to getting it up." Kirby's teasing was hesitant.

Gwydion laughed. Dick jokes made most situations lighter. He squeezed her hand and pointed her toward the stones. "Sometimes a guy just needs a little extra build-up to find that magic feeling."

Kirby gave him a look that was all feigned shock. "Are you suggesting what I think you are? Here?"

"When was the last time you fucked on sacred ground? There's a charge that comes from that." Gwydion hadn't meant for teasing to take this turn, but with the tug of the stones and the pulse of Kirby's aura against his, want spilled inside.

"That's quite a line." Kirby's tone slid toward playful. "You going to buy me dinner first?"

He dragged his nose up her neck, drawing in a deep breath of her scent mixed with earth and magic. "This will be more filling than a meal."

She relaxed under his touch, and tilted her head, exposing more of her neck. "Not sure if you're talking about *the charge* or your dick. Or is one a euphemism for the other?"

"You know I love to brag, but my cock can't compete with this."

"But you are needed to complete the experience. Or could I take care of things myself?" Her playfulness was as intoxicating as the hum in the air.

The combination of sensations was like being drunk, without the loss of reason. He could throw that away without alcohol, though. "You *could*. I love watching a good show as much as participating. But the physical connection is where the real spark comes from." He danced his fingers lightly up her spine, every tap running far below his skin. "This is sex plus eternal adoration and love, plus magic. The experience will blow you out of the water."

Kirby raised an eyebrow, as if looking for the right joke to reply with, but he wasn't teasing this time.

He could drown in the love that flowed between them. It was a tangible caress against his skin, everywhere he made contact and even where he didn't. It wrapped around them in a faint, shimmering mist.

Gwydion cupped her face and stroked his thumb over her cheek. "It seems so implausible that two beings could have what we have, and that it's lasted across lives and centuries." He spoke quietly, needing to be a part of their surroundings rather than disrupting them. "Each time I lost you, each time I went searching for you, I swore I was losing my mind. I was in love with a ghost. But the high each time I found you, it soared."

She leaned into his touch. "When you found me this time, the first time we met again, I *was* losing my mind." The conversation sounded somber, but it wasn't bad. This was another degree of how Kirby connected with Gwydion. They could be anything they needed with each other. "Because I'd just seen a ghost," she said.

"Brit."

Kirby nodded. "You weren't supposed to be there that day."

"I was never supposed to know where you were. I couldn't stand waiting anymore, and Min took pity on me."

"If you'd stayed away… If you hadn't found me in that hotel bar… I don't know what would have happened." Kirby moved her hands to his chest, and gripped his shirt with both fists. "It terrifies me to dive into that possibility, knowing the outcome would've been bad."

"You don't have to dive in, though. A wise woman once told me that playing the *what if* game leads to insanity."

She rested her cheek against his ribs, over his heart. "That's not was I was talking about, and it's not quite what I said."

"But the lesson is the same." He trailed his fingers through her hair. The magical light caught the highlights, making them look like real gold. "Dwelling breeds madness, and between the two of us, we already have enough crazy."

"Not sure if you're talking about—"

"My dick or my life?" Gwydion teased.

Kirby laughed and pulled her head back to look him in the eye. "I love you. Not just for anchoring me but for being you. Strong. Funny. Smart. Loyal."

"Well hung?"

"Are you bored with being serious?" She sounded amused rather than upset.

Gwydion searched her face, smiling softly. "I've never been more serious about anything— anyone—than I am about loving you." His voice came out gravelly. "Never doubt that. If you do, ask me and I'll remind you." He brushed his lips over hers. "I love you so completely. I'm your loyal servant, for all of eternity."

He kissed her again, tenderly, marveling at her soft gasp and the distinct spark that flowed between them. The moment, the place, and the woman drew him in, and he deepened the kiss, diving his tongue into her mouth. Pressing her back into a nearby stone, so their bodies molded to each other.

Magic swelled inside, replenishing him, but at this moment it was the last thing he cared about. He was connected to Kirby, and that bond was tangible. Their kisses blended into a flurry of desperate hands, stripping away clothes so they could be closer. So skin could meet skin.

The more of *her* he felt, the stronger the bond grew. The more he swore he could sense everyone she was connected with. Starkad. Min. Brit. The tug of their presence was ethereal. Potent.

As Gwydion drank in her body, Kirby's wings were extended, stark and stunning against her pale skin, and she literally glowed. He did too. The light cocooned around them.

He felt other threads too, spreading out from her. Faint. Tied to people he couldn't name. A dozen or more. But it wasn't the same kind of bond. It was an unrealized love, but not physical or romantic.

Gwydion and Kirby's feet no longer touched the ground. She draped her arms around his neck and her legs around his waist, and he swallowed her sighs of joy.

He brushed her hair from her face. "I love you more than should be possible," he murmured against her lips as he slid inside her.

She arched into the penetration. He understood the meaning behind her drawn out moan because he felt it too. That sensation of being complete mixed with ecstasy.

Nothing was purer than this.

CHAPTER THIRTY-FIVE

KIRBY

This was the first time Kirby had ever seen literal sparks during sex. But this was more that fucking. This was belonging. With Gwydion buried inside her, the air rushing around them, they were one.

A torrent of magic spilled through her veins, coming from him, flowing to him, and laced with him. Flying during sex wasn't new for them, and she loved the weightlessness, but this was *more*.

Kirby wrapped herself around him as tightly as possible as he thrust, pushing her desire and pleasure higher, farther. Being this close, this intertwined, shouldn't be enough. But the way their souls, hearts, energy, and bodies were intermingled, it was everything.

Gwydion slammed into her harder. Faster. Murmuring *I love yous* in half a dozen languages against her skin, bathing her in kisses and ancient words, and she replied in kind.

As she drew closer to climax, the sensation was new. This wasn't the high of endorphins that she'd sought in pain for so long. That she still dove into with Starkad and lost herself in. This was something she didn't have the words for in any language. *Incredible* felt too tame.

Her body flushed and shuddered and tingled with the wash of orgasm, and she let the pleasure flow. Like this, she could be anything. She could conquer or save the world. Nations would fall at her feet and she would serve them in kind.

None of that mattered when Gwydion came, spilling inside her, filling her. The people she loved, who loved her, were her only thought. With this power, she'd never lose them.

That security was the ultimate high.

Their gasps and moans slowed to heavy breathing as climax ebbed, and they sank back to the ground.

Kirby was intently aware of the grass tickling the bottom of her feet, and then her shins and knees as she and Gwydion sank to the ground, still wrapped in each other.

Gwydion pressed his forehead to hers. "I love you," he said softly, in English this time.

"I love you too. For eternity." Kirby was everything and nothing at the same time at this moment.

"Told you it was a rush." A familiar playfulness slid into Gwydion's voice.

She needed that. To be eased back into reality. "A girl could definitely get addicted." As the words passed her lips, she half expected him to reply with *to my cock?*

"A guy could get addicted to you. Wait, hang on... Too late. But you're a habit I'll never break. I'll never even try."

Kirby's smile grew. That was far sweeter than what she'd expected. She rested her head against his chest, listening to his heartbeat mingle with her pulse. "I feel energized. But also exhausted."

"It takes the body a little while to process this kind of power. Close your eyes. Relax."

Something warm and damp nuzzled Kirby's shoulder and her eyelids fluttered. She hadn't meant to fall asleep, but she felt incredible and better rested than... ever in this life.

Was that a snout? She forced her eyes open.

A horse stood next to them in the clearing, fur blue-black and glistening in the moonlight.

"You're gorgeous, aren't you?" Kirby kept her voice low, and swept her gaze over the horse. Correction, those were wings. "*Oh.*" She couldn't hide her awe. She knew Pegasus were real, but had never seen one, not even in her first life.

Pegasus were something the older Valkyries had told stories about. The winged creatures had hidden themselves long ago, not liking the direction gods and humans were taking the world.

"Someone has a fan," Gwydion said softly.

Kirby laughed. "Yes she does." She stroked the creature's nose.

The Pegasus flattened her ears against the side of her head and reared back, hooves stomping impatiently. She unfurled her wings and took flight.

"You scared her away." Kirby watched in awe as she vanished into the night sky.

Gwydion jumped to his feet, his nudity stunning, scarred and glorious. "That wasn't me."

Instinct overtook Kirby before her mind caught up, wrapping her in Valkyrie armor.

The air whipped around them, and a dragon landed in front of them. Unlike the other day, this one was white and platinum, like a knight before battle.

"There's another one?" Kirby's heart sank.

"There are three. Isn't this the same one—Fuck." Tendrils of vibrant green coiled around Gwydion, highlighting his form making him look terrifying.

A focused stream of flame struck the ground where they'd been standing, but Kirby was already in the air, looking for an opening. She needed Gwydion to be all right, but she had to survive long enough herself to check.

The air next to her whistled, and a wooden stake as large as her flew past, slicing through the dragon's wing. The beast's roar of pain was ear splitting and terrifying, but Kirby's relief overrode fear.

Gwydion was fine.

There was no struggle here to maintain shield, armor, weapons, and wings. Kirby might feel the drain later, but right now being in this form was energizing. She ducked under a swipe of a tail, soared straight up, and plummeted in a controlled dive toward the dragon's back.

"*Enough.*" The voice that filled Kirby's thoughts was that of another dragon.

Fuck. They couldn't even hold off one. She didn't deviate from her vector, and plunged her sword into the first creature, where wing met shoulder.

It howled with a fury that made her teeth chatter. She let the sword vanish, rather than pull it free, and summoned it again.

"I said stop." The new arrival spoke aloud this time. The second dragon had vanished, and a woman stood next to Gwydion. She was as pale as the moonlight, as though she'd been cut from marble.

"*I won't let her be.*" The man's voice in Kirby's head must be the other dragon.

The woman rose in the air without moving, and placed herself between Kirby and the dragon. "Then you'll go through me to get to her," she said.

What the...?

"*Then I'll return when you're gone. We're not done, Valkyrie.*" The white dragon vanished.

Kirby hovered in the air, sword at the ready, facing the woman down. This didn't make sense, which was exactly why she couldn't drop her guard.

"I won't hurt you." The woman floated back to the ground, gaze never leaving Kirby's.

As her feet touched earth, Gwydion knelt in front of her and bowed his head. "My lady."

"No, really, what the actual fuck?" Kirby shouted. She descended as well, still on full alert.

"She attacked me—us—earlier, and you're bowing to her? *My lady?*"

Though under any other circumstance, Kirby might do the same. This woman was pale with a faint glow, as though she'd been carved from moonlight, and so beautiful it was impossible to believe.

"You said you fought a dragon." Gwydion rose and looked at Kirby. He put any Greek statue to shame right now, her stunning warrior, proud and unashamed in nothing but his glory.

"I did. She attacked me." Kirby pointed.

He frowned. "I thought you meant Lance... Guinevere?"

The names clicked in Kirby's thoughts. She hadn't been in that part of the world when it happened, but history had remembered their names in myth. "Guinevere? Lance... alot? You're..."

The woman nodded. "We've had many names through history. That's the one people remember most, but *you* know me by my original name. Urd."

Kirby lowered her sword into an attack position and flew straight toward Urd, fury and centuries of frustration propelling her.

Gwydion stepped between them.

Kirby pulled up short and stared at him, unable to hide her hurt. "I don't fault anyone for the gifts they were created with, but she wrote those visions down. She drove centuries of death and quiet war. And she tried to fucking kill me less than a day ago."

"Once upon a time, we worshiped them the way humans worshiped us," Gwydion said. He moved out of Kirby's way and stood by her side instead. "And our gods treated us just as poorly as we did our followers."

Kirby's smile was bittersweet. She shouldn't have doubted for a second that Gwydion would side against her.

"I'm sorry." Urd sounded sincere. But a lot of people did when they believed they were in the right. "I wasn't trying to kill you; I wanted to push you toward your destiny. Or rather, I needed to know you were worthy."

Kirby stalked closer. She rested the tip of her sword at Urd's throat. "I'm real sick and tired of people testing me *for my own good*. Fuck your opinion of my worthiness."

"Would you have fought the same if I weren't a threat? Because you've met Skuld now, and they're a far bigger danger than I am."

Frustration and irritation spilled through Kirby, at Urd's unflinching posture. "I assume I failed your stupid test?"

"Not at all. You're compassionate, fierce, and you only fight if you have no other choice, or to protect those you love."

Urd's goal was trite, her assumptions and approach arrogant. Gwydion had a point—she was another deity who thought she knew better than those *beneath* her.

"Great. Do I get a participation trophy?" Kirby asked.

Urd frowned and bowed her head. "My apology is sincere. I should have approached this differently. Testing you was a mistake—yes, even those of us who have visions of what could be can be in error. Especially when it comes to things I haven't seen."

"Mhm." Kirby crossed her arms.

"Hey, are we good here? Safe for about thirty seconds? I'm going to put my pants on." Gwydion squeezed Kirby's arm.

Damn him. She almost cracked a smile. The tension hanging in the air thinned, but didn't vanish.

"Do you also wish to change?" Urd asked.

Kirby shook her head. "Thanks for your concern, but I'm good like I am." Fully armored in magical gear that was as intimidating and intricate as it was effective at protecting her. "You can do something for me, though, as the woman who apparently set every one of my lives in motion—you could give us some fucking clarity." Yeah, right.

Gwydion rejoined them, and Kirby gave him a glance. He had limited himself to just putting on pants, and the visual was no less tempting than before.

"That's reasonable. I'll tell you anything you ask," Urd said.

No way. Too easy. "What if I ask you to tell me everything?"

"Then I will do so, and you should be prepared to be here for several days, possibly weeks."

Given that Kirby would rather be kicking down someone's door *right now* that wasn't going to work. But which question should she ask first?

"The prophecy everyone's talking about--the newly discovered one—did you see Kirby's death. Again?" Gwydion's question was tight.

Urd sighed. "It wasn't my vision, but no. Skuld—Lance—is letting everyone believe they wrote *The last Valkyrie will be no more*. It's a fairly direct translation, but it misses the meaning. The original text is more like *The Valkyrie will no longer be the last*."

The words rolled around in Kirby's head, and if she'd been a cartoon a little light bulb would have appeared above her head. "There will be others?"

"Yes."

Kirby swallowed a spark of hope. A whisper of longing from her first life that she hadn't known still existed. "Will my sisters return?"

"Not quite." Urd winced. "You are so much more powerful than you realize, and your strength grows each day. With Odin gone, there's no one to create more like you, but you have the ability to share your gift. To choose who else can do what you do. There are battles coming, and you cannot be there for all of them."

"Oh." *Wait*. Kirby could make more Valkyries? How was she supposed to choose? Where was she supposed to find them? Why was this her responsibility? Did that mean she wouldn't fight anymore? She never had before. She and her sisters saw the fallen to the afterlife, rather than standing by their side in battle.

The flood of questions lodged in her throat, and she didn't know what to ask next. "What if I want to be more than… What? A queen on a throne? A glorified clean-up manager?"

"Prophecies is such a misleading term. The things we saw were only one path. You are never bound to your future unless you choose to be," Urd said.

Fury spilled into mingle with Kirby's confusion. "Are you kidding me? People kill because of those words. Your friend just tried to kill me. Or was that another test? And you're going to stand here and look me in the eye and say *you're not bound by the prophecies?*"

Gwydion rested his hands on Kirby's shoulders and pressed his lips into the top of her head. "I think we started too late in the story. Why do I not know you as Urd? Why doesn't anyone know you and she are one and the same?"

Urd sat and tucked her legs to one side. "This won't take days, but it could take a while. Join me?"

Kirby clasped her hands behind her back and set her feet shoulder-width apart. "I'll stand, thanks." She was talking to a being who could become a dragon in the blink of an eye—this stance wouldn't make enough of a difference in her reaction time if Urd or anyone else attacked. But the armor wasn't made for sitting in, and Kirby was already committed to keeping it on. It was like a security blanket, but sword and bullet resistant.

Gwydion stood by her side.

"Suit yourselves." Urd looked unconcerned. "The three of us, Verdandi, Skuld, and myself, are old enough we don't remember where we came from. To us, we always have been. Throughout the ages, different peoples have called us different things— sisters, fates, crone, mother, daughter—but they all blame us for their lives."

"Go figure. What with you writing down all these prophecies and such." Kirby let the sarcasm drip from her voice.

Urd frowned. "We didn't know what we were doing. Argue if you want, but we were the same as any artist. We saw vivid visions of things we didn't understand, and we wrote them down. We drew them. We made them into song. Anything to capture and understand the horror and beauty that danced in our thoughts. Your story was always one of my favorites, and Skuld told it in such amazing detail. It was the tale that always seemed to end in tragedy, but then you were back. Reborn, glorious, and with the most loyal lovers."

Kirby had never thought of her history as romantic before, but Urd painted a simple and stunning picture of the past.

"As time passed, we met creatures like those from our stories—small, bipedal, and mostly hairless," Urd said. "We took their form so we could walk among them. So we could pretend to live the lives we'd dreamed up. We shared the stories we'd told each other with all new audiences who listened in awe. Then the tales we thought we'd created from nothing started to come to pass.

"Coincidence became more. The people—humans and those they worshipped—thought of us as prophets. Gods. They modeled their lives after our stories. They looked for parallels." Urd stared at the ground, but Kirby doubted she saw the grass. "They granted kingship and godhood and death based on the tales we'd told."

Kirby couldn't ignore the sadness and regret in Urd's story. "But there's an entire organization that holds your name. What changed? Why are you pursuing making these things happen?"

Urd met her gaze, thousands of years of grief etched on her face. "There's a legend that people cling to. A story that's been propagated for centuries. Of a sword in a stone. A lady in a lake. A fated king and the wife and friend who betrayed him. At least, that's the way things are told now. We thought we'd show the people the prophecies were nothing more than tales. We would play those roles. We'd do things differently.

"And we did, but it tore the three of us apart. We couldn't agree. Verdandi wanted to walk away and let be what would be. I wanted to remove our stories from their lives. Twist and warp the tales until they were unrecognizable. And Skuld—who decided they were happier as Lance—wanted to let people keep the stories and influence which ones came true. The *good* ones of course.

"The Followers of Urd bear my name to taunt me. And Lance wants you dead, because they assume you're a pivotal point in what comes next. If there's no Valkyrie, no court of life and death surrounding her, the war—the final destruction of the world—won't happen."

No. Kirby and those she loved were not going to be responsible for Ragnarök.

CHAPTER THIRTY-SIX

KIRBY

"I won't... I can't..." How was Kirby supposed to deny some ancient dragon's vision and interpretation of it?

Urd rose, crossed the short distance between them, and looked Kirby in the eye. "You were always my favorite in Skuld's stories because you were so strong and loved so much. Your heart and soul are immense.

"You're supported by life and death. A balance between the two like only a Valkyrie could be. Worshiped and worshiping a god with a passion that consumes you and him. An equal and opposite to one who adores you and who you adore and who was never meant to be you." Urd looked at Gwydion. "Lover to the one who would live for you, and the one who would die for you. Because they're two sides of the same coin, they'll never see eye-to-eye, but they're as much a part of each other as they are you."

Urd rested her palm on Kirby's cheek. "You don't have to do any of this. You will choose your path. Not all of our prophecies come true, regardless of outside interference. But don't deny who you are, what you have, what you can be, to spite a series of stories three lovers told each other before humanity even learned to speak."

"If you're such a fan of Kirby's—of ours— you'll help us fight."

Thankfully Gwydion had a response, because Kirby had no idea which part of this entire story to focus on or pick apart or cling to.

"No." Urd moved away again, head bowed and sadness in her reply. "You know how potent love can be. I loathe what Skuld has done with our tales, but I can't destroy them. I'm sorry."

Kirby let out a barking laugh. "I hope that decision haunts you for eternity." She turned away and headed for her clothes. "I'm calling Magnus. You ready to take off, Gwydion?"

"Kirby," Urd said.

Nope. This conversation was over. There were too many thoughts. Doubts. Pieces that added up to betrayal. Not quite Urd's fault, but if she refused to take this stand, she was complicit.

Gwydion squeezed her hand. "Let's go."

Kirby placed him between her and Urd, let the armor fall away, and pulled on her clothes quickly, never taking her eyes off the goddess for more than a second or two.

Magnus sounded relieved to hear from Kirby—interesting thing to pretend—and joined them in the clearing almost immediately. She took their hands, and the world blinked away to be replaced with the sidewalk a block or so from NEON.

"Thank you." Kirby meant it. Whatever everyone was hiding, lying about, trying to use her for, this had been straightforward. "I'll call you again when we're ready to discuss strategy. I promise." She turned away.

"Kirby. Can I talk to you, just you, for a minute?" Magnus's tone was almost pleading.

Kirby just wanted to get back home and process. She'd fought for FU, thinking they were on the side of right, and they weren't any better than TOM. It was confirmed. Who was she supposed to trust? "It's been a long few hours, and I'm not in the mood for more bullshit."

"Please?" That was definitely begging sprinkled with desperation.

True, Magnus knew how to lie with the best of them, but Kirby's gut insisted this was okay. She sighed, and looked at Gwydion. "Take your time walking back, and I'll catch up? That way Starkad doesn't run out here."

"All right." He dipped her head near her ear, brushed her earlobe, and whispered, "She's wielding fae magic."

Kirby started at him in wide-eyed shock, and his faint nod confirmed he was serious.

Gwydion turned and walked away, slowing his pace significantly when he was a few meters away, out of hearing range.

"What?" Kirby turned back to Magnus. "What's with the sweetness and demureness and the fake *need*."

Hurt whispered across Magnus's face but vanished quickly. "That's fair. No one's telling you the truth. I don't like it either. I never have. But what I'm about to say next is genuine. It's the most sincere thing you're going to hear today."

"Uh-huh." Kirby had to put up the front, because she wanted to believe the words and that would be a mistake.

"I know life with Hel sucked. Believe me, I know. I never wanted to compete against any of you. You're the only brothers and sisters I had. I'm your family. You forgave Brit, and its different with you two, I get it, but..." Magnus let out a shaky sigh. "Don't do what Dahlia did. Don't leave me because a bunch of creepy old guys said you were special."

Except that unlike everyone else, the men she loved were as out of the loop as Kirby was. "Creepy old guys like Vidar?"

"Like immortals you've known for fewer cumulative years than you've known me. You and Brit—and Dahlia too—you belong with us. With me." Magnus sounded so sincere it ached in Kirby's bones.

This conversation needed to go faster, so Kirby could catch up with Gwydion, but there were still so many questions. "Why does Vidar want me?"

"He doesn't think the prophecy means you'll die. He thinks it means you can make more, and he wants you to turn some of us. Me."

Wow. Someone else wanted to use Kirby. Huge surprise. Not. "And you believe he'd just do that for you."

Magnus turned her gaze to her feet as she kicked a loose pebble on the sidewalk. "Yes."

"Come on. You can lie better than that."

"It doesn't matter if he'll do it or not, it's your power. And I don't care." Magnus looked up again, eyes bright and unguarded. "I mean, it sounds like a really cool idea on the surface—a Valkyrie, holy shit. But it's sucked for you, and I'm not great in a battle. I'm brilliant behind the scenes."

Kirby wanted so badly for this to be true, and she couldn't say why. Maybe it was because so many lies in the last few days threatened to crush her soul. "So come with me. Walk away from Vidar."

"And trade the god I know, the friends I know, for those creepers that have stolen the three of you away? No."

"That's why *I* can't leave. I love those *creepers*, and yeah I kind of thought that same thing when I met them, but that's not who they are. They're genuine. They're safe."

"Even Starkad? Who lied to you in school. Who broke your fucking ankle to keep you in line." Magnus's sweetness was gone. "Yeah, I know about him. Their history with you. At least enough to know it's not a healthy obsession. Why do you think we tried to kill him? He'll destroy you."

No. That was one thing Urd said that Kirby couldn't argue—he'd die for her, like she had for him. "You're not even going to make up a story about what happened to him? Pretend your goal was something else?"

"Nope. We sent him to face Fenrir because we thought it would kill him. When they decided to talk instead, we shot him. Except that bullet—it seems you really do have the power to make people immortal."

Magnus's raw honesty was as refreshing as the information was disconcerting. "I'd never forgive you if he died," Kirby said.

"I see that now. It wasn't my call, but I agreed with Vidar's logic. I'd rather we all just walk away, but I don't think we can ignore a life like this. We know too much. I want us all back together, and I won't give up my security blanket."

Kirby didn't know what to think. What to say. There was too much to process, and not enough information to do so. "I'll call you when we're ready for next steps. Promise."

She turned her back on Magnus—at least there was enough trust there to do that—and strolled away quickly to catch up with Gwydion.

So many manipulations. So many agendas. So many lies.

One thing Kirby agreed with Magnus on— having a family Kirby trusted was the only way to get through this. It would be nice if that trust could extend a little further, but she didn't see how that was possible.

CHAPTER THIRTY-SEVEN

STARKAD

Centuries.

That was how long Starkad waited.

This last decade or so was the hardest.

And now that he finally had the one person he'd been waiting for, he had to wait some more.

Min and Brit had gone to fetch some books from a nearby library, and Starkad was left in this strange place, surrounded by magic he shouldn't be able to feel, to wait for Kirby and Gwydion to return from what should have only taken few minutes. Maybe an hour.

The time alone had given him time to bring the raging wolf inside to heel. He almost felt like himself again, which didn't make him any less impatient for her return.

The scents in the air changed, and Starkad smiled. A moment later, Kirby walked through the front door with Gwydion. She smiled when she saw him, despite a frustration that lingered in her eyes and clung to her.

Starkad knew how to get rid of that. He moved closer, pressing her into Gwydion, and dragged his nose up the side of her neck. The sharp scents that greeted Starkad painted a vivid story of what took so long. "Blood and sex. You two had fun without me."

"You've got some real bad timing." Gwydion rested his hands on Kirby's hips.

She leaned back into Gwydion, and rested her palm on Starkad's chest. Rather than pushing him away, her touch was light. Almost tentative. Frustration splashed across her.

The pair of touches screamed to be grounded. Of being desperate for clarity. Starkad had seen this lost and drifting Kirby so many times when it was only them.

It was different now, though. The desire to give up was gone.

He nipped her neck enough to leave a sting but not break the skin. "What do you need?"

Her laugh had that same lost and floundering feeling. "I need my world to make sense. I need to know that at least here, everything is exactly what I expect."

"We can give you that." Starkad glided his hand up her stomach, over her sternum, to loosely wrap around her throat.

She managed a smile that didn't reach her eyes. "You and Min have something in common. Who knew?"

Besides her? "We both like to see you tied up?"

"Close enough." She clenched her hand, grabbing a fistful of his T-shirt in the process.

"One distraction, coming up." He let the growl slide into his voice. He pressed into Kirby, memorizing everything about this moment. Scent. Heat. The sound of her soft breaths. The way Gwydion's presence mingled with it all, overlapping and enhancing like just enough sugar.

"Why can't this be life?" Kirby's question was soft.

Gods forbid. Starkad loved this, but he'd wither from boredom. "You'd get bored so quickly. You went stir crazy in Aeval's cabin."

Gwydion might be happy to heal the conflict from the back row, and Starkad didn't fault him, but Kirby'd never be able to step back.

"Maybe." She sighed and shifted her weight to rub her body against his.

"As brilliant as this is"—Gwydion was hesitant—"while it's just the three of us, we need to talk."

They did. The thought had been gnawing at Starkad's thoughts for weeks, and amplified when he'd run into Fenrir. It was easy to ignore it when he let the wolf drive his thoughts, but this needed to happen now, before—

Kirby was gone again. The words haunted Starkad. He wouldn't let it happen. His desire was muted with the onslaught of thoughts.

"Fenrir nearly left me in the woods to fend for myself, when we encountered TOM." Starkad hated to kill the moment, but they'd have more of those. This needed to be said. Kirby went rigid under his touch. "And I wouldn't have blamed him. I had a patch of a few centuries, that span of time when it didn't feel like I'd ever find you again, where the only thing that mattered was the fight.

"I'm not talking about those wars I joined to see how real the immortality was. This was more focused. I fought for anyone who would have me. Whatever it took to spill blood again and lose myself in the fight, it didn't matter the cause."

Gwydion's sigh was quiet. He'd seen this coming.

The way Kirby met his gaze, her expression impossible to read, she hadn't. "That's why no one trusts you. I thought Vidar was just being a TOM asshole, but these people toss your name around like..."

"I'm a wild dog?" For the longest time, that was his intention. "That thirst is still here. That lust. When the fight starts, I lose the desire to contain it."

Kirby's expression softened. "When the fight starts, that's when you shouldn't contain it. There are days I don't know if I can face the world as it is." She drew in a long breath, shuddering as she exhaled. "Days I still want life to end. I don't give in, because those are only temporary moments. Is it the same for you? Or would you rather nothing—no one—was keeping you... tame?"

She meant herself.

"Would I surrender you so I could lose myself? No. Never. I shouldn't need you to keep my humanity, but I can't deny I do things because of you. I wouldn't be me without you, and not just for the obvious reasons."

Gwydion was surprisingly quiet. Both a blessing and a concern.

"I get it," Kirby said. "I do. All of it. You're not him anymore, but that voice still exists."

How had he ever doubted? "I can't promise I can keep the urge at bay, especially if you die again."

"I'd be lost without you as well. So don't let me die."

He nipped at her shoulder. "Never again."

"Are we all good now?" Gwydion finally spoke. At least he didn't open with a joke.

"Yes." Kirby was stunning in her confidence, radiating a power that whispered *don't underestimate me.*

"Because we should talk about what Urd told us," Gwydion said.

They'd seen Urd? Talked to her? And they'd let Starkad waste time baring his soul?

CHAPTER THIRTY-EIGHT

KIRBY

Everything Urd said rushed back, tossing Kirby into doubt and frustration.

"I'd rather wait until Min and Brit were here to tell most of the story." Kirby's mind was already into an irritating number of reruns.

But what she'd learned about Starkad and Gwydion—there was no doubt they were they were the coin—Starkad needed to know. Between the three of them, maybe the words would mean more than being a prettily phrased tale of love and loss.

Starkad looked between her and Gwydion. "Well? What's she like? Is she sorry at all for the shit she puts the world through?"

"Yes. And no. She said you and Gwydion are two sides of the same coin. Connected through more than just me."

"Lovely. Poetic." Starkad's voice was flat. "But what does it mean?"

"I don't—" A loud, steady hammering on the door cut Kirby off. She ran toward the sound, her Valkyrie hovered near the surface, ready to emerge in a blink if needed.

Starkad and Gwydion were by her side as she jerked open the front door.

Frey stood on the porch, Dahlia unconscious in his arms. A dark wet spot covered her black T-shirt, focused around a hole in her stomach, and red stained his hands.

Kirby's gut sank.

"Thank Eternity you're here." Frey's eyes were wild. "Tell me you still heal people."

The panic and hope were enough to snap Kirby into action. "There." She pointed to the couch. Whoever owned the place could throw a fit later about stained upholstery.

Frey laid Dahlia down so very gently, and Kirby had to nudge him aside to kneel next to her.

Kirby hovered her hand over the wound, mentally searching for the best place to start healing. A spark tugged at her memory and dragged up concern with it. She hadn't been able to heal Brit. What if this was the same?

"She's still human, right?" Kirby asked Frey.

Frey furrowed his brow. "Yes. Most people don't just magically become otherwise."

Unless Kirby was around. She shoved aside the hesitation and let the magic flow through her. The energy was sharper, fresher than it ever had been before. Was that because of the trip with Gwydion? Did that impact her, too?

211

She closed her eyes and concentrated on knitting the wound. Healing the tissue. The skin. Pulling life back.

It wasn't working. What was Kirby doing wrong?

"Is everyone— Oh." Min's voice tickled the edges of Kirby's thoughts, but she was focused on Dahlia.

An arm rested against hers, and the presence told her Min was next to her. He covered her hands with his.

Kirby didn't dare open her eyes, and confirm what she already knew. "She's not getting better." Her voice caught. "I can't— I don't know why not."

"She's gone," Min said softly.

Dahlia wasn't. Kirby still felt *something*. Desperation clogged her throat. "There's a spark. She can get better."

"There is, but it's so faint." Min had the decency to sound regretful. "Even if I help her cling to it, she won't last with that wound."

There had to be a way. What Magnus did after Kirby healed her... Maybe? "If you can help her and I can't, what I give you that power? What if I can share?" Even as Kirby spoke, she summoned her healing and let the magic bleed into the connection with Min.

"I will try." Min went quiet. In fact, the whole room seemed frozen in anticipation.

Kirby didn't dare look. She focused on the bond with Min. The faint glow she knew was there from Dahlia. She kept her attention turned inward, on the same need before to close the wound and heal the tissue.

If she had encountered Dahlia in the field, months ago when Kirby was tracking down Nobles, would she have flinched? Probably. Kirby liked Dahlia, and the decision to continue doing so was made easier by the fact that Frey and Fen trusted her. She couldn't watch Dahlia die.

"Huntress," Min said gently. "I believe it worked. She's alive."

Kirby's breath hitched and she finally dared. Dahlia still lay unconscious.

"Now we wait." Min squeezed Kirby's hand.

Brit had joined them, knelling at Kirby's other side, worried gaze fixed on Dahlia.

Kirby looked at Frey. "What happened?"

"We went to Aya's for any information we could find about Gluskab. We were coming out and someone opened fire on us. I didn't stick around to ask questions, I just brought her back here."

Kirby swallowed a hysterical and not at all amused laugh. No wonder she was the one to do all the dirty work when she did FU jobs. "If it was FU, they have *the* worst shooters in history."

"Storm troopers in training, am I right?" Dahlia asked.

The familiar voice and light teasing made Kirby laugh-sob and tears of relief pricked her eyelids. She was almost knocked on her ass when Dahlia threw her arms around Kirby's neck.

"You're alive." Dahlia squealed, stealing Kirby's line. "I mean, a lot of people said so, but seeing you in person is so much better than hearing rumors. Gods, you're alive." Dahlia slid onto the floor in a controlled fall and shifted her hug to Brit. "And you're here, too. Oh my god. I can't believe it. And you're together. Are you *together*? I'm so glad you're both here. I missed you so much." She pulled away and looked around the room. "Why is everyone staring at me?"

This was so different than the guarded greeting Magnus gave them. And Kirby welcomed it. "You were shot."

"Oh." Dahlia looked down and poked at the hole in her shirt. "Yeah. That sucked. But I'm better now." She jabbed her stomach again. "How...?"

"Him." Kirby jerked her head toward Min.

He squeezed her fingers. "Us. You made her whole."

Warmth and gratitude spilled through Kirby.

Dahlia gave Min a brief nod. "Thank you. Both of you."

How much did Dahlia know about Kirby? At least the concern was minimal that Frey and Fen had told bad stories.

Dahlia stood and they joined her. She looked completely better, aside from the drying blood on her clothes and skin. She tugged the hem of Brit's shirt. "I got you guys all gross. I'm sorry. I really need a shower. *Oh*. They have a bathhouse here. An honest-to-god bathhouse. You should come with me." She grabbed Kirby's and Brit's hands. "We can catch up. Compare notes on immortal dicks." Dahlia looked at Brit. "Sorry. Or you know, whatever."

"We have a lot to talk about," Starkad said sharply. "The gossip session should wait."

Dahlia's posture shifted in an instant. It was subtle, but years of training with her made the stiffening of her back and the way her shoulders went back obvious. She faced the rest of the room and moved closer to Frey.

A bath sounded like an incredible idea, and since Kirby should be cautious, it also sounded like a great way to catch up with Dahlia and at the same time gage who she was. Like Magnus, like any of them, she could lie. But Kirby could at least get a sense of how guarded Dahlia was in a longer conversation.

Kirby also wanted to compare notes and make plans.

"Fifteen minute debrief to determine next steps and decide how critical they are." Kirby hated the practicality of the decision, especially after spending the last several hours fucking and fighting and fooling around. But this was the moment they'd been waiting for. If their plans included fighting now, a shower wouldn't matter to Kirby and Dahlia wouldn't be going with them.

Dahlia jammed her hands in her pockets. "We never really get out, do we?"

The implication raked over Kirby. "This is necessary, and it's not just a product of TOM. I've fought in wars—"

"Yeah. Past lives. I've heard. Were you Bad Ass Sergeant Kirby in Charge in any of those lives?" Dahlia's tone wasn't accusatory, simply... sad? "I was hoping after a few years, I could put it all behind me."

215

"I don't know if I ever will." The confession startled Kirby. Under the surface she'd always known she couldn't remove herself from any of her pasts, including this one, but she'd hoped she'd be able to at least lock it away. That didn't seem like the best idea anymore. "I'll let go of some parts of it, maybe. But war is coming. It doesn't stop because I want it to, and I can't sit back and watch."

Shit, that sounded judgey. "Not that I mean... I don't expect anyone to take the same stance or fault them for making their own choices. Play to your strengths. I hated what Hel put me through, but I can't ignore the useful things I learned."

"I'm curious if Urd told you anything useful," Starkad said. He might be saving Kirby from the fumbling, or he could be getting tired of the tangents in a critical time. Probably a bit of both.

"You met Urd." Frey's tone was flat disbelief.

Brit looked skeptical too. "You sure it was her? I mean, anyone can say..."

"Positive." Gwydion stood next to Starkad, both of them in T-shirts. They wore scars and tattoos. Were well muscled with a presence that hung over the room. How did Gwydion manage to convey kindness where Starkad was so fierce? And how did both look safe? "Not a lot of dragons left in the world," Gwydion said.

Dahlia's eyes grew wide and her defensive posture wilted. "Dragons are real?"

"Right? It's so cool." Brit cut her own laugh short. "Until one attacks you."

Min cleared his throat. He lingered behind Kirby, dwarfing the corner, but being the opposite of imposing. In the best way possible. A large folder was tucked under his arm. "Tall, slender woman? Pale as moonlight? Tends to be vague and leave out important details even when she's being direct?"

Kirby had almost forgotten he met Urd once. "That's her."

"What did she say?" Starkad was getting impatient.

"Tl;dr version? She doesn't have anything to do with FU, and they do want me dead," Kirby said. "To prevent a prophecy, not fulfill one." How much more could Kirby say in front of Frey? Dahlia? She didn't want to dive into Urd's revelation about Kirby being able to create more Valkyrie with such a large group.

"I told you guys so." Dahlia pointed a glare at Frey. "Queen Motherfucking Valkyrie. She won't be the last anymore because she'll build a new... army? Pack?"

Kirby struggled to fight a smile at Dahlia's certainty. "Sisterhood."

Dahlia grinned. "I like it. But he"—she jerked her thumb at Frey—"was all like *We know how to read. That's not what it says.*"

"According to Urd, that's what it says." No reason for Kirby to hold back now. "Problem is, even though she defined the prophecy for us, and told us what Lance—FU—wants, she didn't give us any information that will help us stop them."

"We have something." Dahlia looked smug. The rapidly drying blood seemed to be an afterthought. "I used Min's tech for trend tracking, and I found... Frey tells it better."

Frey met Kirby's gaze. "Welcome back, by the way. I'd love to catch up when this is all over."

"I'd like that." Kirby was as happy to see him as she had been Fen.

"As you know, the now-stopped disasters were focused in cities where the gods are who bound Malsumis. We suspect Gluskab has the remaining seven," Frey said. "But the magical activity hasn't stopped. It's centered in Mexico. We've been going through Aya's things, making calls and visits, and we know where Malsumis was sealed away. Min?"

Min stepped more into the room, and flipped through the folder he held, revealing several folded sheets of paper. "One of my companies has tech that uses satellites and drones to map tunnels and similar things that are underground. These are printouts of the region where they believe Gluskab and Lance are holding everyone."

"That was where we were, and missing all the fun, apparently," Brit said.

Starkad's smirk was almost feral. "You were the one who didn't want to stay here."

"Because you're unbearable at the best of times, and when Kirby's gone, you're a beast."

"I won't apologize for that." Despite his stance and expression, Starkad was lightly teasing rather than verbally attacking.

Nice change. "Next steps," Kirby said. "We need to be rested, and not all of us are. Dahlia needs a bath and I wouldn't mind one either." Time to get a better idea of who Dahlia was now. "We need a plan, and part of that will include how much we tell Vidar."

"We're not—"

"We are," Kirby cut Starkad off. "We'll plan for the contingency of betrayal, but we need people for this mission. If what Frey says is true—Gluskab has all of the original gods—then Grytha is there with the others, and Vidar has as much of a stake in this as we do."

Starkad clenched his jaw and stared Kirby down.

Kirby didn't want to go into this disagreeing with him, but she wasn't backing down. She'd given her word and this was the right way to go.

She hoped.

Chapter Thirty-Nine

BRIT

There were a lot of terrifying creatures in the world, but Brit still counted Starkad as one of the most frightening. She wasn't so concerned these days about him hurting her. When he was high-end irritated though, it still scared her.

Another reason she loved Kirby—who stared Starkad down unflinchingly. If this was a romance novel, they'd be the ultimate alpha couple, and Kirby was stunning in that role. Dahlia was right—Kirby really was Queen Motherfucking Valkyrie.

Brit was in awe, rather than envious.

"All right." Starkad yielded and the tension in the room deflated.

The corners of Kirby's mouth twitched in an unformed smile. "Eat, sleep, or do whatever you need to be frosty. You have four hours." She grabbed Brit's hand and Dahlia's. "We're going to take a bath."

"We're set then?" Dahlia asked.

"Lead the way," Brit said. This situation was a lesson in contrast. Then again, so was life with Kirby in general. A least a few of them were about to go into battle, against an insane god, a dragon, and whatever soldiers they had. And first, Brit was going to have a girls' afternoon out with the friends she grew up with. Yes, Kirby was more than a friend now. But in this moment, Dahlia tugging them down a disconcertingly suburban street, it was almost possible to pretend that the three of them were just girlfriends, looking to catch up.

Why didn't it feel this way with Magnus? Because Brit and Kirby were greeted by being kidnapped and Brit being shot? That definitely added to it, but Magnus had been more guarded from the moment they saw her. Dahlia didn't have those walls up. Okay, she was the one who was shot and dying. She seemed to have made a full recovery though, and this Dahlia wasn't any different from the one Brit remembered.

They reached the bathhouse. A simple counter sat out front, and the woman behind had fox-like features and vibrant red hair.

Dahlia handed her a small stack of bills. "Three, please."

The woman nodded, tucked the cash away under the counter, and set three buckets out in return. There was a washcloth, small bar of soap, and small towel in each.

Dahlia gave a short bow, and Brit and Kirby mimicked the movement.

The three padded along wood flooring, down a long hallway lined with rice paper walls and doors. Intricate details were carved and painted on everything.

"Is this a real onsen?" Brit couldn't drink in the details fast enough.

Dahlia led them through a curtain, to reveal a room with individual shower heads and stools along the wall, and lockers in a row down the middle. "Depends on your definition. Those are real hot springs out there. We're expected to scrub down completely and enter them nude. The woman who owns the place is actually a brownie, and I don't know if she's ever been to Japan."

Brit hadn't either. "I've always wanted to go."

"Japan?" Dahlia looked surprised. "You've never been?" She stripped off her shirt, wrinkled her nose, and tossed it in a wastebasket.

Kirby undressed as well, but folded her clothes in a neat pile. "What are you planning to wear when we're done?"

"Check this out. Bag of holding." Dahlia opened the wristlet she was carrying, and reached her arm in, all the way to the elbow. She showed them a hint of T-shirt before shoving the clothing back down into whatever invisible pocket held it. "You guys can borrow something if you need. Help me get the blood out of my hair?" She settled on a stool and turned on the water next to her.

"I will." Brit stripped out of her clothes and set them next to Kirby's. The three of them naked in what was essentially a communal shower was nothing new. Another throwback to growing up that felt natural.

Kirby took the stool next to Dahlia and started scrubbing clean as well. "When this is over, I don't care what comes next, we're going to Japan," Kirby said. "I can't believe you never had a mission there."

Dahlia's snort of laughter was bitter. "You're kidding. *Everyone* knew she wanted to go. Of course Hel made sure she never did."

That sounded about right. Brit soaped and rinsed the tips of Dahlia's hair until the water ran clear, then took her own seat and washed up. The *bath* part of the building was more for soaking and relaxing. The three of them needed to be clean before they stepped into the springs.

They strolled into a room with rock walls and six large baths cutting a straight line to the one farthest from the entrance. The water was a hair too warm when Brit dipped her toes in, but she sank in and let the heat embrace her. Kirby settled next to her, with Dahlia on her other side.

The silence, aside from the ambient trickle of water, was soothing, and they sat for a moment not speaking.

"What happened with Magnus?" Brit asked softly. Meditation was all well and good, but things needed to get done.

Dahlia sank so low only her head was exposed, and leaned against the rocks with a sigh. "We had different definitions of what *getting out* meant. We were free and clear. We had the money and connections to hide for the rest of our lives. Or, I thought so. Vidar found us."

Not quite the same as Magnus's story, but the core sounded similar enough. Dahlia seemed more willing to talk about it, though.

"Did he threaten you? How'd you get away?" Brit couldn't ignore the memory of how Hel required she prove her loyalty.

"He promised us things were different without Hel. That he didn't believe in rule by manipulation, and that we were welcome back into the fold, no questions asked."

Kirby made a soft *hmm.*

Would Brit have gone back if she were promised the same? Not enough of those people gave a shit about her for her to feel safe there. "Magnus gave us the impression you left for another god. Frey? Fen?"

Dahlia's laugh was light and genuine. "No. I left for me. I've gotten to know them over the years, and I'm not sure if you've noticed, but I love to talk, and since I can't talk about most things TOM, I talked about Kirby. How much I missed her. Imagine my surprise when they told me they knew her from previous lives. I mean, what in the what? So when I found a prophecy about her, I figured they were the best people to tell."

There was something unspoken in Dahlia's story, and Brit grasped to pull the pieces together. It was right there at the edge of her thoughts.

"I was *so* pissed when they wanted to use the information in exchange for helping Aya," Dahlia said.

Kirby frowned. "I would have helped them regardless."

"That's what I told them." Dahlia was indignant. "Just because you only loved Brit in school didn't mean you only protected Brit. Aya didn't believe me. I never should've let them tell her."

There it was. Brit knew what was missing from the story. "How long have you known Kirby was alive?"

Dahlia worked her jaw and ducked her head. "A few years." She spoke so softly it was difficult to hear.

"You said hours?" Brit knew she hadn't. "There's no way you've known for years."

"Yeah, so, when Frey told me you weren't dead, it rocked my fucking world." Dahlia looked at Kirby. "It was like Yule, my birthday, and Spring Equinox all in one."

Brit's hurt grew. *Years* meant Dahlia had known long before things visibly fell apart at TOM. "And yet, you kept it to yourself," Brit said.

"I didn't like it. It was another secret. But Frey asked me to, and it seemed smart." Dahlia finally met Brit's gaze. "I wanted to tell you so many times, but I also didn't think you'd ever see each other again. Knowing wouldn't have helped you heal and... I didn't know if it would be safe for Kirby." Dahlia's voice dropped off at the end again, before her expression brightened. "But look, you're together. You're both happy. It all worked out."

Except Brit couldn't ignore the ache inside. Had she wasted so much time? What would have been different if she found out sooner? Would she have gotten out sooner?

"Thank you." Kirby's sincerity was tangible.

Would Kirby have died before she became a Valkyrie?

"It all worked out, but you couldn't know," Kirby said. "Thank you for keeping my secret, especially given how much you hate them."

It didn't matter what could have been. This was what was, and Brit was happy with the current situation. It was simply going to take a little while for that sting of *what if I'd known* to go away.

A somber cloud settled in around them as silence descended again.

"You're really going to be Queen Motherfucking Valkyrie, aren't you?" Dahlia's cheer was too-bright as it shattered the still.

Kirby shrugged. "Urd says so. I've never been a big fan of what Urd says, and meeting her didn't change my opinion."

"You'd pass up a chance like that to spite her?" Dahlia's disbelief mirrored Brit's.

"The spite is a pleasant side-effect, but there's more to my hesitation than that," Kirby said. "What if I can't do it? I'm barely capable of taking care of me. I can't make more Valkyries."

Brit's disbelief grew. "You're kidding. Aren't you? You just stood in a room full of gods, garnished with one borderline psychotic wolf, and told them what their plans were for going to war. You didn't so much as flinch."

The steam that floated up around Kirby, combined with the soft lighting, cast her in an unearthly glow, and didn't hide the fact that her already flushed cheeks darkened. "It was the right decision to make."

"Which is why you're the queen." Dahlia spoke as if there was no room for argument.

And Brit didn't see any reason to. "You shared your power with Magnus."

"You did?" Was Dahlia hurt?

"*Temporarily.*" Kirby emphasized. "It wore off in minutes."

"What if you meant it?" Dahlia asked.

Good point. "You don't trust Magnus with that kind of power." Brit thought for a moment. "Do you trust anyone that much who doesn't already have their own?"

"You."

Brit's heart snagged on the confession. "Yeah?"

"Yeah." The corner of Kirby's mouth tugged up in a half-smile. "I still have things to work through, with myself and with you. I don't think I'm the only one. But I want you here while it happens."

It didn't feel odd to have Dahlia here for this conversation. Maybe Brit should be more suspicious, but this was family. And she'd ached for so long to have Kirby's trust again, even though she still wasn't sure she deserved it. "I'm willing to work. I'm willing to do anything."

"No you're not." Kirby shook her head, but her smile grew. "*Anything* is fairly all-encompassing, and I wouldn't ask that of you. It's like we said before—I want us to be equals. Not identical. Not competitors. Partners. Lovers."

"Aww." Dahlia's squeal was soft. She hid her face when Brit and Kirby looked at her. "Sorry. It's so sweet."

It was. "Like chocolate cake with strawberries," Brit said.

"Exactly like that. So, um…" Kirby chewed her bottom lip.

"I know you don't want to hear it again, but I'm sorry." Brit's voice cracked on the apology and a lump formed in her throat. "For every doubting you. For betraying you. For not knowing what love was, and throwing what we had away. Odin may have cursed you with the multiple lives, but how many people get the kind of second chances you've had? I'm pretty much the luckiest person ever to be one of them. I love you." She poured every ounce of feeling and emotion into the words. It had never been more important to her to be believed.

"I love you, too. What happened wouldn't have nearly destroyed me if I didn't." Kirby pressed her forehead to Brit's. "But just as important, I trust the things you say. That it won't be a problem again. That whatever comes at us—monsters, gods, or assholes—we're strong enough to conquer it together."

"I'm full up on all of the above, thanks. Maybe someone could throw jelly donuts at us instead?"

"I will." Dahlia's cheer was welcome.

Brit laughed through the tears pricking her eyelids. "So, not to push the issue, but since we're on a timer… how do I get me a set of those nifty Valkyrie powers?"

Kirby kissed her on the nose. "I don't know?"

"How did you do it with Magnus?" Dahlia asked.

"I focused on sending the power through her."

"Sounds like a good starting place," Dahlia said.

Brit shook her head. "Kirby already tried that with me."

"But now you're both completely on the same page. In love." Dahlia's sigh came with a soft smile. "It's so sweet," she repeated.

"I'm not declaring my love to everyone I turn into a Valkyrie," Kirby said as she took Brit's hand, closed her eyes, and exhaled slowly.

A sharp shock, like a live wire, struck Brit. "*Ow.*" She yanked her hand away. "What was that?"

Deep creases lined Kirby's forehead. "It's the same thing I felt when I tried to heal you, after you were shot. My magic clashes with whatever makes you immortal."

"I can't be a Valkyrie, then?" Brit expected a surge of disappointment. There was a trickle of hurt, but was it tempered with relief?

Kirby looked upset. "I don't think you can. I'm sorry."

CHAPTER FORTY

KIRBY

"I promise I tried. I'm sorry it didn't work."
Kirby hated that she couldn't share this with Brit. If
Kirby couldn't gift this to the one person she *knew*
would use it right, what was the point?

Brit's smile was sweet. Forgiving. "It's okay. I
promise." She was sincere. "I'm not you. I know for
the longest time I wanted to be, but I don't anymore.
I love you for you, and I need to be me."

Kirby didn't know how to respond. "I still
wish…"

"Don't." Brit brushed her lips over Kirby's.
"Wish for something else for me. Not sure what, but
just as good and very different."

"All right." Kirby could do that.

When their time was up in the bath, they
climbed out, patted off the excess water, and padded
back to the dressing room.

Kirby stared with distaste at the stack of neatly folded TOM clothes. She so badly wanted to leave those people behind. Working with them was a necessary evil, but the thought of wearing things they'd given her filled her with ambivalence.

"Here." Dahlia nudged her and handed her a pile of mostly black fabric.

Kirby unfolded a black T-shirt, leggins, and a sports bra.

"I'm not loaning you my panties, sorry." Dahlia sounded anything but.

Kirby smiled. "Thank you." She was a little taller, flatter, and Brit shorter and curvier, but with Dahlia falling somewhere in between, this worked, and the leggins would be much easier to fight in than jeans.

Another thing to do when this was all over—have Min take them shopping. The bucket list of *when we survive* was growing. They'd better survive.

"Can I see it?" Dahlia asked as they dressed. "You as a Valkyrie?"

There was still no one else here, and Kirby didn't know if that mattered anyway. This was a village of supernaturals, wasn't it? "Sure."

With zero effort, she let the wings unfurl. It was energizing, rather than draining. That was new, and it felt good. She didn't summon the armor, though. That felt a bit like overkill in a bath changing room.

Dahlia stared at her with wide-eyed awe. "So gorgeous. I've always wanted wings."

"Could you give it to her?" Brit's question was hesitant.

Kirby trusted Dahlia in few ways, especially knowing she'd kept the secret of Kirby being alive. But making someone a Valkyrie wasn't a *I don't think you'll shoot me in the back today* kind of thing. It was a potential eternity of power. "How about we start with temporarily, like with Magnus, and then go from there?" If Kirby could even do it again.

Dahlia frowned, but nodded. "That's fair. Plus, wings, even for a few seconds, *wow*."

Kirby took Dahlia's hand, and focused on letting energy flow between them. There was an invisible wall. No, thinner, like paper? The same thing Kirby felt when she'd tried to heal Dahlia earlier.

"This shouldn't hurt," Kirby watched Dahlia's face, looking for any change in expression, any hint that this was going badly, as she nudged the barrier then pushed through. She expected a shock, like she'd felt with Brit. Instead, the resistance tore. Wings flickered into view, spread from Dahlia's back, and then vanished, like a bad horror movie special effect.

Kirby tried again, pushing harder this time. The after-image of wings stayed longer, a second or two, and then disappeared. "It's not working," Kirby muttered.

Dahlia pulled her hand away and let it drop limply by her side. "It's okay. I get it. You don't trust me as much as you do Magnus. I can earn that. That's fair."

"That's not it," Kirby said. "I promise I don't trust her more than you. But I also don't know how this works. Maybe it doesn't. Maybe she was a fluke.

Maybe I'm not this great and mighty being people think I am." Disappointment she didn't expect welled inside. She didn't want this to be true. Her reaction to Urd's revelation had been shock and disbelief, but the idea was growing on her. She could be more than a lost soul, rescued life after life. She could make a difference. She could take a stand. "Do you think if I told Lance that I can't do what their vision said, that they'd back off?" Her joke was weak.

Brit shook her head. "Unlikely."

"Yeah." Kirby sighed. "But you know me— eternal optimist." Eternal punching bag for the fates, and she was sick of it. She was going to figure this out, and anyone who didn't like the way she did it could fuck right off.

Dahlia headed back to NEON, and Kirby and Brit to their temporary house. No surprise, no one was resting. Gwydion, Min, and Starkad sat in the living room, their presence making the space feel cramped, despite there being plenty of room and furniture.

Starkad raised an eyebrow at their clothing. "You join the goth girl club?" His tone was light.

"Shut it," Kirby said playfully. "Do you want to go over blueprints before we all get together again?"

"Are you done *relaxing*?" Starkad asked.

Probably until this was over. Another thing for the bucket list. *Relax.* "Yes."

Kirby, Starkad, and Brit spread Min's printouts across the kitchen table, linking them together as best as possible to form a big picture. It would be easier to go into the next meeting with the start of a plan, rather than let the committee make a decision.

They circled caverns that looked large enough to hold multiple people—those were the targets and warning spots. They found the entrances closest to each.

"Four teams, myself, Brit, Starkad, and Magnus," Kirby said. "Any soldiers Vidar provides split evenly among us."

Brit shook her head. "Vidar's not going to go for that. Not with Starkad."

True.

"I agree," Starkad said. "But you're not letting him lead."

"Fen." Kirby didn't hesitate. She didn't know if he had formal combat experience, but he was a warrior, and he had been a mostly neutral party for centuries. "Starkad can go with him. Gwydion with Magnus. Vidar with me. Frey with Brit." They weren't taking everyone, but those were the parties who could fight or get them out."

Starkad shook his head. "No. Vidar with Brit."

Kirby stared at him, waiting for an explanation beyond *Because I don't give a shit what happens to her.*

"Give me some credit." Starkad might as well have read her mind. "She's more immortal than you, and you've got the shield. Frey isn't a fighter."

Kirby couldn't argue that.

"Vidar's going to see this pair-off for exactly what it is—a way to keep an eye on him and his people." Brit drummed her fingers on the table.

Kirby didn't care. "He insists he needs us, and these are our rules. They're not unreasonable."

"So sexy when you take charge." Brit grinned.

Starkad raised an eyebrow. "Can't argue that. Unless you're naked and begging."

Kirby rolled her eyes, but she loved the affection and that the two weren't completely clashing. Could she really do this Queen Valkyrie thing? She had no idea how she'd find people who were worthy, but there had to be a way. If there wasn't, they'd make one.

While they planned, Min left with Frey and came back with clothes for everyone, since they'd lost most of what they were traveling with in the quakes.

As the clock ticked toward mission time, Kirby's tension cranked higher. A new feeling crept in. A haunting sensation that everything was about to change. She was walking into the situation with the people she trusted more than even herself— Gwydion. Starkad. Brit.

Her gaze landed on Min. It felt odd doing this without him. He'd been crucial in each of the big fights they'd been in, but he wasn't a fighter. If she left him here, would something happen only he could have helped with?

She hated second-guessing her decisions, and this was the worst time to have more than the normal level of doubt.

Kirby settled next to Min on the couch in the sitting room. Everyone else was doing other prep-work. Mentally steeling themselves in their own way. "I don't want to leave you behind," she said softly. "It feels like the right decision, but the past says maybe it's not."

"I'll be crucial here." Min's tone was kind. Reassuring. "I'll be monitoring everything with Dahlia. When you return, I'll be here." He rested his hand on her leg and the heat of comfort flowed between them. "You know what you're doing. I have absolute faith in your plan."

That made one of them. But the assurance warmed her, and realization surged inside. This was what she'd wanted from him, when they first met in this life. She'd wanted—needed—him to understand and accept who she was. The things she knew and the way she thought. And at the same time, she understood now why he wasn't and couldn't be the same.

"I'm sorry I took so long to see it," Kirby said. "Who you are and what you stand for. It's one thing to say the words, but I finally *get* it." As she spoke, the spark inside grew to a flame, hot and all-consuming. "I love you. And even though I have in every life, this is the first time I feel like I truly understand who you are, and what you stand for. I'm so very grateful you're here, balancing me. Believing in me. Strong in your convictions and what you represent."

An ache pinged behind her ribs. A happy longing in her heart that threatened to burst with joy.

Min faced her, placed a finger under her chin, and drew her gaze to hers. "I feel the same."

Kirby raised an eyebrow at the simply underwhelming version of *me too*. He was typically so much more poetic. "About which part?"

CHAPTER FORTY-ONE

MIN

The woman watching Min, question, playfulness, and adoration all reflected in her crystal-blue eyes, was so much more a huntress than he'd thought possible. As he searched Kirby's face he saw a warrior and a queen.

Yes, she was a fighter, and sometimes she had to kill, but she wasn't a killer. Aya was right—Kirby wasn't the cause of the wars she found herself, she was the balance. He'd loved her for long, but he'd never loved her this deeply before.

"All of it," Min answered her question. She opened her mouth, and he pressed his finger to her lips, so he could finish the thought. "In the past, in your other lives, it's been so easy to love you."

Kirby pulled from his touch, her mouth twisted in a not-quite smile. "You're saying it's not anymore?" She didn't sound annoyed, simply curious.

"Right at this moment? No. I've never loved you more or been more certain of that love. You're the most amazing creature in existence. You're beauty. Grace. Vulnerability. Strength. Power. Kindness. You love so much because you are so much. And I sold you short before this life. I saw a beautiful, kind girl, lost and in need of guidance."

"That does sound like me. *All of it.*" She laughed lightly.

"But you're so much more. Before now, I didn't recognize the woman who's strong enough to stand on a battlefield, but kind enough to do so to keep others from having to. I see now the power and determination it took to surrender yourself for a berserker. And I see a queen who wants to save the world, and is one of the few who can."

Min cupped her cheeks. "As you leave for this mission, I won't send you with the wish that I hope you come back. You will. I have the kind of faith in you that people reserve for gods. You're my huntress. I worship you. I adore you. For as long as the world turns, and even after it stops, I'll continue to love you."

CHAPTER FORTY-TWO

KIRBY

When it was time, everyone gathered at NEON. It was less crowded than the house. Kirby explained the plan and pointed everyone to their assigned routes. "Memorize the layout," she said.

Everyone nodded.

"Now. There will be a quiz." She needed this to go as perfectly as possible from their side. This wouldn't be like the rescue mission for Aeval's people. "We expect to be ambushed, and the odds are as high it will come from Vidar and TOM as from anywhere. At the very least, he and Magnus have the ability to make entire sections of the world vanish from magical detection, and they can keep Frey from teleporting us out of there."

"It's fae magic," Gwydion said. "I didn't recognize it at first, but after the recharge... I don't know how she's wielding it, but she's literally making entire sections of the world fade into the fae realm. It's how she's teleporting as well."

"Can you stop her?" Kirby wanted to know how that worked, but those answers needed to wait. When this was— Fuck it, she'd get to it all when she got to it.

Gwydion nodded.

"And Kirby can shatter the shell," Brit said. "She did it in Salt Lake and against the dragon."

Kirby hadn't... Not consciously. But a lot of things she did with her Valkyrie power were instinct at first. "Dahlia and Min will be here, monitoring everyone's signals. We'll keep two channels, one to let us talk to TOM and one specifically for us. If anyone needs backup, when you find hostages or gods, or dragons, or anything, holler. We all clear?"

Everyone nodded. Kirby ran them through the details again, asking random people random questions to make sure everyone had the plan cemented. "We'll bring TOM up to date and meet everyone at the rendezvous point. I'll call Starkad as we leave. Be prepared to go in the instant we arrive."

"Only one thing left to do before we go in," Starkad said.

Kirby nodded, dragged in a deep breath that did nothing to soothe her, and called Magnus.

"Hey." Magnus was as cheerful as last time. "We're starting to make this a habit."

Except this may be the last time the connected this way. Kirby didn't want that to be the case. Though some of Magnus's choices made her difficult to trust, Kirby wanted things to be otherwise. "I have information. We're ready to fight if you are."

"Down to business. That's so you." Magnus's cheer faded. "Pick you up in the same spot?"

"Yeah. We'll be out there in five." Kirby disconnected and looked at the room. "We're in. Wait for my call."

Brit checked the magazine in her Desert Eagle .40, chambered a round, and holstered the weapon again. Extra magazines were stashed in a pocket.

Dahlia pushed back from the table. "I'm going with you." She held up a hand when Kirby opened her mouth. "Not to fight. That would be a disaster. I want to see Magnus. Please?"

Kirby nodded. She didn't want to drag out *goodbyes* because she'd be back with everyone soon. She gave Min, Gwydion, and Starkad each quick kisses, and walked out the door with Brit and Dahlia.

The short walk didn't take long, but Magnus was already waiting. She gave Dahlia a tentative smile as they approached. "Are you going with us?" Magnus asked.

Dahlia hung back about five meters. She shook her head. "No. I wanted to see you. Say *hello*. Hopefully not *goodbye*."

"Vidar has a place saved for you. I do. We're sisters. You can't pick them over me."

Dahlia dropped her gaze to the ground. "I'm picking me. You can come back with us, when this is over. My terms aren't nearly so restrictive as TOM's."

Sadness and hope flowed between them. Kirby understood both perspectives—that overwhelming need to belong to a bigger whole, and the just as potent desire to not be beholden to any god. Dahlia

241

and Magnus weren't lovers. They didn't have the same kind of relationship Kirby had with Brit, but they really were sisters.

"So you're staying." Magnus's tone went flat.

"And you're leaving. In that case, *goodbye*." Dahlia turned back toward NEON.

Magnus growled as she roughly grabbed Kirby's and Brit's hands. The city street vanished, replaced with an outdoor firing range.

The three of them were on the shooter side of the dividers, looking downrange. This wasn't the same setup they'd had at TOM.

"Ladies." Vidar greeted them. "Welcome back. Magnus tells me we're a go?"

There were twenty soldiers behind him, standing in rank and file formation. They wore heavy body armor and were equipped with assault rifles. Appropriate. And a mildly terrifying considering they had bullets that could kill immortals.

Kirby faced Vidar, stance unyielding and expression blank. "We're ready. We have a plan, layouts, and team divisions." She handed him a tablet with the information on it that they'd agreed to give him. Magnus moved to stand next to him.

He glanced between the screen and her. "What aren't you telling me?"

"Saying would defeat the purpose, wouldn't it?" Kirby asked. "You trusted me to carry out my half of the agreement, and I will. Keeping important information from you hurts us as well. I need you backing us up."

Vidar focused on the tablet. "These are half of my best. I can't afford more. I don't care what you're hiding as long as they come out of it alive."

"That's fair." Kirby was grateful to have Brit by her side. A reassuring hand squeeze would be nice, but Kirby would settle for knowing someone here was on her side.

Magnus pulled on her own body armor, and loaded and checked her gun.

Vidar frowned. "I don't care for the way your teams are broken up."

"That's the best you get. We need each other."

He nodded and handed the tablet back. Kirby set it on a nearby firing counter. It was a throw-away device, and she didn't have anywhere to keep it.

"Do you need time to prepare?" Kirby asked.

He shook his head. "I've come up short in my searches. You're right, I need your help. But I'm not afraid to take my people and make a tactical retreat, if it comes down to it."

Which meant leaving Kirby and her people behind. It was better than her Worst Case Scenario. Not that she'd tell him that, on the off chance that it hadn't already occurred to him that turning on her team was an option.

Chapter Forty-Three

GWYDION

The earth in this tunnel was fresh. Damp. Untouched by human hands for decades, possibly centuries.

Gwydion would love the chance to linger. To breath deep and appreciate the beauty of it. Under other circumstances he wouldn't even care that it was cramped in here, but walking with a team of five heavily armed and armored soldiers, and Magnus, there was no peace or beauty.

The high, almost imperceptible hum in his hear helped shatter the serenity. The earpieces were set to a shared channel, so Gwydion's group and Magnus's could all communicate.

They made their way through their section of tunnels at an astronomically slow pace, checking each blind corner and pausing to listen. Gwydion didn't like having a squad of neutral at best—and more likely enemy—soldiers at his back, but he was the shield in this group, and he wouldn't let them be fodder, either.

There was supposed to be no chatter on the earpieces, so the single tone in his ear startled him. He hid the reaction as they continued the cave sweep.

"This channel is only our group." Dahlia's voice greeted him. "Receive only. Anything you say, everyone still hears, including TOM. They have a similar channel, but I've patched us in. Even if they think their conversations are private, they won't be."

Neat trick, but what was to stop TOM from doing the same thing?

"Magnus *could* do the same, if she weren't with you. But no one else is as good as she or I," Dahlia said.

The confidence in her specific skill set was the most obvious indicator Gwydion had seen that she was TOM trained. True, plenty of people were confident, but she didn't radiate that until it came to her ability to hack.

They continued their journey inward, roots and moss brushing Gwydion's skin. The buzz from his recharge lingered, and the contact with the plantlife hummed under his skin. He could put up a physical barrier if needed. With a little luck, the action wouldn't bring these ancient paths crashing down around them.

Magnus came up short, arm in the air and fist clenched, indicating the group should halt.

They'd reached the cavern.

She tapped ear three times, and the beeps echoed in Gwydion's ear. Her silent signal to the group that this team had reached their destination.

She pointed to the soldiers with them, gesturing two should stand on one side of the entrance and three on the other, and stepped into the room with Gwydion to clear the cavern

It didn't take much. The space was the size of a medium room, maybe three meters each long, wide, and high. Shadows lingered along the walls, but nothing was hidden

"Gwydion." An eerie, androgynous tenor greeted them. Lance appeared from the shadows. "You could still leave."

"Fire at will," Magnus barked.

Gwydion summoned wooden embrasures in front of the squad, and bullets flew. Gunfire echoed over the earpieces.

"We're pinned down," Kirby shouted.

Starkad's growl grew feral and distant, as if his mic had fallen away.

"Who has Gluskab?" Kirby's shout was difficult to make out over the chorus of weapon fire.

Lance's dragon filled the room. The flame that shot from his mouth incinerated the embrasures.

Gwydion summoned another wave of defenses, and his entire body protested. The new walls were too thin. How the fuck was he already drained again?

"Target found." Vidar's voice came over the ear piece.

"Only Grytha. Where are the others?" Brit asked.

Something to worry about when Gwydion and his squad were out of immediate danger. His defenses were useless against flame regardless of their density. He needed to go on the offensive. He formed and fired spikes at Lance, one after another. Each shot drained Gwydion further, and most bounced off the dragon's chest and shoulders.

The bullets weren't doing any good either. The only thing keeping the squad alive is most were outside the room and Lance was too large to maneuver in here.

"We're done," Vidar said.

Familiar magic licked over Gwydion. Magnus was trying to leave. He pushed out everything he could to keep her here. The fight wasn't over.

She vanished anyway, as did the dragon.

"*Fuck.*" Kirby's shout in his hear was drowned out by the roar of a dragon.

CHAPTER FORTY-FOUR

KIRBY

This was *pinned down* at its worst. Kirby wanted a shelf a story up to pick off the soldiers shooting at her and her squad. She had a shield around her soldiers, and Brit had located the target.

If Kirby had Frey take her there, her squad would be open. Unprotected. True, they were trained for this kind of firefight, but she didn't have a full read on any other immortals here, and leaving was abandoning her team.

"We're done." Vidar said over the earpiece.

The TOM squad with Kirby vanished.

Fuck.

She turned to Frey, to have him do something similar.

Lance as a dragon appeared in the middle of the room, with Magnus in front of them.

Magnus looked at Kirby with wide, terror-filled eyes, and sprinted in her direction.

Kirby expanded her shield.

Flame erupted from Lance's mouth,

"*Fuck*," Kirby shouted.

Magnus's scream of agony was the stuff of nightmares. The fire deflected off Kirby's shield, but Magnus's forearm was scorched almost to the bone, with the severe burn extending most of her right side.

"I can't leave," Frey said. "Something is stopping me from getting us out of here."

"Come out and play, Valkyrie." Lance's voice echoed in Kirby's thoughts and off the cave walls.

The gunfire in her ears had stopped. "Everyone's gone but us. On our way to you," Starkad said.

Magnus alternated between screams and whimpers, as she rolled onto her back.

Kirby wasn't feeling the strain of having her shield up on top of everything else, but the weight of pressure was immense. She couldn't focus on healing Magnus and fight at the same time. If everyone else was where they should be, they were at least a few minutes out.

"Watch her," Kirby barked at Frey. "As in, make sure she doesn't die." Her feet left the ground, though she stayed low as she flew in a straight line toward Lance's gut, zipping at the last moment to fly straight up and come down on one of their wings.

Lance knocked her aside with his tail. She expected the counter, and twisted in a controlled fall, coming up with her sword pointed at what she hoped would be less dense armor under the arm.

As she swept up, her target vanished.

She pulled up short before she hit the ceiling of the cave, but a clawed hand grabbed her, squeezing until she thought her bones would shatter despite the shield. Lance flung her across the cave.

She slammed into the wall with a grunt, grasping to catch her breath and recover before she hit the ground. It didn't work.

"How far out is everyone?" Magnus's pained question overlapped itself in Kirby's ear and the cave. "She can't do this alone."

"Three minutes, at least," Brit replied.

Kirby stumbled to her feet, and attacked again. This probably wouldn't kill her, but it was going to hurt.

Each attack was rebuffed, either on purpose, or as she bounced off dragon scale. And that vanishing and reappearing trick was really fucking irritating.

None of the countless battles Kirby had been in over the centuries prepared her for this. As with the last two dragon fights, she wasn't making any headway. This was far worse than before, being unable to maneuver in this tight space and having to protect two others at the same time.

Magnus's whimpers of pain, like she was trying her best to suppress them and couldn't, only made things worse.

Kirby needed help with this fight. Another person to pick up Lance's feints and pin them down. She dove for his belly.

They swiped at her, one claw penetrating her armor and going clean through her shoulder.

Kirby couldn't hold back her scream of pain. She dropped to the cave floor on one knee, losing precious seconds as the wound knit itself shut.

Lance turned his attention to Frey and Magnus.

Kirby pushed past the lingering agony, and charged at Lance's back, aiming for that same spot under their arm. There had to be a weak spot on this creature.

Flame filled the cavern. Kirby felt the intense heat, despite the fire bouncing off her shield.

Magnus screamed again, but the energy wasn't there.

Kirby hit her mark.

Lance howled and their dragon form flickered toward human, like bad movie special effects.

Kirby landed next to Magnus and Frey, her back to the wall. "We'll be out of here soon." As soon as she could stop fighting long enough to focus on pushing her shield outward again to shatter this magical cage.

"I wasn't going to leave you behind." Magnus's voice was weak. "That was the order, but I couldn't." She dragged in a strained breath. She wouldn't last much longer. "I meant everything I said. You're my sister."

Lance was a solid dragon again.

None of them would survive long enough for backup if something didn't change *now*. Kirby knew what to do. "Fight by my side?"

Magnus's laugh ended in a wet, hacking cough. "You're insane. I can't even stand up."

"Don't," Frey warned.

It wasn't his decision, and they were out of time. Kirby had no idea what she was doing, but instinct took over. She knelt next to Magnus. "Sisters always? In life and death? In battle and peace?"

"Sisters always." Magnus grasped her hand.

"What are you doing?" Starkad's question echoed in Kirby's ear.

She'd explain herself when they were out of danger. The spark that flowed between Kirby and Magnus was a flash of blinding white that filled the room. When Kirby's vision cleared, Magnus stood next to her, healed and wearing stunning auburn wings and Valkyrie armor.

"Don't let him get hurt." Kirby nodded at Frey.

She and Magnus launched at Lance.

The two front attack forced Lance's attention in multiple directions. Kirby drew his fire while Magnus charged from behind. She bounced off dragon scale, and swept back into the air.

She was catching on quickly. Good.

Lance's tail flicked toward Magnus, and Kirby swept under, aiming for anything tender. The dragon vanished, and Kirby swooped straight up, colliding with Magnus as Lance reappeared.

Kirby shook off the crash and pointed Magnus toward the wings, before gliding in front of the dragon's face again, making a more direct attack.

Kirby couldn't expect Magnus to fight like Brit. They all had the same training, but the familiarity wasn't there. Magnus had never been on a field assignment with Kirby. But they both new the basics.

"Delta pinch, high seven," Kirby shouted.

Magnus's blank stare faded into recognition, and she took point on the maneuver.

The distinctly different snarls and growls of two wolves greeted Kirby, and she knew without looking that Starkad and Fen had joined the attack on the ground.

Lance wouldn't think twice about stepping on them, but they were another distraction.

A large stake struck the dragon and splintered, as a gunshot echoed off the cavern walls. Brit and Gwydion were here too.

"Get us out of here," Kirby shouted at Frey.

"I can't until you do your thing."

Right. She focused more power into her shield, pushing out.

Fen dodged a foot, and collided with Starkad, who rolled with the mistake and leaped up, teeth bared, and bouncing off Magnus as she swept in to spear an arm.

All three of them clattered in different directions, shook it off, and charged again.

Kirby wove between them, familiar with most of their moves, but not Fen's. Each time a breath of flame or a claw caught her, the wound took too long to heal, and the pain didn't evaporate. The way Fen's attacks slowed, Magnus's dives faltered, and Starkad spent longer pausing than running, it was the same for them.

Kirby needed to coordinate. She also needed to clear the path for Frey to get us out of her. "I'm falling back," she shouted.

Lance fired another blast of flame at her, and she deflected it. The heat singed her skin, despite not making contact, and left blisters in its wake.

She hated to do it, but she let the other's draw the dragon's attention, and focused harder on pushing out her shield.

As she had when she and Brit were at the café with Magnus, Kirby met resistance. Unlike that morning, though, she couldn't push past it.

"Still stuck here," Frey shouted.

Kirby clenched her jaw. "*I'm trying.*" She cut in a straight path toward Magnus, and hovered near the new Valkyrie. "I need you to push out your shield," Kirby said. "When you meet resistance, keep pushing. But don't stop fighting."

Magnus nodded, and Kirby felt something new. A caress of magic. A second wave of protection. Neat trick. Too bad there was no time to dwell on it.

Whatever Lance was doing to keep them here was still up, though. No matter how hard Kirby pushed, she couldn't force her shield past it.

"It's still not working," she said.

If they were stuck here much longer, someone was going to take a hit they couldn't recover from.

CHAPTER FORTY-FIVE

BRIT

"What's different about now?" Frey shouted.

Brit reloaded, and opened fire again. Each shot was deliberate, hitting a new spot. Watching for any flinch from the dragon. None of it made a difference. She flicked quick glances to Kirby and Magnus, and tried to ignore the envy muttering inside. It was true, she didn't want to be Kirby, but Magnus was a Valkyrie now. Stunning. Immortal. Powerful.

Magnus ducked under a claw and soared up, her gaze landing on Brit. "You," Magnus said. "You were the difference." The tail slapped her in the chest and sent her flying into the wall.

"*Focus.*" Kirby was in full combat mode. *That* was stunning.

Was Magnus right? Kirby was the one pushing at the cafe, but she'd warned Brit something was coming. The only thing Brit wanted at the time was to leave. To find their friends and go back to them.

Starkad snarled and leaped for the dragon as Kirby tried to draw their attention. Flame encased him anyway, but magic kept him from so much as a singe.

Even him. Brit had missed the grumpy asshole as much as she had everyone else. Well, maybe not quite as much.

Brit recognized the maneuver as Kirby and Magnus sped toward Lance in another attack. Brit and Kirby practiced an on-ground version all the time as a sniper team. Kirby would go high, draw Lance's attention, Magnus would hit with a soft blow, and Kirby would strike harder when Lance turned away.

Magnus jumped the gun, striking a fraction too soon, and Kirby fumbled mid-air to recover.

In the field the other day, Kirby's attention had been solely on Vera—Urd—and again, Brit had wanted so badly to leave.

She could shoot and pray to get out of here at the same time. She'd been praying half her life to an asshole god, why not to some mysterious power she may or may not have?

Brit wished, prayed, pushed for all she was worth, past the suffocating buzz of magic in the air. The same sensation she'd felt with Urd, but corrupted.

Something shattered in the field of energy.

Magnus vanished. *Blink*, she was gone.

The fuck?

"To me. *Now*," Frey shouted.

The dragon roared, and fire erupted from their mouth again, striking something and billowing out around them like a wall—a magical shield—kept it from progressing.

Everyone grabbed Frey, and they blinked out of the cave, landing back at NEON.

The bottles behind the bar rattled as six individuals dropped to the floor or onto the nearest piece of furniture. Brit ached places she didn't know she could ache, and that was saying a lot based on her past.

Everyone was covered with sooth and dirt. The group's collection of deep scratches and burn marks were healing slowly, but they were healing.

Except for Gwydion. Blood continued to trickle from a large gash across his arm, and he was pale.

"She's gone. I'm such an idiot." Kirby raked her fingers through her hair.

Brit pointed her toward Gwydion, and Kirby sob-gasped.

"Fuck, fuck, fuck." Kirby muttered over and over as she rushed to Gwydion's side and focused on healing him.

Brit echoed the sentiment. They'd survived, but they hadn't rescued Aya or the other gods, and there was no way they could take that dragon down. If they had Gluskab with them next time—a god who could summon deadly earthquakes and typhoons, one after another—they were fucked.

CHAPTER FORTY-SIX

KIRBY

Fucking idiot. Kirby wanted to slam her head into a wall—the one near the stage, in NEON's main room looked good. That had to be brick. How could she make such basic mistake? She wasn't any sort of Queen Valkyrie. The first chance she had to share the gift with someone else, they bailed. She was shit at reading people, and her instinct lied.

"What the *fuck* were you thinking?" Frey's angry question mirrored her thoughts and drew her attention.

Starkad stepped between them, anger flashing in his eyes. "She made what she thought was the right call, in the heat of battle."

Starkad's defending Kirby actually made her feel worse. Why didn't he see how big a mistake she's made?

"What happened?" Dahlia asked. She was seated at a nearby table, where they'd been left to monitor.

Min had left her, to approach the group. When he reached for Frey, Fen growled menacingly.

"She made Magnus into a Valkyrie." Did Brit sound sad?

Kirby tried with her first. She really had. Grief and self-loathing bubbled inside, threatening to overwhelm in a feeling she was all too familiar with.

"Hey." Gwydion's voice was soft, only meant for her. "Stop."

Not this time.

"Is Magnus here?" Dahlia's face lit up, and her tone was hopeful.

Frey kept his glare focused on Kirby. "Of course not. She bolted the instant she had the chance. You were idiotic, irresponsible—"

"It's not your decision." Min's voice was hard. "This is Kirby's power, and she made the call."

"That's a bullshit excuse." Fen stood next to Frey, a united front of judge and jury against Kirby's mistake. "Next you're going to say *fate wouldn't have given her this ability if she wasn't capable of using it correctly.*"

Gwydion squeezed Kirby's hand with his now-healed one. "Show of hands," he said. "Who here has *any* faith in the fates at this point."

Starkad reached behind him, to grab her other hand. "I trust Kirby."

Their support would be comforting if they were right.

"Such a loyal lapdog," Frey taunted.

259

Starkad growled, his canines and jaw extending as he bared his teeth

"Everyone step back. We need to stop." Wonderful Min. Always the voice of reason.

"We *need* to go back now, maybe with someone who doesn't give everything up to our enemies, and get my sister." Frey spoke through clenched teeth.

Gwydion stepped forward, closer to Starkad, forming a wall in front of Kirby. She wanted to stop him, remind him she didn't need protection, but she also wanted to hide. She shouldn't feel this way. She was better than this.

"Aya wasn't there. No one but Grytha was." Gwydion wasn't pale anymore, but he didn't look like he was at full strength.

"She—Grytha—told us the others were somewhere else," Brit said.

Fen focused on Starkad. "You're not this gullible. How are you buying that any of this is right?"

"I trust the people I keep company with. Their word, instinct, and choice." Starkad was half-wolf by now, but his tone was clear, human, and hard.

"You want to prove how reliable and bad ass you all are? Let's go back. Now. I can't abandon Aya," Frey said.

Dahlia made the tiniest, most unobtrusive cough. "I want her back too, but if you guys came back in this condition, how does running back there now make things go better?"

"You're welcome to leave without us." Gwydion tossed the words out like it didn't devour him to pretend he didn't care about another life. This had to be eating at him, though.

Frey let out a long hiss. "You swore—"

"To help you protect Aya," Min said. "We will."

Indignation snapped inside Kirby. "As a matter of fact, you came to us as friends. Doing us a favor. *Information about the prophecies*, you said. *All to protect Kirby*, you said. And I've believed the two of you were the same friends I've always known. But if you were, you would have approached me. Asked me. I would have helped you, Frey, because I know you. I thought I did. I made a mistake. Don't be stupid by adding to the list."

"Don't be—" Fen stared at her with disbelief. "You insisted we work with Vidar and his band of little killer soldiers. Now that it didn't go well, do you need to rest your broken ego, and come up with another naively stupid—"

Starkad shifted to full wolf in a blink and lunged.

"Excuse me." Magnus's voice was like pressing *freeze frame* on the room. It would have been humorous if any of the tension evaporated.

Kirby's brain froze too. She came back. To taunt them?

"You swore you'd never set foot in here." Dahlia was the first to speak.

Magnus ducked her head and stayed near the doorway. "I meant what I said in the cave, Kirby. I wasn't going to leave you. Vidar pulled me— I was so furious. I told him to fuck off and I walked away."

Dahlia squealed and sprinted across the room to wrap Magnus in a hug.

Wait. What? Magnus was back? Kirby didn't make a mistake? "What about them being family? Things being different? Every reason you gave for not coming with us before?"

Dahlia stepped aside, but Magnus didn't look up. "None of these decisions have been easy for me. I didn't want to leave them or you all. But he left me there, and you saved me. I made you a promise and you trusted me with this." Her wings appeared, stunning auburn, before they vanished again. "That says a lot."

"Great. Get the fuck out." Frey clipped off the words.

Dahlia scowled.

"Duckie…" Fen's tone was one of warning.

So much for things being better.

"Then I leave with her." Dahlia grabbed Magnus's hand.

"We can all go, since I'm responsible for this. Or do you need our help too much for that?" Kirby was tired of the pressure and accusation from all sides, but especially from those who were supposed to be her allies.

She still wasn't completely secure with Magnus's about face, but did see any reason for her to be here if her story wasn't true. Magnus and Vidar had what they wanted.

"Do you blame us for being suspicious?" Frey asked.

Kirby shook her head. "I blame you for not trusting me. Dahlia. If you don't trust us, why are we here?"

"She can stay at the house on Cottage Street." Fen was resigned. "You know the one."

Dahlia's grin was back, wide and bright and genuine. She skipped across the room to give Fen a hug and kiss him on the cheek. She cast a glare at Frey when she pulled back.

"You're getting soft in your old age," Starkad muttered without malice.

Fen rolled his eyes. "You're one to talk."

This didn't solve everything. Magnus could still be lying, but after so many twists and turns, the deception would become too complicated. Everyone at TOM knew the best lies were simple and closest to the truth. Having Magnus be reluctant to be here before, then throwing her into danger, then pulling her from the fight, then sending her back to beg forgiveness? Too many steps. Too many places for something to go wrong.

Kirby had bigger concerns, though. Like walking back into a dragon's cave, where they were expected, and they still didn't have the best intel in return. "You want us to save Aya? We take a small strike team. Most of us have already fought together. We go in fast and get out the same way."

"*No.*" Magnus's vehemence was startling. "You can't go back. Period."

"Why not?" Min asked.

"It was a setup."

"Big surprise," Starkad and Fen spoke at the same time.

Kirby shot them a raised eyebrow look.

"Vidar traded Kirby for Grytha," Magnus said. "He realized Kirby wasn't going to side with him, which meant she wouldn't be turning any of our— his—people into Valkyries. None of you were supposed to be able to leave. If you go back…"

"Why Kirby?" Brit asked. "She wasn't involved in sealing Malsumis away. She's powerful, but she's not the ultimate in power. Why?"

Magnus shook her head. "I don't know. Hand to heaven, I have no idea. But you can't go back there."

CHAPTER FORTY-SEVEN

STARKAD

Fury and bloodlust spilled through Starkad's veins. He didn't want Dahlia here. Or Magnus. Or anyone from any secret organization. But he was a soldier, and happy to be such. Somewhere along the way, Kirby had become a brilliant general.

No.

Dahlia was right—Kirby was a queen. Capable of mercy, justice, and when needed, punishment. In the cave, the way Kirby fought was glorious.

The caves. "I know why Lance and Gluskab surrendered Grytha for Kirby," Starkad said. "Fen saw it too."

"Holy shit, you're right. The sigil carved in the floor." Fen's eyes grew wide.

Starkad yanked a stack of napkins from the holder on a nearby table and laid them out in a grid on the flat surface. "I need a pen." He knew a sacrificial seal when he saw one.

Min handed him a pen and he drew. Occasionally, Fen would take over, filling in missing bits. It wasn't an intricate or ornate mark, but the details in something like this were important in understanding it.

They finished and stepped back.

"Oh, fuck," Dahlia muttered. "Does anyone else see what I see?"

Kirby was pale. "That's a TOM campus map. Infirmary. Firing range. Classrooms. Administration. Housing." She pointed at each of the corners of the pentagon.

"That explains why Vidar only reconstructed part of the place," Magnus said.

"Blood sacrifice to break a seal." Frey sank into the nearest chair. "We have to get back there."

Kirby nodded. "We will. Soon. We're not going to let them take Aya's life."

"Or release a goddess of destruction on the world." Brit's words had an edge. "I'm just learning to like it here. No one's fucking destroying it."

Killing the gods who created the original seal, letting their blood wash the mark away, would break it. But Hel was already dead, and Grytha had been let go.

"You heard what the young lady said, didn't you?" Min asked. "If Gluskab doesn't have his full contingent of original gods, there's a reason he wants you instead. If you go back there of your own will, if you're ready to die to save people, that's a willing sacrifice."

Gwydion pinched the bridge of his nose and took the seat next to Frey. "Coincidence they've been pushing Kirby to become more powerful? The more strength running though her, the stronger Malsumis is when she emerges."

This could be a battle to best all battles. Starkad couldn't help the thrill in his veins.

"You're not going back." Min sounded as if the matter was settled.

Kirby gave him a grim smile. "The *let's sacrifice the Valkyrie* idea only works if they win. I'm not the only one who's more powerful."

"Than half an hour ago?" Dahlia asked.

"Yes." Kirby moved to the center of the room and pushed a table out two meters. "Brit. Starkad."

She wanted a big enough clearing to spar. Starkad knew it without question. It only took a moment for the three of them to push aside enough furniture to leave the floor clear.

Kirby crooked her finger and motioned for Magnus to join them. "Us versus them," Kirby said to Magnus. "Three minutes. He won't hold back."

"Excuse me. *Do* hold back." Frey was cold. "Don't wreck this place."

Kirby shrugged. "Tag team only."

Magnus whimpered, but squared her shoulders and set her stance. "You realize we weren't coordinated in the cave. *I* shouldn't be the one pointing that out to *you*. I'm not your partner. We never trained together."

"But we did. You saw every time Brit and I were collaborating over the past few days. Every word. Nudge. Look. You *knew*. I wish there was time for more. To build your confidence and to practice together. There's not. You have the ability now to do everything we were ever taught. Lean into it," Kirby said.

Magnus hesitated, then nodded. "Okay. Let's do it."

This was going to be fun.

"Dahlia, count us down," Kirby said.

Dahlia frowned and jabbed at her watch. "One. *Go.*"

Starkad let the wolf out. This was new. He had full clarity and control. He could wait for Magnus to make the first move. To so much as twitch.

Kirby would be upset if he hurt her new Valkyrie. Fortunately, he recognized the line was between *don't hold back* and *kill*. He also couldn't go nearly-all-out against Kirby. Brit would.

Brit swept a kick at Kirby's legs, not bothering with a feint like she had last time she sparred with Kirby.

Fight was on, and Magnus was open. Starkad liked Brit's approach, and Magnus's fear was on his side. He lunged at her.

Terror splashed across her face, and she vanished as he swung a fist. At a tap on the shoulder, he spun to find her behind him, tentative smirk in place.

Irritation and intrigue flooded his veins. Not just fun. Challenging.

The four exchanged taps and near misses. Endurance was a distinct perk of this brand of immortality. Starkad found the pattern to Magnus's blinking out of sight, and backed her into a corner.

Each time he pinned her down, Kirby switched, mixing up the patterns and stalling Starkad in his tracks.

He wasn't sure how much time passed, several minutes at least, when Magnus called "Time. It's a draw. Seriously, guys."

Starkad ran his tongue over his canines before retracting them, savoring the lingering flavor of a good fight.

"Not sure that proves your point." Frey didn't sound impressed. "Kirby sacrificed herself repeatedly, knowing Starkad wouldn't hurt her."

It very much proved the point. "Because she knows our strengths and weaknesses," Starkad said. You wanted to see that we're stronger than half an hour ago, and we are. You want to go back now, this is what you get."

Magnus nodded toward Gwydion. "Is Gwydion joining us? He knows some pretty neat tricks." She shifted her weight, her body language radiating discomfort. "What about Fen?"

Starkad didn't know if Gwydion should be fighting again, not out of some sense of disdain, but he'd been wrecked after both of the recent fights. Starkad wouldn't admit it in this group, but he was worried about Gwydion.

No one else answered, either.

"I think I should sit this one out," Gwydion finally said.

Fen stepped forward. "I'll join you."

"To keep an eye on us?" Starkad wasn't even half teasing. Maybe a quarter.

269

"No. We all have to be focused on the real fight."

Interesting. What turned him around? Desperation? Reason?

"Dumb question." Brit drew everyone's attention. "If this Lance guy wants Kirby dead, because supposedly her army of Valkyries will destroy the world, why would he use her death... wait for it... as a means to free a goddess who wants to destroy the world?"

Fair point.

"He's not trying to stop Kirby from destroying the world," Min said. "It all makes a twisted, god-logic kind of sense. Lance saw her and other Valkyries involved in deadly battles, but Aya said it best. Kirby doesn't cause the wars, she's drawn to them, to help those who need it. And she inspires others to do the same."

Also true. Starkad looked around the room, his gaze lingering on each face for a moment before moving on. It didn't matter why each of them joined this specific battle, Kirby unified them and pointed them toward a common goal.

Dahlia clucked. "So if they use her blood for the sacrifice, they get rid of a major obstacle and instead of fighting for the world, her death helps destroy it. That's fucked up."

"God-logic. Just like Min said." Brit sounded disgusted. "What do you expect from an ancient psycho who lets people worship them based on visions they had before humanity existed?"

Now that everyone was on the same page, Frey was right. They should go back sooner rather than later. "It's unlikely Lance expects us to return immediately," Starkad said. "Who votes for waiting on our asses and losing the element of surprise. Show of hands?"

He wasn't surprised when no one voted for that option. "Good. You have thirty minutes to get your heads in the right place."

"After that, we'll take another fifteen to solidify the plan. Magnus, I assume you can teleport us in there?" Kirby said.

"Yes."

"What if they block you from entering, the way we were kept from leaving?" Frey's question might have made more sense at the start of this discussion.

Starkad wouldn't blame him, though. His business was pleasure, not death. "They want Kirby there. They won't stop her."

"Any other questions? Comments? Concerns?" Kirby paused. "No? Break. Back here in thirty."

Starkad grasped Kirby's fingers to draw her attention. "A moment in private?"

She nodded, and the two of them moved to another room.

Mirrors lined one wall, with a counter running underneath, and chairs pushed up to them. Lockers ran along the opposite wall. Dressing room.

Starkad caught his reflection, and the person who stared back was foreign. His nose was sharper and longer than it had been his entire life. His injured arm looked like a blacked, gnarled reproduction of an arm and hand, if it had been carved from wood. Wildness stared back.

He was terrifying.

"You're beautiful." Kirby's reverence dragged his attention from his reflection. "Frightening. I can't say handsome, that sounds too clean. But you are breathtaking as you. I don't know how else to say it. It's like you've shed a costume that wasn't right for you."

He felt the same, but that wasn't quite why he'd pulled her aside. Or perhaps in a way it was. "I was lost without you. For so long. Even when I got you back, and had to watch you grow up in that place. Not knowing the student, but remembering and missing the woman I knew before, was torture."

Kirby stepped closer, and he grasped her hands. She tilted her head up to meet his gaze. "I realize that the first few decades of my life—this life—were nothing compared to how long I've lived. But while I was at TOM, I'd never felt so alone. Even after I—we—left. After you saved..." She drew in a shuddering breath.

This vulnerability from a woman who had just stood in front of gods without flinching and told them what to do, was breathtaking.

Could Starkad ever atone for the secrets he kept when he took her from TOM? "I'm sorr—"

"I'll never forget how much I ached. I doubted everything in my world, myself most of all. I asked myself every day why you weren't as obsessed with me as I was with you. Why I was the only one who couldn't stop thinking about what we could be."

Starkad gripped her chin tightly enough to convey he wouldn't let her go, but not so much it would ache. "I never stopped thinking about that. Not over the last thousand years. Even when I pretended otherwise."

"Magnus wanted us to go back with her. To stay with Vidar and TOM." Kirby's words weren't a surprise, but they still sliced through Starkad. "Growing up, even though I hated it there, I thought they were family. She's my family. Dahlia. If I didn't love and trust you completely, I'd consider Magnus's request."

There was so much more in Kirby's words than showed on the surface. He hadn't known how to help her, truly help her, through the years of doubt and depression. Through the trauma. He offered what he had, but being unable to heal her devoured him. He didn't have to ask *what about the others*. Min and Gwydion would hate a decision like that, but they'd let her make the decision. Brit would most likely join her.

But that wasn't the important part here. Kirby was giving Starkad so much trust. So much faith. And he felt the same about her. "I love you." He poured the emotion into the words. It didn't matter that they'd said them to each other hundreds— thousands—of times over the centuries.

Today it meant more. The promise was more vast. They were the couple fucking before battle again. The berserker and the Valkyrie who would always be together. "I love you wholly, eternally, and obsessively. I'd watch the world burn to save you. To ensure I never lose you again."

"I don't want the world to burn. So don't let me wind up in that situation." She rose on her toes to brush her lips over his.

273

Starkad slid his hand to the back of her neck to grip possessively, and crushed into the kiss. He swallowed her gasp of surprise, and drew out her whimpers. He feasted on each sigh and moan and the sensations and flavors that were distinctly Kirby, and didn't pull away until both their mouths were swollen and red.

He rested his forehead against hers, still holding on for everything he had. "You're mine. For eternity. I don't care who else you fuck or love. I know which part of your heart belongs to me."

"I *am* yours. Forever."

CHAPTER FORTY-EIGHT

GWYDION

"I *am* yours. Forever."

Kirby's words drifted out to Gwydion as he approached the dressing room. She was so sincere. So certain. It warmed him from the inside and made him smile.

Gwydion hated to interrupt the moment, but she'd put them on a timer, and he suspected she didn't like to be kept waiting. He knocked. "May I join you?" he asked when she and Starkad looked up.

Starkad beckoned with his good hand. *Good* wasn't really the right word, though. The other hand seemed to work fine, despite its twisted and rotted appearance.

Doubt stalled Gwydion. He'd been considering this longer than he realized, but couldn't put all the right words to it until they came back from the caverns. From a fight that nearly killed him and his entire team. After watching Kirby share her power with Min, Gwydion understood what Urd meant, about he and Starkad being connected. He knew what he had to do next.

"Do you want me to leave?" Starkad didn't sound like he would, regardless.

Gwydion shook his head. "I need to talk to both of you. Mostly you." He looked Starkad.

Kirby approached Gwydion, grabbed his hand, and pulled him further into the room, so the three stood close. He would never stop being amazed that her strength and vulnerability coexisted so beautifully.

Best to get this over with. It was the right decision, as foreign as the idea felt. "The last thing I want—that any of us wants—is to see Kirby hurt. Since we all met again, months ago, I thought that meant physically fighting by her side. Being there for each battle." He dragged in a deep breath. Was what he wanted to do possible? He believed so. "I see now it means being here after that fight is over. For the other struggles. As an anchor. A healer. I wasn't created to destroy, and being in so many wars has torn me apart for centuries."

"I understand." Kirby squeezed his hand. "And I don't fault you."

Gwydion smiled. He didn't expect any less from her. "There's more to the thought. I know when my power started fading. It was after Starkad was shot, when he shifted and arm became a part of his arsenal of death, instead of TOM's." The pieces all fit. It could be coincidence, but Gwydion thought it was more.

"It doesn't make any sense, but I also think you're right." As Starkad spoke, he flexed the fingers on his infected hand.

"How do we fix it?" Kirby asked.

Gwydion shook his head. "We don't. Not in the way you're asking. I think we can change it, though. When you changed Magnus, how did that work?"

"It's mostly instinct?" Kirby sounded uncertain. "I kind of will it to happen."

Gwydion did want this to happen. The longer he stood here, the more certain he was. "In that case, Starkad, I give you everything I have that you need to keep Kirby safe. I'll be here when the fighting is done, but take what you need to make sure you all are too."

Gwydion expected to feel weak as the power flowed through and from him. Instead, life and hope filled his veins. He was refreshed. Stronger than he'd felt in... he didn't know the last time he'd felt so right in his own skin.

At the same time, Starkad's arm was changing. The gnarled, knotted bits faded then vanished, replaced by a jet black fur that was almost midnight blue in the flash of the mirrors' lights. The wolf-like appearance faded and blended farther down his arm, vanishing near the wrist, and leaving his hand looking human.

Starkad's chuckle was low and threatening as he clenched his fist. He spun and drove a punch into the nearest locker, piercing the sheet metal and the cinder block wall behind like they were tissue paper. The screeching of shredded metal and shattering rock pierced the air. "Nice." He pulled his hand free, and flexed. There were no visible marks on skin.

"What the fuck?" Frey asked from the doorway. The others stood behind him, varying degrees of awe and shock on their faces as they looked past him, into the room.

Starkad laughed again, more easily this time. "I'll pay for the lockers."

Frey joined them, gaze on the new hole the entire time. He tugged the edges of the metal, and they didn't budge. "You did this? With your bare hands?"

"Hand." Starkad was smug.

Frey's eyes grew wide, and he looked between Gwydion and Starkad. "Fuck. Why didn't I see that sooner?" Frey's question was soft, as if he were asking himself.

"Don't keep us in suspense," Gwydion prompted.

Frey hovered his hand over Starkad's arm, never making contact. "The thing about being a twin is it's given me a unique perspective on how everything—everyone—is connected."

"Okay, so, Urd already told us that about the two of them," Kirby said flatly.

"What she didn't tell you is that they've been fighting it." Frey stepped back. "I'm making an assumption, but its based in experience. Starkad is immortal. That's Kirby's gift and Odin's curse. The bullet couldn't kill him. Wouldn't have killed him. But it would have kept devouring his flesh if he hadn't pushed the way he did."

"When I shifted, after I was shot, I felt something inside snap," Starkad said.

Frey nodded. "That wall you put up that keeps the two of you apart. You broke it. But you didn't know it was there, so you repaired it again the instant you could. You stopped the decay, but the damage was done and your immortality, your power, isn't life."

Understanding flowed through Gwydion. "When I opened the connection again, the connection I share with nature made a change."

"Exactly. And now the energy is flowing however the two of you allow it, which is currently manifesting itself in the strength in that arm." Frey shook his head so hard, Gwydion expected to hear something rattle. "I don't give a shit about the lockers. Bring everyone back safe, and we're good."

Part of Gwydion, the bit that was ingrained with centuries of *fighting is the only way to save what I love,* hated the idea of sitting this out. But he wasn't really. Like Min, he'd be here when they returned, to comfort. Heal. Protect in a different way.

Chapter Forty-Nine

BRIT

There were so many variables in this plan, and no way to resolve them before arriving. If they were going now though, there weren't a lot of other options. The only thing making it seem like the ritual couldn't be done without Kirby was that it hadn't been yet.

But Lance also wanted Kirby dead. Would he kill the gods and find another way to her? What if the other gods weren't there? What if this group was killed the instant they appeared? What if they were completely wrong about this entire thing?

Too many variables.

Brit stood in the still cleared space in the middle of NEON, with Kirby, Magnus, Starkad, and Fen.

"Their plan is complicated. Ours is simple," Kirby said. "I'm the bait. Magnus will drop us in the room Starkad and Fen are in. If the gods aren't there, she'll take Brit, blip through the caves. No gods? We leave. Otherwise, we destroy Gluskab and Lance. Questions?"

Brit kept her avalanche of concerns to herself. Asking them aloud wouldn't serve any purpose.

"Wait." Magnus sprinted toward her bag where it sat next to Dahlia. "I can't believe I didn't think of this." She pulled out a full magazine for a Desert Eagle. She thumbed out the top bullet and handed it to Dahlia, then jogged back to hand the clip to Brit. "These are TOM's secret weapon. What they used on Kirby and Starkad. And the only ones I have left." Which was why she'd given one to Dahlia—reverse engineering.

God killing bullets. Brit was bringing two guns, but had planned to stick mostly with the AUG on full auto, but these couldn't be wasted. She re-loaded her Desert Eagle .40 and chambered a round before tucking it back into the holster on her right hip. Normally she'd hide the miniature arsenal. No reason today.

"Thank you." Kirby gave Magnus a tight smile. "Anything else?"

Nope.

Everyone reached for someone else's hand, so Magnus could teleport them.

The tension in Brit's gut coiled to impossibly tight. Every mission she'd done for TOM, she said a quick prayer to Vidar. Kirby had done the same, but in Freya's name. Brit would never again pray to a god to guide her or secure her path.

Instead, she focused on Aya. On her face and power and how glorious she'd looked firing off magical spears in Salt Lake as Brit called out targets. *We're coming. Be ready.*

"No one lets anyone die," Brit said as she took Magnus's hand.

They appeared in a vast cavern. An immersive, invisible weight pressed in on Brit, crushing her toward the ground. Her joints creaked under the pressure. She kicked her legs out, toes and palms on the ground, to make herself as small a surface as possible, but still allow her to get up quickly.

"This sucks," Magnus said.

A pair of growls, wolves, said Starkad and Fen agreed.

Brit was already pushing back. She had no idea how she'd shattered the fields before, but this had to be a smaller version, and if she could just focus...

"Visitors. Delicious." Lance stood a few feet away, in human form.

Next to them was a man—god, from the presence he radiated—with wild eyes and a twisted smile. He had short dark hair that was mussed, and a sturdy, thin frame. The fact he could've been a super model really added to the I'm-a-Hollywood-super-villain vibe. "I know you. Most of you anyway. You were there when Loki woke me." He crouched in front of Kirby, who was pinned in the middle of the room, in a similar position to Brit. "Now you can do the same for my sister."

"I don't know. My calendar's booked for a few centuries. Can we reschedule?" Kirby's voice was tight, as though she struggled to breathe, but she still managed flippant.

"No. I'm so tired of humanity. Over people fighting over prophecies and visions I never asked for." As Lance spoke, the charge in the air grew. Magic, maliciousness, and madness clawed its way over Brit.

They were summoning something bigger, and as they did so, Brit felt where the fields pinning them down stopped, and the rest of the magic began. She followed it back to a blend of auras. Other gods.

Gluskab crouched next to Kirby, and Starkad's growls grew louder. More threatening.

Brit didn't blame him.

"I wanted to bring you here the instant Lance told me what your blood could do." Gluskab's voice was smooth and seductive. "I'm glad I was convinced to wait. Your power, your drive to save the world, is tangible. And the best part is, you're here willingly. A sacrifice made of your own free will. My sister will be so stron—"

"Shut. Up." Lance cut him off.

The charge in the air grew stronger, and some of the weight on Brit decreased. She knew how to break through. The instinct was there. But if she did so before the other gods were brought in, the mission failed. "Wait." She need a little more time to summon her strength. "You're supposed to tell us all about why you're doing this."

Lance focused a glare on her. "Insignificant. Even as an immortal. How about this? I'm tired of this world, and Gluskab and Malsumis will get rid of the irritation."

The air was so heavy with magic now, Brit could taste it. There was no reason to draw things out once the other gods were here. She'd have the slimmest moment to act, and the others needed to be ready.

"You're not going to give them any last words?" Gluskab asked.

Brit was going to take them regardless. "Hey. Remember that mission we did together in Salt Lake?"

Lance frowned. "What?"

"You're such a moron." Magnus's words were carried on a heavy sigh.

"Don't listen to her," Kirby said. "She doesn't realize that you die enough times, and last words become overrated."

They both understood Brit was about to do what she and Kirby did with Magnus. That they said anything beyond expressing confusion was enough confirmation.

"Idiotic children," Lance spat.

The charge in the air surged. Please let her hit this at the right point.

Brit forced her will out, and felt cracks, spread, and summon chaos.

The pressure pinning them down vanished as a group of gods appeared in the circle next to where Kirby had been.

But she was already flying directly at Lance and Gluskab.

Magnus vanished and appeared next to the gods. Then the entire group disappeared as Lance became a dragon, and slashed the air with his claws.

Blood splashed across the ground from thin air. He'd hit someone.

Two wolves, one as large as a truck and the other humanoid, charged past Brit. As Kirby ducked under Lance's attack and drove toward his side with her sword drawn, Starkad pounced, teeth bared and aimed at the dragon's neck.

Fen tackled Gluskab, pinning him to the ground.

"Help." Magnus's plea came from beside Brit. "I got everyone out but her." Aya lay on the stone, bleeding freely from a large gash that ran from her shoulder to the opposite hip. "The shields went up again."

Damn it. Brit hadn't noticed in the bedlam. She pushed out, to recreate the shattering trick from a moment ago, but the pattern had changed. She needed to recalibrate?

"She's dying. She won't stop bleeding." Magnus was near panic.

Kirby was a little busy. And may not be able to heal a god anyway. But if she could, was Magnus capable of the same? "Heal her," Brit said to Magnus, her attention split between this and the fight.

Magnus pressed her hands into the gash. "I can't. I don't know if it's because I've never practiced or I don't know how or... I'm trying."

"Work together." Aya's words were as fragile as paper. Her eyelids fluttered, and shut.

So not helpful. Apparently even dying gods were infuriatingly cryptic. As Brit fumbled with the words and her frustration around them, she covered Magnus's hands with her own.

This was how Kirby did things right? How she and Min had shared their power?

A new energy flowed over Brit. Calming. Liquid. Deadly, but in a good way? It was Aya's magic, and it was weak. Was that keeping Magnus out? Breaking the flow completely seemed like a bad idea. Brit needed to disrupt it, like water around a rock, long enough for Magnus to heal Aya.

The battle echoed off cave walls and screamed in Brit's ears. Lance roaring. Gluskab laughing. Fen and Starkad growling. Kirby's soft grunts each time she was struck.

That last one was the hardest for Brit to hear. She should be part of the fight, but could do more good here.

"It's not working. I don't know what I'm doing wrong." Magnus was panicked.

Nobles weren't supposed to panic, but the two of them weren't Nobles anymore, and this was a unique situation. Brit turned inward, trying to block out the world. Difficult, given the situation. She wasn't sure how she knew, but she knew her priority was giving Magnus an opening.

"*Shield.*" Kirby's shout sliced the edges of Brit's focus.

Intense heat blasted around her, and Magnus screamed.

Brit jerked from her meditation, to see Magnus kneeling between the fight and Brit and Aya, wings at full spread and flame scorching away feathers and cartilage and skin.

A yelp reached them and Fen slammed into the cave wall to Brit's right. He wobbled on his feet as he stood, before straightening and charging back in.

The dirt glistened with the dark red of blood. Kirby was in flight and looked uninjured, but Lance and Gluskab looked as fresh as when the fight started. As fresh as a dragon could look anyway.

"Whatever you're doing, do it faster," Kirby yelled.

Magnus had recovered from the burns, and she pressed her hands back to Aya's chest. "I'm trying," Magnus muttered. "It's still not working."

CHAPTER FIFTY

KIRBY

At the sound of Magnus's scream of pain, Kirby's insides curdled. She'd asked too much too soon from someone new to these powers. But what choice did she have?

Lance had sized themself small enough to maneuver but large enough to be threatening in the cavern the size of a two-story home.

Kirby would celebrate the fact that they weren't as big as in the field, but size didn't matter if they remained invulnerable.

Gluskab remained himself, but superimposed over him was a double-sized vision of decay. The twisted, transparent visage resembled the damage to Starkad's arm before Gwydion stepped in.

A series of five magical blades sliced through Kirby, striking her biceps, thighs, and stomach. Gluskab had thrown several attacks like this at her. They were clean cuts that healed a moment after they were made, but they hurt like hell, and each slice caused a momentary falter.

Starkad charged up Lance's tail, claws using scales for purchase and teeth bared. He dove for Lance's throat, and was knocked aside. He slammed into the rock with a thud and a sickening crunch that made Kirby cringe.

Fen attacked Gluskab. He was flung back and whimpered as he met the cave at high speed.

Kirby needed her full team. "Whatever you're doing, do it fast," she shouted at Magnus. She hated to push, but again, what choice was there? The divided attacks made progress impossible, but if she and the wolves focused on one god, the other was free to strike unprohibited.

She swooped in for another attack, sword aimed at what she hoped was sensitive skin under Lance's arm. She was flung back, and Gluskab's blades caught her mid-air again, inflicting another round of deep wounds.

The ground rumbled and tiny rocks clattered from the ceiling and fell around them. A faint glow formed at the edges of the seal on the ground, cracks splitting out in various directions.

"You're bleeding all over the mark," Brit called.

Kirby looked down. *Fuck*. Lance and Gluskab didn't have to kill her to draw her blood. They just needed to pierce her over and over, and her natural healing would provide them a potentially endless supply.

That explained why Fen and Starkad were being knocked into walls, rather than being carved up the way Kirby was.

She and her team were no more ready for this fight than they had been a few hours ago. What had she been thinking?

"*Got it*," Magnus said.

Kirby didn't dare look, as another round of knives flew in her direction. She dodged, flying under and back up, directly into Lance's claws. As blood flowed freely from her wounds, the ground shook harder and the glow grew brighter.

An ethereal wave passed over Kirby. It was soothing and familiar, like herself, but not quite.

Gluskab roared and the illusion around him flickered.

"*Incoming,*" Brit shouted.

Magical spears—Aya's—flew past Kirby and pierced Gluskab, before he could stabilize.

Magnus had healed Aya.

There was no time to stop and make a drawn out plan, but Kirby needed to regroup now that she had her full team.

She landed at the far edge of the seal, near Brit and Magnus. If Kirby was the target, she'd stay clear of the mark. One problem sorted.

"Joining the others," Aya said before she blinked out of sight, appeared behind Gluskab, and drove a spear through him.

She, Fen, and Starkad would keep the gods distracted, but Kirby probably didn't even have thirty seconds.

Magnus said, "So the undead in D&D—"

Kirby silenced her with a look. None of them had played those games except Magnus and Dahlia.

Magnus rolled her eyes. "God of death. Healing magic is a weakness."

That made a disturbing amount of sense. Kirby should've brought Min after all. "Odds that magical immortal-killing bullets will work on him?"

"Not high." Magnus shook her head.

Fantastic. Not. "Unless healing him hurts us, trying doesn't make us worse off than we are now. Magnus, hit him hard. Brit, save the good ammo for the dragon, just in case. Otherwise, target practice time. Go."

Kirby swooped in a wide arc around the circle to rejoin the others. Lance caught her with their tail and flung her over the seal as lance made of darkness pierced her shoulder and pinned her to the ground. She was immobilized for precious seconds, bleeding freely, as she fought to free herself.

Starkad sprinted toward her, his human-wolf hand reaching for the weapon. Lance knocked him aside with a wing.

Kirby worked herself free, and the spear vanished. The damage was done. The ground shook harder now, and the glow around the seal was bright.

Gluskab chanted in a language Kirby didn't speak, and she had to take to the air to keep from stumbling on the rolling ground.

Starkad's normal arm was tilted as a bad angle, and he struggled to keep his footing.

Another blade, similar to the one that had caught Kirby, nailed Brit to a far wall. Her scream was agonizing, cutting Kirby to the quick.

291

Fen tumbled to the ground, and his wolf form flickered before vanishing. He was moving, but it was slowly.

Magnus was focused on Malsumis, but like before, she wasn't making headway.

Kirby needed to help her. Weaken one god long enough to destroy him. Hopefully. She dove straight toward Gluskab.

Lance pierced her thigh with a claw, pinning her to the center of the seal. They'd gone through the bone, and she couldn't move. She was bleeding worse than before.

The room might as well have been on rockers. The glow as bright as sunshine, and ground cracked all around them. The madness in the air was tangible and vile.

Could Kirby break free without tearing off her leg? Would it matter if she opened a gash large enough to spill the entire contents of her veins? They were so fucked.

Chapter Fifty-One

KIRBY

Gluskab roared in pain.

Was Magnus making headway? Kirby needed to get to her. To help her.

Starkad charged toward Kirby again, teeth aimed Lance's claws. He clamped his jaws around Lance's finger, and tore the claw free, knocking it from Kirby's thigh at the same time.

Gods, her leg hurt, but it healed in a blink, and Kirby was already joining Magnus.

The glow flickered, casting the room in a strobe effect.

Kirby poured her healing magic toward Gluskab, joining it with Magnus's. The god howled as his larger visage flickered. He was more human than illusion.

"*Brit, Aya, now,*" Kirby screamed. Bullets and spears flew at Gluskab.

His roars of pain and fury threatened to split her eardrums. He collapsed, body far outside the circle.

Silence blanketed the cave. No more screams or glow or sounds of battle. There was nothing.

"Gross," Magnus muttered as Gluskab's body shriveled to a husk.

The chanting resumed, but in Lance's dragon voice, echoing in everyone's thoughts. The quakes resumed, and the near-blinding glow was back.

"She can't get free. If her brother wreaked havoc on the world in just a few days, and he was the sane one..." Everyone knew how critical this was, but Kirby had to drive home the point.

Deep fissures ran along the ground. The exhaustion on everyone's faces reflected Kirby's. Rapid healing didn't matter if they wore themselves out taking hits from Lance and not doing any damage in return.

But they had done damage. Starkad had caught Lance off guard.

"There has to be a reason he's afraid of *you*. A lot of people will be on both sides for Ragnarök," Fen said.

Kirby shook her head. "I haven't been able to get close enough. I need a way to pin..." She trailed off as pieces clicked in her mind. "If Lance can pin us in place with a shield, Magnus and I should be able to do the same, especially if we work together," Kirby spoke quickly and quietly. "Coordinated attack, all of us. I'll break off last minute."

Everyone nodded.

Starkad and Fen darted in front of Lance, while Kirby and Magnus lingered against the outside wall, overlapping magical shields pressing in on their target, rather than surrounding them.

Lance swiped at Starkad, but hit an invisible wall.

"Press harder," Kirby said. It took an extra layer of focus, but she worked the shield into a net, leaving openings for projectiles to get through, but not enough room for Lance to move.

Brit fired one round after another, and Aya did the same with her spears.

The ground split open under Kirby, and an aura of madness licked at her senses.

Starkad and Fen crossed and came back in from opposite sides, striking Lance and splitting the dragon's focus.

Now or never.

Kirby rose into the air, dropping her portion of the shield at the last moment, before slicing down at Lance's neck. Her sword cut from shoulder to hip.

Lance howled in agony. The sound was ear-splitting and soul rending.

The ground stopped shaking. The madness evaporated. Silence settled in again.

A faint *thank you* filled the air, and Lance vanished in a gust of sparks and glittering dust.

"Is he dead?" Brit asked softly.

"*I don't think anyone's ever seen a dragon die.*" Fen's voice was in their heads, as Lance's had been.

A single sheet of parchment fluttered to the ground, landing at Kirby's feet as she touched down. She picked it up, and it took her mind a moment to adjust to the ancient language. This wasn't a pretty poem, it was a short tale of a Valkyrie who slayed a dragon.

A bittersweet pit welled in her chest. "Beholden to their own visions until the very end." Kirby felt bittersweet about the whole thing. "Let's go home."

The group appeared in the middle of NEON, exhaustion gnawing at Kirby all the way to her core. Her clothes were torn—magical armor hadn't stopped fabric from being shredded any more than it prevented the now-healed wounds underneath. But they'd done it.

"You're all back." Dahlia's squeal was sunshine in the darkly painted room. She wrapped Magnus in a tight hug.

Frey embraced Aya, who returned the gesture.

Gwydion pressed into Kirby's back, wrapped his arms around her waist, and rested his forehead against her skull. She didn't need to hear words to understand the meaning. She was so grateful to be here.

Min stepped in front of her, rested a hand at the base of her neck, and kissed her deeply. Possessively. Lovingly. "Welcome back."

"Feel left out at all?" Fen asked.

Kirby glanced past Min to see Starkad shake his head. "Nope. None of you assholes get to see the celebration I have planned."

Heat flooded Kirby at the implication, and she grinned.

"We heard from the others," Dahlia said. "One of the other gods called Frey as soon as they were out, to ask if Aya made it back. We were worried when you didn't."

"I wasn't." Min's words were soft against Kirby's lips. "I knew you had things under control."

Gwydion snorted with amusement. "He was terrified."

Min raised an eyebrow. "I was deeply concerned."

Aya broke away and approached Kirby. "Thank you. You didn't have to come for me, and I realize you would have stepped in regardless of being coerced into it, and regardless of the risk to your own life."

"To be fair," Frey said, "if any one of you had been in a situation you considered as big a threat, you would've done what you needed to, in order to secure help."

Kirby couldn't argue that.

"I seem to remember we did make a similar request. With Hel." Starkad's tone was hard.

Aya kept her gaze on Kirby. "I'm sorry. I wanted to help. I would've given you what you requested, if I'd had any choice. I'm grateful you were able to do more. Someday, I hope to return the favor."

"I don't trade in favors," Kirby said. "It's a nasty spiral."

"But maybe be a little less insulting when you ask for help next time." Brit glared at Frey and Fen.

Aya turned to her. "I don't believe we've been formally introduced."

Brit gave her a short bow. "Brit. World unrenowned assassin and bad ass immortal, even without super-powers."

Kirby couldn't fight her grin. She loved seeing Brit own her strengths.

"But that's not true, is it?" Aya studied Brit.

Seriously? Irritation surged through Kirby.

Aya cast her gaze around the room. "In fact, the group of you are a fascinating dichotomy, woven so tightly with fate and love and magic and defiance that it radiates from you. Potently when you're all together. I can't believe Frey didn't see it."

"I did. But you were more important than explaining it to them."

"*Excuse me.*" Kirby let irritation bleed into her voice. "You don't get to insult Brit like that then move on like it never happened."

Aya looked surprised. "It wasn't an insult. Brit, has no one told you what you are? What gifts you have?"

What?

Brit flexed her fingers and rolled her shoulder blades. "I've been trying to shoot fire at people, but it's not working. Is that a trick you can teach me?" She was sarcastic.

Aya sighed. "The others forget, because it's been so long and was outside of their realm. Odin's Valkyries accompanied fallen warriors to Valhalla, but it was my privilege to choose one-half of the heroes slain in battle for my great hall in the Fólkvangar."

"I didn't forget. I just..." Suddenly *it's been a few lives* didn't seem like a good excuse to Kirby. She'd totally forgotten.

"Odin had an entire army of battle maidens to do his bidding." Aya grasped Brit's fingers and looked her in the eye. "I did the choosing with the help of one or two others. History calls them Valkyries as well, but they were unique. Like the Valkyries, they all vanished, and I've never met anyone worthy and capable of carrying the mantle. Until you. You do have power. The power to shatter bonds. To bolster the fallen. To stand for those warriors who get overlooked because they're not clubbing people over the head for glory."

"I've never used a club," Starkad said.

Kirby elbowed him.

Aya shook her head, but her attention stayed on Brit. "In the coming battles, I'd be honored if you'd assist me."

"I swore I'd never work for a god again." There was no apology in Brit's tone.

"Think of it more as a partnership."

The corner of Brit's mouth tugged up. "I may be more amenable to that."

"Yay." Dahlia squealed with happiness and clapped.

Her joy mirrored Kirby's. Brit deserved this.

Aya stepped behind the bar and grabbed a bottle from the top shelf. "Let's celebrate. A victory. A partnership. Old and new friends."

Honestly, Kirby just wanted to sleep for a week. She needed to burn off a little adrenaline first, but drinking with a group wouldn't do that.

"I think we're going to take a raincheck, and head home," Gwydion said.

Kirby was pretty sure the only home she knew had been destroyed. Not that she was going to miss the imitation of suburbia that she and Starkad had lived.

"Yours?" Min asked.

Gwydion nodded.

Oh.

Brit wrinkled her nose. "I always pictured you as more of a vagrant type."

"I prefer the term nomad, but I do actually have a house."

House was an understatement. "Is it still...?" How much should Kirby say? It shouldn't be a secret, but if no one here knew about it, maybe he preferred to keep things under wraps.

"Castle big enough for at least five," Gwydion confirmed.

"You own a fucking castle." Dahlia probably meant her tone to be flat, but the awe was evident.

Magnus sighed. "Of course he does."

"But how the hell did he hide that from me?" Dahlia asked. "Not that I was stalking you or anything. I mean, I kind of was, but... How did you hide a castle?"

Built it centuries before computers existed, and never transfer ownership.

Gwydion smirked. "It's what I do. How 'bout a ride, love?" His question was spoken in a heavy brogue.

"Ugh." Magnus sounded disgusted. "Do you have to make it sound dirty?"

Kirby laughed. "That's also what he does. But we could use a lift, please?"

Magnus bowed. "Anything for you, boss."

As Kirby gathered into a small group with her lovers—her new family—and took Magnus's hand, contentment blanketed them. A decade ago, even a year ago, she never thought she'd have this kind of peace. It was incredible.

CHAPTER FIFTY-TWO

KIRBY

The outside of the castle was exactly as Kirby remembered, from hundreds of years ago.

The inside was a completely different world, visually. Gwydion had modernized the place with windows, rugs, heated floors, and comfortable furniture.

"There's no dust in here." Brit trailed her finger along a nearby table. "Magic?"

Gwydion shook his head. "Grounds crew. Grand tour starts upstairs, if you'd all like to join me."

He led them to the hallway where the rooms had been, once upon a time, and swung open the door to the one he and Kirby had shared.

Her heart skipped when she took in the décor. Trinkets from her previous lives. Gifts from each of her loves. And in the center of it all was the most ridiculously large bed she'd ever seen, as though someone had shoved two queen-sized mattresses together.

"Your room," Gwydion said to her.

Kirby suspected it would become everyone's room, unless someone needed privacy. She moved inside, tentative at first, unsure where to focus. There was a locket from France. A figurine from Russia. A dagger, similar to the one she wore from her first life, but more ornate and less made for battle.

Starkad stepped in front of her, wicked smirk dancing on his face. "I think we should test out the bed." He nipped at her bottom lip and nudged her back with his full body, until she collided with Min.

She remembered this—the lust that came with a battle. Before. After. Anytime a fight was involved.

Starkad's kisses were hungry as he sucked along her jaw and widened the tears in her shirt. He dragged his tongue over fresh scars left by magical wounds, devouring her as though each of her gasps was more fuel for his need.

This wasn't the same as her first life, though. Not only because Min stood behind her, tracing his fingers along her spine, and kissing along the back of her neck.

Kirby had more now. More to look forward to. More responsibility. More love. She grinded into Min, her body molding tighter to his with each fresh kiss or lick or nip from Starkad, and desire flooded her senses.

She was intently aware that Gwydion and Brit were watching, which they both enjoyed.

Starkad drew his tongue along her collar bone, up her jaw, to nibble her earlobe. "Never thought I'd get to fuck royalty."

Kirby flushed at the implication. She could accept the ability to make others like her, but wasn't sure how she felt about the title *Queen*.

"He's blind, then. I've always known you were meant to sit on a throne." Min's tone left no room for argument.

Kirby expected a sneer or other retort from Starkad.

Instead, he'd resumed tracing along the fresh, pale while lines that scarred her right bicep and shoulder. "This body is less than thirty years old. I can't keep you safe, can I?"

"Not the way you're talking about. Kind of surprised you're still talking," Kirby teased.

He held her gaze. "You're complaining?"

"Making an observation." She enjoyed the conversation, but this wasn't like Starkad. Not when adrenaline was high and victory lingered on his tongue.

Starkad dragged a finger down the front of her shirt, easily slicing that and the bra underneath, without nicking her skin. "Let's leave the observation to others."

His kiss was reckless and sloppy, more concerned with happening than with form as the feeling wrapped her in abandon. He moved his hands to her breasts, kneading and pinching as he dropped his head to suck on one nipple.

Each nibble-laced circle of his tongue sent desire coiling through her. The cool air against her back said Min had moved away, but she was too focused on Starkad's touch to linger on any other thoughts. Too consumed by pulling his mouth back to hers... Stripping off his shirt and shoving his jeans to the ground... Pressing her bare chest into his... Dragging her nails up his back.

Starkad gripped her hips and lifted. She wrapped her arms around his neck and her legs around his waist, lost in kisses and passion and raw need.

He turned and in a controlled fall, landed on the bed, Kirby still tangled around him. His erection pressed through the thin fabric of her leggings, teasing her already damp core. She needed to wear these more often.

Starkad kept his mouth pressed to her lips, her collarbone, her chest, and back to her mouth, as he scooted them back on the mattress. He fell to his elbows. The way he raked his gaze over her flooded her with heat. He pressed his thumb into the seam of her leggings, teasing her clit through the stretchy fabric, until she was grinding and moaning.

A sharp *rip* filled the air when Starkad ripped the leggings apart, exposing her and leaving her bare pussy to rest against his cock. She rocked her hips, back and forth, slipping easily along his length and teasing them both.

The mattress shifted when a now-naked Gwydion knelt next to them. He gripped her chin and slanted his mouth over hers, swallowing her gasps of mounting pleasure.

A mouth wrapped around Kirby's nipple. Brit had joined them as well, on the other side, and was focused intently on sucking along Kirby's chest. So much for the two of them being content to watch.

Not that she was complaining.

Brit rested a palm on Kirby's cheek, drawing her attention from Gwydion to lay a series of soft kisses along her lips.

The air around them was charged with a tangible, delicious desire that she wanted to lose herself in. Each new caress demanded savoring.

Starkad dug his fingers into her hips and lifted her. When he penetrated her, his, "*fuuuuck,*" mingled with her groan. Gods, he felt incredible, buried inside her.

Gwydion stole her mouth again, knotting his fingers in her hair and holding her captive, as Brit slid her fingers down Kirby's stomach, to tease her clit.

Starkad was still inside her, except for the occasionally twitch of his cock, but he gripped her thighs tightly enough to leave marks.

Kirby broke away from Gwydion to lean in over Starkad, and brush her lips up his chest. She clenched around him, to tease, and met his gaze, bottom lip caught between her teeth. "Wearing you out?"

"Testing my limits," he growled. "I want this to last, but I won't much longer." With his palm on her chest, he pushed her upright again, driving himself deeper inside her.

Brit crushed her mouth to Kirby's and pressed harder into her clit, while Gwydion teased her breasts. With Starkad buried in her, orgasm sped up on Kirby, pushing out the rest of the world, and reducing her thoughts into *Gods, this feels good.*

Min kissed up her back, and bit her shoulder. The stimulation from so many places was too much. Kirby plummeted into climax, losing herself in everything, milking Starkad.

He gripped her tighter.

Brit brought her fingers up to suck them clean, pressing them between her lips and Kirby's, sharing the taste and twisting their tongues together. Brit finally broke away with a sigh and a light smile. "I'm going to step back." Her voice was breathy. "I may not be interested in fucking any of them, but I do like watching you."

Another layer of want wrapped around Kirby. She enjoyed being on display. The confirmation that it was mutually beneficial made the moment even better.

Starkad rolled, and Kirby squealed in surprise. He pinned her arms above her head. His expression was hungry, almost feral, and so enticing. He released her wrists, straightened, and pushed her thighs to her chest. There was a desperation to his pounding, his groans becoming punctuated grunts, and then a drawn-out howl when he came, spilling inside her.

Though Starkad slowed to a less frantic pace, the intensity didn't ease up as Gwydion still worked his touch over her, tweaking and pulling in all the right places.

Kirby needed more. Of him. Of Min. She reached for Gwydion's cock. "I want to taste you. Please." She pouted for effect.

He crawled higher on the bed, and she wrapped her hand around his shaft. She drew her tongue in circles around the head, before drawing him into her mouth.

Min pressed his lips to her ear. "You're so stunning, my huntress. Flushed and aroused. Let me worship you." He took Starkad's place between her legs, and glided large, tender hands higher.

Starkad laid next to her. He danced his fingers over her body, the light touches adding to her euphoria.

Kirby groaned around Gwydion's cock when Min slid inside her, stretching her out. An incredible buzz—dizzying and electrifying—enveloped her mind and body. She fell into the fluffy clouds of ecstasy as she straddled that line between just enough and too much.

Gwydion's grunts blended with Min's. Starkad's fingers played her moans in harmony. Even the sound of Brit's heavy breathing, that *almost there* gasp, added to the chorus.

A salt spurt hit the back of her throat, and she let Gwydion spill into her mouth, sucking like he was he favorite candy. Licking him clean as he pulled away with a shudder. Driving her tongue into his mouth when he pressed in to kiss her.

Min paused, and the world seem to do the same, before emptying himself inside her with a long groan.

The haze hovered in her thoughts and in the air as the song of passion faded. This was the high she'd chased for so long, and it was incredible.

As everyone pulled away, left long enough to clean up, Gwydion made her stay put, and returned to make sure she was clean as well. Within moments, the group was back in the bed, collapsed in a happy, satiated pile.

This felt like home, tangled up in the people she loved. She should be exhausted, but a fresh energy thrummed inside.

"What's next?" Brit lay with her head on Kirby's thigh.

Starkad dragged a single nail up Kirby's stomach. "Round two in about five minutes?"

Gwydion chuckled. "I need at least seven. Call me old if you want."

"You're old," Brit teased. "But I meant outside the bedroom."

"There has to be a way to find these other Valkyries outside of stumbling upon them day to day." Leave it to Min to be the voice of reason.

And he was right. "I think I can feel them. Like invisible strands connecting me to all these other beings. They're faint. A splash of water. Some are more distinct tugs." Kirby closed her eyes and focused on the sensation, following one of the stronger threads. "I can almost see faces in some instances. Names."

"We can find them. We've spent years tracking potential gods," Starkad said.

Stalking. Hunting. Killing or saving based on the whim of the god pulling the strings. Kirby didn't like the association.

"And then what?" Disdain hung heavy in Brit's voice. "Stick them in a safe house? Promise them they can be a superhero and save the world, if they just come work with this small group of gods?"

Kirby knew that pitch. It was similar to the one Loki gave her when he pulled her from a group home as a teenager. "We're definitely not doing either of those things."

"So, buy 'em a pint and tell 'em the truth." Gwydion made it sound like *problem sorted.*

Brit glanced up at them, face scrunched in doubt. "Maybe don't get people drunk before you tell them a story like this."

"But it's a good plan otherwise." In fact, the longer Kirby thought about it, the more it felt right. Approach them, gauge the situation, and get to the truth as quickly as possible. See what happened from there.

Okay, it wasn't actually a good plan, but it was a starting point. And Kirby loved the idea of *see what happens next*. Not because some secret organization was pulling strings to make or prevent prophecies from happening. But to stop that from happening nearly so much in the future. To give the world back to the people who lived in it.

And in Kirby's off time, to be here, *home,* with the people she loved.

When Odin cursed her, centuries ago, she never questioned she'd made the right decision in saving Starkad.

When she remembered the past in her next lives, she loathed the idea of her next death. And when Loki recruited her, and Hel turned her into a killer, Kirby just wanted everything to stop.

Holding out was worth the wait. *This*, love, support, family, was the kind of ideal future she never imagined. And it was hers.

310

Epilogue One

Three Months Later
Kirby

Kirby sat in a booth at the back of a coffee shop, Starkad next to her.

To the outside observer, they looked like the kind of cuddly cute couple who was so enamored with each other, they couldn't stand to be separated by so much as a table as they shared a muffin.

Really it was because this was the perfect spot to see the entire café, and neither of them would sit with their backs to the door.

Not that Kirby minded being shoulder to shoulder with Starkad.

Starkad popped a piece of muffin in Kirby's mouth. When she dragged his finger in and sucked playfully, a low, contented growl rumbled from his chest.

If twenty-two year old Kirby could see her now… she'd think she was drugged and heavily hallucinating. The realization drew a dark laugh from her.

"Something funny?" Starkad asked.

"No. Just a bit fucked up." Kirby handed him her cup. "More coffee?"

He pressed his lips to hers in a drawn out kiss she felt in her heart, toes, and tonsils. "Sure."

Supposedly, one of the people Kirby was connected to would be here this morning. Mia stopped in for a coffee most mornings before she went to work. Starkad was with Kirby, because based on what they'd seen about Mia online, Starkad's presence should make her feel secure rather than scare her off.

Brit was going with Kirby in a few weeks to approach a single mother.

This entire situation was odd, though. Walking that line between needing to know about a person before approaching them, and not wanting to be a stalker. Kirby didn't want to lie to anyone, but approaching them with an opener like *I'm a Valkyrie and you could be too,* would come off as completely wacked.

Starkad returned and set the drink in front of Kirby. A sip of scalding liquid told her it was the perfect level of sweet and hot.

He glanced at his watch. "She's late. Next steps?"

"Regroup. Replan." Maybe come up with an approach that didn't feel so…TOM-like.

Starkad slid from the booth again, offered Kirby his hand, and tugged her to her feet. The way he tangled his fingers with hers was all real. No *just for show* here.

They headed toward the door. "Shit. My coffee." Kirby turned back to the table.

"Watch out." Starkad wrapped an arm around her waist and tugged her closer.

Kirby looked up as a shoulder jarred into hers, and met the gaze of a girl in glasses and a ponytail, who miraculously managed to keep the stack of books in her arms from tumbling to the ground. A snake tattoo peeked up above the collar of her shirt, the creature's fangs sinking into a wine-colored birthmark shaped like an apple.

Mia.

"I'm so sorr..." Mia's eyes grew wide when she saw Kirby. "I had a dream about you."

Me too, didn't seem like an appropriate response. Kirby's brain stalled.

"Except—you're going to think this is nuts— you were wearing armor, like video game armor but cooler, and you had wings." Mia shook her head and stepped back outside, leaving the doorway open. "Sorry. I didn't mean to get in your way."

Kirby and Starkad joined her on the sidewalk, and Kirby extended her hand in greeting. "It's not as crazy as you think. I'm Kirby."

EPILOGUE TWO

DAHLIA

Apartment hunting. Dahlia couldn't believe she and Magnus were doing something so benign. So *basic*.

It was fantabulously glorious.

Frey and Fen were happy to let them stay in one of the NEON properties, but as much as Dahlia occasionally enjoyed their company, she was a bit burned out on gods.

She wanted a roommate and ordering pizza whenever they wanted and late night movies and *knock first if there's a sock on the door* awkwardness and everything they should have been doing a decade ago as part of early adulthood.

Dahlia and Magnus stood on the sidewalk outside of a small apartment complex, surveying the layout before heading into the leasing office.

"All the units have windows facing front and back. I hate that the corner unit are blind on the open walls," Magnus said.

Kirby had been right—some training would probably never go away.

"Maybe we need a house instead. Then again, I like the second-story view." Dahlia could see at least three different spots to hide cameras. It shouldn't be too big a deal though—the magic on Magnus's ring would keep them hidden. Specifically from TOM.

"It's a nice neighborhood. I think you'll like it here." The new voice chilled Dahlia. Bragi was a member of the TOM board, and one of the gods who specifically should *not* be able to find them. "I hear you ladies left the fold."

Dahlia steeled herself and faced him, emotionless expression in place. "We did."

"I always felt the two of you were wasted as part of Hel's little army." Bragi's voice was smooth and seductive, rather than condescending the way his words implied. He was a few inches taller than them, with eyes so dark they were almost black and matching hair, that were a stunning contrast against pale skin. "You could've been so much more if she'd let you spend more time with us."

"We *are* so much more." Dahlia ticked through a list of things they needed, in order to vanish more completely. He shouldn't have found them so soon. No one should have found them at all.

"Mmm." Bragi turned to Magnus and lifted her chin to look her in the eye. "We have our fingers in more than you realize. It's a world so very different than the disgusting one you were subjected to."

Magnus stepped back, breaking the contact between them. She liked Bragi. Had flirted with him on occasion. She called him *friend* when she talked about him. "We're good with the choice we've made. Thanks."

Bragi raised an eyebrow. "We'll see. Happy house hunting, ladies."

Dahlia maintained her confident posture as he strolled away, but her shoulders sank the moment he was out of sight.

"No one's supposed to be able to find us." Magnus's words echoed Dahlia's thoughts.

Something told Dahlia hiding wouldn't be the option they hoped for.